MURDER MANSION

JESSE DYLAN YOUNG

Murder Mansion

Copyright © 2026 by Jesse Dylan Young

The following is a work of fiction. Any names, characters, places, and incidents are products of the author's imagination. Any resemblance to actual events or persons, living or dead, is entirely coincidental.

ISBN 979-8-9948906-1-5 (ebook)
ISBN 979-8-9948906-0-8 (paperback)

Published by Cosmic Cat Publishing
5318 E 2nd St. #4109
Long Beach, CA 90803
United States
info@cosmiccatpublishing.com

www.cosmiccatpublishing.com
www.jessedylanyoung.com

CHAPTER ONE

The girl died beautifully.

She stumbled into the ballroom, one hand clutching her throat, blood seeping between her fingers in dark rivulets. Her French maid outfit—black and white, absurdly pristine except for the crimson spreading across the collar—made her look like she'd wandered out of someone else's fever dream.

Her mouth opened. No scream came. Just a wet, gurgling sound that seemed to echo off the high ceilings before dying in the heavy air.

She crashed into a table. Dishes exploded across the floor—glass shattering, porcelain splintering, roses scattering their blood-red petals like secrets spilled at a funeral. The white tablecloth drank up the fake blood in slow, spreading blotches.

Then she collapsed, dragging the cloth down with her in one final, graceful surrender.

Silence.

Three heartbeats of perfect stillness.

"CUT!"

The girl groaned—very much alive, very much annoyed—and propped herself up on her elbows. Corn syrup blood dripped down her neck, pooling beneath her in a sticky mess that smelled faintly of vanilla.

"I'm going to be finding this stuff for weeks," she muttered, examining her stained fingers with disgust.

Sam Scury strode into view, a worn paperback of *Carrie* peeking from his back pocket. He scratched his head, grinning. "That was great. Really sold the terror. But next time, aim for the aisle, yeah? Keep the carnage off the china."

The girl shuffled out, leaving red footprints across the pristine floor.

Sam turned to his best friend, Curtis Garlan, who stood watching the whole scene with the expression of someone witnessing a miracle and a train wreck simultaneously.

"Pretty awesome, huh?" Sam asked.

Curtis nodded slowly. "Still can't believe you're running the whole operation. Last year you were just helping with props."

"Yeah, well." Sam's grin turned wry. "My aunt had a vision. Guess she figured I'd know how to pull it off."

"No one's more macabre than Sam Scury," Curtis said. "You're like Stephen King if he threw house parties."

Sam laughed and slapped Curtis on the back. "Come on. I want to show you something."

He led Curtis to a door at the back of the ballroom—one that blended almost invisibly into the wallpaper. With a flourish, Sam pulled out an old-fashioned brass key and twisted it in the lock.

The door swung open, revealing a dim space crammed with shelves, mannequins, and an unsettling array of props.

"Welcome to the props room," Sam said, sweeping his arm wide. "Also known as my happy place."

Curtis peered inside. "This is like stepping into your brain. Creepy, chaotic, and way too organized all at once."

The room was a macabre wonderland.

Grotesque masks lined the walls—plague doctors with impossibly long beaks, cracked porcelain faces, theatrical tragedy masks frozen in eternal sorrow. Shelves groaned under fake severed limbs, jagged weapons, bottles of blood in varying shades from bright arterial red to deep venous black.

A guillotine stood in the corner like a monument to mankind's creativity in death, its blade dulled but menacing. Costumes spilled from boxes—tattered cloaks, bloodstained dresses, pristine suits waiting to be ruined.

The air smelled of latex, paint, and something faintly metallic.

Curtis picked up a retractable knife from a nearby table, pressing the blade into his palm. It retracted with a satisfying click. "This is insane," he murmured. "How much did all this cost?"

"It's everything we need for this weekend." Sam grabbed a noose hanging from a hook and yanked it apart, revealing the Velcro seam. "My aunt was... thorough. Obsessive, even."

Curtis grinned, lunging forward with the fake knife and plunging it into Sam's stomach.

Sam staggered back, clutching his chest. "You bastard!" he groaned, stumbling into a shelf. "That's it—you're on cleanup duty."

Curtis doubled over laughing. "Okay, okay. But seriously, this is going to be epic. When do we leave again?"

"Tomorrow morning at ten. I have my team making sure everything's perfect right now." Sam leaned against a shelf, crossing his arms. "Or at least functional."

Curtis picked up a prop gun, examining its weight, the textured grip, even the fake serial number on the side. "So... was this really your aunt's dying wish? To host a murder mystery in her honor?"

Sam hesitated. Something flickered across his face—grief, maybe, or guilt. Then a sly grin spread. "Maybe. Or maybe it's just a good excuse to throw the bloodiest Valentine's Day party ever." He smiled. "Either way, she'd approve."

Curtis rolled his eyes. "So what are the rules? No sex and drugs? Gotta keep it PG?"

Sam barked out a laugh. "Oh, you sweet summer child. Even if that *was* a rule—which it's not—this crowd would break it before we got through the welcome toast." He grinned. "Most of them are theater kids, Curtis. All grown up and still desperate for attention."

Curtis laughed. Then had a thought.

"Wait. Are sex and drugs part of the storyline?"

Sam paused, his hand hovering over a pile of chains, a grin sliding into place.

"That's the fun of it, right? You never know what's real and what's part of the game." His eyes gleamed. "That's what keeps people coming back. The uncertainty."

They left the room, Sam pulling the door shut with a decisive click. The lock engaged with a sound like a coffin lid sealing.

The ballroom was silent as they walked out, much like the mansion would be when they arrived tomorrow.

CHAPTER TWO

Zoey Hopkins stood by the king-size bed, folding a fitted black blouse with the precision of someone who found solace in order. Each fold was crisp, mathematical—the kind of perfection that came from using control over small things to manage anxiety about bigger ones.

Her apartment was in chaos. Clothing covered every surface. Tops draped over chair backs, shoes scattered in mismatched pairs, an abandoned scarf hanging off a lampshade. The city hummed through the cracked window—car horns, subway rumble, someone's music bleeding through the walls—mingling with the upbeat pop playlist Zoey had put on to keep the mood light.

Despite the mess, she worked methodically, placing items into her suitcase like puzzle pieces. Outfits grouped by scenario, accessories tucked where they wouldn't wrinkle.

Across the bed, Chelsie Turner sighed dramatically. In one hand, a sequined top glittered in the afternoon light. In the other, impossibly high red-soled heels dangled from two fingers.

"Ugh, Zoey," Chelsie groaned, tossing the top onto a growing pile of discarded options. "I give up. Can I just bring the whole closet? Would that be weird? I feel like that would be weird, but also practical."

Zoey looked up, a teasing smile tugging at her lips. "Bring that pink dress. You look super hot in that. Like, criminally hot."

Chelsie paused, her frustration momentarily forgotten. "Really? Hot?" A slow, playful smirk spread across her face. She leaned forward, draping herself across the bed like a perfume commercial. "How about we just stay here, then? Forget the murder mystery. I can think of better ways to spend the weekend."

Zoey rolled her eyes, but her soft laugh betrayed her amusement. "No, Chelsie Turner. We're going. We already RSVP'd, and you know how important this is to Sam. It's basically his debut as company owner."

Chelsie collapsed onto the bed with dramatic flair, burying her face in the duvet before rolling onto her back, one arm flung over her eyes. "Yeah, yeah. Okay, but only because he's your brother. And because I love you. But mostly the brother thing."

Zoey arched an eyebrow. "You should want to go because I do."

Chelsie lowered her arm, her eyes meeting Zoey's with a mixture of mischief and sincerity. She reached out, her fingers brushing against Zoey's hand. When she spoke, her voice dropped to barely a whisper. "I want to be wherever you are, babe."

Zoey's expression melted, her earlier resolve fading into something warmer. "You better," she said, her voice teasing but threaded with genuine emotion.

Without hesitation, she crawled across the bed, closing the distance between them. Her hand cupped Chelsie's cheek, her thumb tracing along her cheekbone. Their eyes met briefly—a silent exchange of all the things they didn't need to say out loud.

And then their lips met.

The kiss was unhurried and sweet, filled with quiet intimacy. It wasn't the kind of kiss meant to dazzle—it was the kind that lingered, leaving behind the unshakable impression of love and trust. The kind that tasted like home.

Outside, the city continued its hum, but for Zoey and Chelsie, the world shrank to just that moment and the unspoken promise it carried—that whatever the weekend brought, they'd face it together.

As their kiss broke, Zoey lingered, her forehead resting softly against Chelsie's. "We're going to have a great time," she murmured, her voice low and almost convincing.

Chelsie leaned back slightly, her brow furrowing. "What's on your mind?"

Zoey hesitated, her gaze darting toward the window before she shook her head, summoning a small smile that didn't quite reach her eyes. "Nothing. Just pre-party jitters. You know how I get."

It was true that Zoey got anxious before social events. But this felt different somehow, heavier, though she couldn't quite articulate why.

Chelsie studied her for a moment longer, searching for cracks in her mask. But she chose not to press—that was one of the things Zoey loved about her, the way she knew when to push and when to let things breathe.

Instead, she slipped off the bed with fluid grace, scooping up the pink dress. She held it against her body and twirled in front of the mirror. "Alright, babe, you win. Pink it is. But if I look washed out, I'm blaming you entirely."

Zoey watched her spin, the dress catching the light as Chelsie's laughter filled the room. For a moment, Zoey's unease melted into quiet admiration. Chelsie had a way of making everything seem lighter, easier. It was a gift.

Chelsie turned back, placing her hands on her hips in a mock-modeling pose. "There. Decision made. Now let's get these bags packed so we can spend the rest of the night doing... other things," she said, her lips curling into a devilish grin.

Zoey laughed, shaking her head as she returned to folding.

"Not a chance. You'll need your energy for the weekend. Sam's events are intense. Like, emotionally draining. You have to stay in character, follow the clues, interact with everyone. It's basically improv theater for twelve hours straight, for two days."

Chelsie arched a perfectly sculpted brow. "You mean like the time he set up that fake kidnapping for your birthday? When I almost called the actual police because I thought you were being trafficked? That kind of intense?"

Zoey groaned, pressing her palms against her temples. "Oh god, don't remind me. But yes, exactly like that. Except bigger. And bloodier. He's got props this time. Professional-grade stuff. It's going to be a whole production."

Chelsie gave an exaggerated shiver, wrapping her arms around herself. "Well, as long as there's no real blood involved, I'm in. Fake blood I can handle. Real blood freaks me out. You know this about me."

"I know, babe. I'll protect you." Zoey winked and pulled her in tight.

CHAPTER THREE

Sam leaned back in his chair, the old leather creaking as his fingers hovered over the keyboard. The monitor's glow bathed his sharp features in pale blue-white light, making him look almost ghostly.

The tiny office was an ode to his dark passions. A replica skull grinned from the corner of his desk, its hollow eyes fixed on him in permanent judgment. A taxidermied raven perched on a nearby shelf, its glassy gaze tilted downward. Above him, a crooked vintage *Psycho* poster—an original from 1960, his aunt's gift—added chaos to the carefully curated space. Janet Leigh's screaming face caught the light at odd angles, her terror forever frozen.

On the desk sat a small nameplate shaped like an open coffin. The inscription read in mock-gothic lettering: "SINISTER" SAM SCURY. A gag gift from Curtis years ago that Sam had kept because it was perfect—self-aware enough to be funny, true enough to make him smile.

He cracked his neck and stretched, the tension between his shoulder blades finally releasing. His fingers resumed their rhythm on the keyboard, making final adjustments to the weekend's itinerary. Every detail had to be perfect—guest lists with dietary restrictions noted and activities timed down to the minute.

Sam didn't settle for anything less than perfection. His aunt had taught him that. "If you're going to scare people," she used to say, "you'd better commit to it completely."

The door creaked open behind him, hinges protesting with that familiar squeal he'd been meaning to oil for months. Heels clicked on the hardwood floor—slow, deliberate, measured. But his attention remained fixed on the screen, scanning through the morning schedule.

Then a familiar scent reached him, cutting through the stale coffee and old paper. Jasmine and leather, expensive and deliberate. The kind of perfume that announced its presence without apology.

His hands paused mid-type. He glanced up, turning slightly in his chair.

Gwendolyn Pierce stood framed in the doorway like she'd been positioned by a photographer, her silhouette backlit by the hallway light. She looked effortlessly poised in her tailored red business suit, accentuating every curve with surgical precision. Her jet-black hair fell in waves over her shoulders, gleaming like polished obsidian, and her crimson lips curled into a smile that was both professional and dangerously inviting.

Sam couldn't suppress the grin that spread across his face. "Hey there."

"Hey, Sam," Gwen replied, her voice smooth and velvety. She stepped further into the room, heels clicking with each deliberate step. "Everything's set. Everyone's confirmed. The yacht leaves at 10 a.m. sharp tomorrow." She pulled a small tablet from under her arm, glancing at it with practiced efficiency. "I sent final reminders to the stragglers and confirmed the catering order. We're good to go."

Sam leaned back, folding his arms behind his head. "Wonderful. Thank you. You're the best. Seriously, I don't know what I'd do without you running point on all this."

Gwen's smile deepened, her eyes flashing with playful glimmer. "I do my best." Her presence was magnetic—a blend of efficiency and allure that made her invaluable and impossible to ignore. She'd been his aunt's right hand for years, knew the business inside and out, and had somehow made the transition to working for him seem effortless.

Sam's gaze lingered on her for a beat longer than necessary, his mind wandering briefly into decidedly unprofessional territory. He caught himself and cleared his throat. "You've earned some rest. I suggest you head out and get some sleep. We've got one hell of a weekend ahead."

"Hokey dokey," Gwen teased, straightening in mock seriousness, giving him a playful salute sarcastic enough to make him laugh.

But she didn't leave immediately. Instead, she lingered, her weight shifting to one hip, her expression softening as she studied him with sudden intensity. "What time will you be at the dock tomorrow?"

Sam considered for a moment, fingers idly drumming against the desk. "I'll meet you there at eight. We'll grab breakfast and go over the details before everyone else shows up. Maybe hit that café you like—the one with the good espresso and terrible croissants."

A flicker of something warmer crossed Gwen's face, her smile losing its professional edge entirely, becoming more genuine. Her eyes brightened in a way that made Sam's pulse quicken. "Sounds delicious. Good night, boss."

The way she said "boss" made it sound like an endearment rather than a title, intimate in a way that blurred the lines he'd been trying to maintain.

"Good night, Gwen," Sam replied, his voice dipping with genuine affection he couldn't quite suppress.

As she turned and walked toward the door, Sam's eyes followed her—he couldn't help it. The sway of her hips was hypnotic, deliberate enough that he suspected she knew he was watching, that this was part of some larger game they'd been playing for months without ever acknowledging out loud.

Gwen was efficient, brilliant, and undeniably attractive—a combination that made her both an asset and a distraction. She challenged him, matched his dark humor beat for beat, and made even tedious administrative tasks feel like part of some elaborate conspiracy. She was dangerous in the best possible way.

The door clicked shut behind her, leaving the room quiet save for the faint hum of the computer fan. Sam exhaled slowly, running a hand through his dark hair as he leaned back, the leather creaking.

His mind drifted to the weekend ahead. He had helped with countless murder mysteries over the years, each more elaborate than the last. But this one felt different. Bigger. More intricate. More personal.

It was his first major event as official owner of the company, his first chance to prove that his aunt's faith in him hadn't been misplaced. If everything went according to plan, it would be unforgettable—the kind of event people would talk about for years.

He knew that things could go wrong, but what could go terribly wrong? He told himself that he was worrying too much.

Refocusing, he typed the last few notes into the itinerary, double-checking every detail. Breakfast: 8:00 a.m. Boarding: 9:30 a.m. Departure: 10:00 a.m. sharp. Introduction and character assignments: 10:30 a.m. First "murder": 8:00 p.m., right after dinner when everyone would be relaxed and unsuspecting.

When satisfied that every minute of the next forty-eight hours was accounted for, he leaned back, the ghost of a grin tugging at his lips.

"Let the games begin," he murmured, snapping the laptop shut with a decisive click.

The room seemed to darken as the monitor's glow vanished, the objects around him casting long, distorted shadows across the walls like grasping fingers. The skull's grin seemed wider somehow in the dimness, more knowing.

Sam glanced at it and chuckled, the sound low and conspiratorial. "This weekend's going to be one for the books," he said to the empty room, to the skull, to himself.

He stood, stretching, and grabbed his jacket from the back of the chair. As he reached for the light switch, he paused, taking one last look around his office—at the posters and props and carefully curated darkness that reflected who he was.

Then he flipped the switch, plunging the room into complete blackness, and stepped out into the hallway.

Behind him, in the darkness, the skull continued its eternal grin.

Waiting.

CHAPTER FOUR

The morning sun bathed Dev's Dockside Diner in a golden glow, its light shimmering across the harbor like scattered diamonds. The café was alive with the hum of life—laughter, clinking silverware, and the sizzle of food on the grill. Waiters bustled between tables, balancing trays stacked with eggs Benedict, towering pancakes, and perfectly golden toast. The warm aroma of freshly brewed coffee mingled with the salty tang of sea breeze drifting through open windows.

It was the kind of morning that hinted at new beginnings, adventures waiting just around the corner.

At a waterside table with a perfect view of the marina, four friends lingered over the remnants of a decadent breakfast. Their cleared plates had given way to glasses of champagne that sparkled like liquid sunshine. Laughter hung in the air between them, easy and genuine—a perfect prelude to the weekend ahead.

Darren and Alice Sarper sat side by side, the image of a couple still deeply in love after nearly a decade of marriage. Darren's hand rested casually on Alice's thigh, his thumb tracing small, absent-minded circles against her sundress. Alice leaned into him, her face glowing with excitement.

Across the table, Norma Batkins and Russell Fremont were their rough-around-the-edges counterparts—less refined but no less affectionate. Russell slouched in his chair, his Hawaiian shirt unbuttoned just enough to show off his gold chain. Norma sat upright beside him, her crimson nails fidgeting with her champagne flute as her sharp eyes darted between the harbor and her friends.

"This weekend has to be awesome," Russell declared, swirling his champagne with a smirk. "It's already off to a great start. Champagne brunch on a Friday? On the water? Who'd have thought I'd be this fancy? Look at me. I'm basically royalty now."

Darren chuckled, lifting his glass in a mock toast. "Agreed. Though I'm pretty sure actual royalty doesn't brunch next to a bait freezer and a sign advertising two-for-one clam chowder."

Details," Russell said, waving him off. He held the flute up toward the sun, admiring the way the light caught the pale gold bubbles. "This is real glass. Listen." He tapped it gently with his fingernail, producing a soft, dignified chime that felt wildly out of place among the gulls and the low rumble of boat engines. "That's the sound of sophistication."

A gull shrieked overhead as if in protest.

Darren grinned. "Yeah. Very regal. Nothing says 'Your Majesty' like seagulls plotting to steal your hash browns."

Russell took a slow, dramatic sip and sighed contentedly. "This weekend I am not a man who Googles marina parking rates. I am a dockside duke. An aristocratic detective. Please address me accordingly."

Alice clapped her hands together, her enthusiasm bubbling over. "Well detective, I'm so excited! A murder mystery on a private island, with great people, and my honey?" She squeezed Darren's hand. "It's going to be the best Valentine's ever. Better than Paris, even."

"Better than Paris?" Darren raised an eyebrow, teasing. "That's a bold claim. Paris had the Eiffel Tower."

"This has murder," Alice replied with perfect logic. "Much more interesting."

Norma leaned forward, grinning. "I know, right? I've always wanted to do one of these mystery weekends! Since I saw that movie—you know, the one with the mansion and multiple endings? But this doofus," she jabbed a thumb at Russell, "never wants to go."

Russell feigned a wounded look, his hand over his heart. "This doofus is too busy working to pay for your extravagant hobbies. Do you know how much your book club membership costs? Books are free at the library."

"It's a wine and book club," Norma corrected with dignity. "The wine is the point. The books are just an excuse."

"Exactly my point," Russell said, though his grin suggested he wasn't actually complaining.

Norma shrugged, used to this routine after fifteen years together. "You're not wrong. So, Darren," she pivoted smoothly, "you've done one of these before, right? Give us the inside scoop. What are we getting into?"

Darren nodded, taking a thoughtful sip of champagne. "Yeah, a couple of years ago. Just the dinner version, though—not a whole weekend. It was one of Sam's aunt's events." He paused, growing more animated. "It was incredibly detailed. She really had a knack for setting the scene. Every prop was perfect, every actor knew their lines, and the clues were clever enough that you actually had to work to figure it out."

"She sounds incredible," Alice said, her voice tinged with admiration. "I heard she was kind of a legend at this stuff."

"She was," Darren agreed, his tone softening. "She made it all feel so real. It wasn't just a game—it was like stepping into a whole other world. She was a genius, honestly. At immersion."

Norma leaned closer, her curiosity piqued. "And Sam? Think he's got what it takes to pull it off? Those are some big shoes to fill."

Russell snorted, swirling his champagne. "Shouldn't be too

hard. The whole thing was set up for him, wasn't it? He's basically just executing someone else's vision."

Alice tilted her head, confused. "Set up? By who?"

"By his aunt," Russell replied casually. "From what I heard, she put everything together before she died. The whole mystery, It's about her death. Like, literally. We're solving the mystery of how she died or something."

The table fell into a brief, thoughtful silence. The café continued around them—clatter of dishes, a child laughing, a seagull crying overhead—but at their table, the mood had shifted.

Darren frowned, his fingers tapping against his glass. "That's... a little weird. Morbid, even. Using your own death as entertainment?"

"Right?" Norma said, her voice dropping to a conspiratorial whisper. "I thought the same thing when I heard that. Like, is this going to be depressing? But I guess if it was her dying wish, it's kind of nice to be part of it. Like... honoring her legacy." She paused. "Still weird, though."

Alice, ever the optimist, smiled warmly. "Exactly. It's a privilege, really. Sam's aunt was an amazing woman—fun, creative, and a little wild from what I've heard. That's what this weekend is going to be: fun. A celebration of someone who clearly loved life and wanted to go out with a bang."

"As long as the bang is metaphorical," Russell interjected, draining his champagne. "I didn't sign a waiver or anything, did I?"

Norma swatted his arm. "You're terrible."

"You love it," Russell countered with a wink.

Russell placed his empty glass on the table with a decisive clink. "Speaking of fun, we'd better get to the boat. I heard it's got three decks and a hot tub. A hot tub on a boat, people. That's living."

Excitement rippled through the group. Chairs scraped as

they stood, gathering their belongings and finishing the last sips of champagne.

Russell grabbed his flute and raised it high with theatrical flair. "To a killer weekend," he declared, his voice brimming with good-natured sarcasm and genuine enthusiasm.

The others laughed, raising their glasses in unison. "To a killer weekend!" they echoed, their voices ringing with anticipation.

The soft chime of glass meeting glass resonated in the salty morning air as seagulls wheeled overhead and boats rocked gently in their slips. The group downed their drinks and made their way toward the dock.

Toward the yacht.

Toward the island.

Toward the adventure that awaited them—one that would prove far more memorable, and far more dangerous, than any of them could possibly imagine.

CHAPTER FIVE

The sun shimmered on the pristine waters surrounding the yacht, its reflection scattering like thousands of tiny diamonds across the surface. The vessel itself was a masterpiece of luxury—sleek and imposing, with polished teak wood gleaming like honey poured over silk. The kind of boat that whispered money and taste in equal measure.

White railings encircled the decks, adorned with garlands of roses intertwined with delicate red heart-shaped ornaments. It was a Valentine's Day touch that would have been charming if not for the small crimson vials shaped like blood bags dangling among the flowers. Each one swayed gently in the breeze, the red liquid inside sloshing faintly, catching the light in a way that made them look disturbingly real.

The contrast was striking—a blend of romance and the macabre. Beauty and death, intertwined.

On the stern deck, Sam and Gwen sat at a table dressed in crisp white linen. A simple but elegant breakfast they picked up earlier lay half-eaten before them—golden croissants, fresh fruit, and cups of coffee that filled the air with their rich aroma.

Sam leaned back in his chair, his gaze drifting across the endless expanse of water. But despite the relaxed posture, his mind raced through checklists, contingencies, potential problems.

"And then," Gwen said, her voice low and brimming with excitement, leaning forward conspiratorially, "we reveal the murderer. Right at the climax, when everyone thinks they've figured it out—boom. Plot twist."

Sam's focus snapped back to her. A grin tugged at his mouth. "Perfect. And no one knows who it is, right? Not even the staff? We kept it completely locked down?"

Gwen's smile widened, satisfaction gleaming in her eyes. "Big secret. Only you and me. It'll hit them like a freight train."

Sam let out a quiet laugh. "Wonderful. Now we just have to pull it off without a hitch. No technical difficulties, no actors breaking character, no guests figuring it out too early."

Gwen raised her coffee cup. "I've got it covered," she said smoothly, before taking a deliberate sip. Her eyes remained on him over the rim, watching, assessing.

Sam studied her—the way the morning light caught in her dark hair, the precise way she held herself, the intelligence that practically radiated from her. He set his cup down, his expression softening. "I know you do. Thank you, Gwen. Seriously. I know this one's been brutal. None of this would be possible without you."

The words hung in the air between them, heavier than he'd intended.

Gwen leaned forward, her crimson lips curling into a sultry smile. "I'll think of a way you can repay me," she said, her voice carrying layers of meaning that made Sam's pulse quicken.

Sam chuckled, heat creeping up his neck. He opened his mouth to respond, but movement on the dock caught his eye. His expression shifted immediately as the first guests arrived.

Darren and Russell led the way down the weathered dock, eager and purposeful. Darren's eyes scanned the yacht with genuine awe. Russell walked beside him with his usual swagger, hands shoved in his pockets, Hawaiian shirt billowing in the breeze.

Behind them, Alice and Norma followed, their conversation punctuated by bursts of laughter as they took in the spectacle.

Darren stopped at the base of the gangplank, his jaw dropping slightly. "There she is," he murmured, his voice tinged with reverence.

Russell slapped him on the shoulder. "The perfect woman. Doesn't talk back and lets you ride her all day."

"Oh my god," Norma said, smacking his arm with her purse. "You're such a child, Russell."

"Forty-two," Russell corrected proudly. "And you love it."

"I tolerate it," Norma replied, but her smile betrayed her.

The group climbed aboard, where a deck hand in crisp white nautical attire greeted them with leis made of roses, hearts, and tiny faux blood bags that clinked together softly.

Norma lifted hers curiously, letting the light catch the crimson-filled vials. "Okay, this is officially creepy. Like, I love it, but it's creepy."

Sam and Gwen approached together. Sam's arms spread wide in a welcoming gesture. "More bodies! Welcome aboard."

He greeted each of them warmly, making each person feel like they were the guest he'd been most excited to see. It was a gift, that ability to make people feel special.

Gwen stood slightly behind him, her sharp eyes assessing each guest as if they were puzzle pieces. She was cataloging them —noting their dynamics, their energy levels, their potential as players.

"This is my assistant, Gwen," Sam said. "She's been the mastermind behind making sure this whole thing doesn't go up in flames. If you enjoy yourselves this weekend, thank her. If anything goes wrong, blame me."

Gwen offered a small, professional nod. "Just doing my job."

———

A SLEEK BLACK car pulled up to the dock just as the first group disappeared up the gangplank. Zoey stepped out first, her movements careful and deliberate as she smoothed down her blouse and adjusted the strap of her overnight bag. Chelsie emerged from the passenger side with considerably more flair, her pink dress—the one Zoey had insisted on—flowing in the breeze. She stretched dramatically, arching her back and lifting her face to the sun as if posing for an invisible photographer.

"Okay, I'll admit it," Chelsie said, her eyes widening as she took in the yacht. "This is actually incredible. Your brother really went all out."

Zoey smiled, though something tight remained in her chest. "He always does."

They made their way down the dock, Chelsie's heels clicking confidently while Zoey walked with more measured steps. As they approached the gangplank, Zoey's eyes swept over the decorations—the roses, the hearts, and then the blood bags. She stopped for a beat, staring at them.

"Creative," Chelsie murmured, reaching out to tap one of the vials with her finger, watching it swing. "Very Sam."

The deck hand greeted them with leis, and as they boarded, Sam appeared from around the corner. His face lit up when he saw his sister. "Zoey!" He pulled her into a tight hug, lifting her slightly off the ground. "You made it."

"Of course I made it," Zoey said, laughing despite herself as he set her down. "Wouldn't miss your big debut."

Sam turned to Chelsie, his grin widening. "And you brought the fun one."

"Always," Chelsie replied, accepting his hug with easy grace. "Nice boat, Sam. Very murdery."

"That's what I'm going for," he said proudly. "Come on, there's champagne inside. Make yourselves comfortable."

As they moved toward the other guests, Zoey glanced back at her brother, catching something in his expression—excitement, yes, but also nervousness. The same look he'd had before every big presentation in school, every performance, every moment that mattered. She wanted to say something reassuring, but he was already moving, already headed to greet the next arrival, already performing.

Curtis appeared on the dock looking exactly like someone who'd been talked into something against his better judgment. His duffel bag hung from one shoulder, and his Hawaiian shirt—clearly a last-minute purchase—still had the fold creases in it. He walked with the slightly awkward gait of someone who wasn't entirely comfortable in beach attire, one hand shading his eyes as he squinted at the yacht.

"Jesus Christ," he muttered to himself, stopping to take it all in. "He actually did it."

Sam spotted him from the deck and immediately waved, his grin infectious. "Curtis! Get up here, man!"

Curtis climbed the gangplank, accepting his lei from the deck hand with visible skepticism. He held up one of the blood bag vials between two fingers, examining it like a specimen. "Corn syrup?"

"What else?" Sam said, appearing beside him and slapping him on the back hard enough to make him stumble. "You made it. Was starting to think you'd bail on me."

"Thought about it," Curtis admitted, but his smile took the edge off. "About five times on the drive here, actually. But some-one's gotta make sure you don't go full Kubrick on these people."

"Kubrick was a genius."

"Kubrick was insane."

"Exactly," Sam said, his eyes gleaming with that familiar manic energy Curtis had known since middle school. "Make sure to go meet everyone. And find me later. There's a props closet below deck you're going to lose your mind over."

"Of course there is," Curtis said, before heading toward the gathered guests.

Sam watched as a taxi pulled up to the dock, and before it had fully stopped, the back door flew open. Shea Colton tumbled out, fumbling with an overstuffed backpack and what appeared to be at least three different camera bags.

He burst onto the dock like a tornado of creative energy, his vintage band t-shirt already rumpled, his dark curls wild from what had clearly been a frantic morning. He jogged down the weathered planks, bags bouncing against his sides.

"Sam!" he called out, waving enthusiastically. "This is insane! The lighting out here is perfect—golden hour is going to be incredible later—"

Sam appeared at the railing, grinning. "Shea! Glad you could make it."

"Are you kidding? Murder mystery on a yacht? I've already got like fifteen composition ideas." Shea reached the gangplank, pausing to look up at the vessel with obvious awe. "Dude. This is gorgeous. Can I shoot it? Please tell me I can shoot it."

"You sure can," Sam said as Shea bounded aboard, accepting his lei from the deck hand. "But mingle first, art later."

Shea held up one of the blood bag vials, his eyes lighting up immediately. "Oh man. The way the light hits these—" He was already framing shots with his hands, his photographer's eye cataloging angles.

"Shea," Sam said, grabbing his shoulder before he could pull out his camera. "Meet people. Then photograph things."

"Right. Yes. People first." But Shea's eyes were still darting around, taking in every detail. "It's just—the aesthetic is so good, Sam. Seriously. Romance and horror? That's like visual poetry."

Curtis appeared beside Sam. "Well look what the cat coughed up."

"Curtis! How the hell is it going?" Shea said, giving him a hug.

"You still photographing weddings?" Curtis asked.

Shea nodded. "Yep. I need to pay rent somehow. What are you up to?"

"Lately, helping Sam not die in props-related accidents," Curtis replied.

"Important work," Shea said seriously, then his attention was already drifting toward the other guests gathering near the bow, his mind clearly racing with photographic possibilities.

"Go mingle," Sam said, giving him a gentle push. "And Shea? No social media until after the weekend. We want to keep the mystery contained."

Shea looked physically pained but nodded. "Fine. But I'm documenting everything for my portfolio."

As he headed toward the other guests, already introducing himself to Norma and Alice with his characteristic enthusiasm, Sam and Curtis exchanged a look.

"Think he'll make it five minutes without his camera?" Curtis asked.

"Not a chance," Sam replied, grinning.

As the group exchanged pleasantries around the ship, Sam's attention was drawn back to the dock, pulled by some instinct he couldn't name. His expression shifted, softening in a way that was almost vulnerable.

Lacy Lovette moved down the dock with hypnotic grace, her bright yellow sundress fluttering in the breeze like a flag of sunshine. The sunlight seemed to follow her, highlighting her every step.

Sam's chest tightened involuntarily, and for a moment, he could do nothing but watch her. The world seemed to quiet—the chatter of guests and cry of seagulls fading into background noise, until there was only her.

She spotted him standing at the rail, and her face lit up with a radiant smile that sent a jolt straight through him. Her hand lifted in a delicate wave, the gesture simple yet strikingly personal, intimate in a way that suggested a history between them.

Beside him, Gwen shifted almost imperceptibly, her sharp gaze darting between Sam and Lacy. A subtle, knowing smile tugged at her lips. She filed the information away.

The deck hand helped Lacy onto the yacht, draping a lei over her shoulders—the roses and blood bags settling against her yellow dress in perfect contrast.

As she stepped fully onto the deck, her eyes found Sam immediately, and he moved instinctively to meet her. "Hey. You came," he said, his voice softer than usual, almost hesitant.

Lacy tilted her head, her smile playful. "I RSVP'd, didn't I?"

Sam chuckled, rubbing the back of his neck. "I know. Just... glad you didn't change your mind. Wouldn't have been the same without you here."

"Yacht. Murder mystery. Weekend on a private island," she replied, counting off on her fingers. "How could I say no? Plus, I've been practicing my detective skills. I'm going to solve this before anyone else."

Sam's grin widened. "Confident. I like it."

Before he could say anything else, Gwen cleared her throat pointedly. "Sam, they're setting off. We need to get the intro ready. Five minutes."

Sam blinked, snapping out of the spell Lacy had cast. "Right. Yeah. Of course." He turned back to Lacy, his smile lingering. "I'll see you later. We're doing the full welcome in a few minutes. Enjoy yourself until then."

"I plan to," Lacy replied warmly, her voice carrying a promise that made Sam's smile widen.

As Sam and Gwen disappeared into the cabin—Gwen leading, Sam following with one last glance back—Lacy turned to join the group of guests gathering near the bow. The others welcomed her with open arms. Alice immediately pulled her into conversation, Norma offered her a champagne flute, and Russell made some joke that earned groans and laughter in equal measure.

As the yacht's engines rumbled to life, a deep thrumming that could be felt through the deck, the vessel pulled away from the dock. The sound of their voices echoed over the water, filled with excitement and anticipation for the weekend ahead.

CHAPTER SIX

The yacht sliced effortlessly through the open ocean, its sleek hull cutting a perfect path through the endless expanse of water. The horizon stretched in every direction, a seamless blend of crystalline blue sky and gently rolling waves. The sun hung high above, its light glinting off the water like thousands of shards of broken glass scattered across velvet.

Above deck, the mood was relaxed and carefree. Guests sprawled on cushioned lounge chairs or leaned against the polished railings, their conversations punctuated by bursts of laughter. Some had already changed into swimwear, soaking up the sun. The breeze carried away snippets of chatter—gossip, jokes, speculation about the mystery to come—mixing with the occasional clink of glasses.

Below deck, however, the atmosphere was noticeably different—quieter, more intimate, somehow heavier.

The yacht's parlor was an elegant retreat of dark wood paneling and plush furnishings that spoke of old money and refined taste. Warm, ambient lighting bathed the space, casting a golden glow over polished surfaces and creating pockets of shadow in the corners. The room smelled faintly of leather and expensive cologne, with an undertone of salt air.

The bar stood as the room's centerpiece—a curved mahogany structure with a granite top that reflected the overhead lights like dark water. Rows of spirits lined the shelves behind it, their labels a kaleidoscope of colors and languages. Top-shelf every-thing. No expense spared.

At the bar, Curtis fumbled with a bloody mary and a martini, his tongue caught between his teeth in concentration. He had the awkward air of someone trying too hard to impress, his movements jerky and uncertain.

As he turned toward the room, balancing both glasses with exaggerated care, the inevitable happened—a splash of red liquid escaped the bloody mary and splattered across the polished bar, spreading like a bloodstain across the granite.

"Shitballs," Curtis muttered, glancing around in panic for something to clean up the mess. With a resigned sigh, he resorted to his sleeve, dabbing at the spill with comical determi-nation. It wasn't particularly effective—his sleeve was now stained red and the bar still had a faint sheen—but it was better than nothing.

Nearby, a crystal vase of flowers sat on a side table. Among the roses—mostly red and white—was a single orange bloom that stood out like a flame, vibrant and impossible to miss.

On a whim, Curtis plucked it from the arrangement. He twirled it between his fingers, admiring how the petals caught the light, as he balanced the drinks in his other hand with precarious grace. A self-satisfied grin spread across his face as he turned toward the lounge area.

Across the room, Chelsie sat with another guest, their conversation clearly winding down. Chelsie's posture was relaxed, one leg crossed over the other, but her eyes were sharp, observing the space with quiet detachment.

When she spotted Curtis weaving toward her, drinks and rose in hand, she let out a subtle sigh. Her lips tightened for a moment—annoyance? resignation?—crossing her features. By the time he reached her, though, she had replaced her exaspera-tion with a polite, practiced smile.

Curtis's face lit up as he extended the bloody mary toward her like a triumphant prize. "Here you go. I got you a drink. Made it myself. Well, mostly myself. The bartender showed me where everything was."

Chelsie took the glass, her gaze immediately drifting to the vibrant orange rose in his other hand. She arched an eyebrow, genuine curiosity flashing across her face.

Curtis noticed her attention shift and, with dramatic flour-ish, held the rose out to her. "Oh, and this. I got this especially for you. You look like an orange kind of girl. Like, your energy is orange. Does that make sense?"

Chelsie accepted the rose, her fingers brushing against his briefly, and found herself studying the flower for a moment longer than she'd intended. It was beautiful, undeniably so. She looked back at him, a faint smirk tugging at her lips. "Do you even know what an orange rose means?"

Curtis blinked, his confident grin faltering. "Uh, no? It means something? Roses mean different things?"

She leaned back, twirling the rose lazily between her fingers. "Yeah. It's an expression of a fervent romance." She let the words hang in the air between them.

Curtis's brow furrowed as he processed this. "Oh. What's a fervent romance?"

Chelsie's laugh was soft, almost involuntary. Despite herself, she found his cluelessness oddly endearing. "A heated passion. A burning desire. Like, intense romantic feelings. The kind that consume you."

Curtis's face brightened immediately. "Oh! Well, I was going for normal romantic, but that could work too, right? I mean, romance is romance." He looked pleased with himself.

Chelsie shook her head slowly, her smile becoming more genuine despite her better judgment. "I don't think so. You've got the wrong hardware." She gestured vaguely at him, hoping he'd understand.

Curtis frowned, the comment sailing right over his head. "Wrong hardware? What does that mean? Like, I should have brought chocolates instead? I can get chocolates—"

Before the awkwardness could deepen, Sam strode through the parlor with purpose, a security guard in tow—a large, professional-looking man who seemed to be taking inventory of the space. As Sam passed, he leaned in briefly without breaking stride. "On the deck in five. We're doing the welcome."

Curtis and Chelsie both nodded quickly, the interruption a welcome reprieve. Curtis looked almost relieved, while Chelsie took the opportunity to take a long drink from her bloody mary.

Silence settled between them once again, heavier and more awkward than before. The ambient jazz playing softly through the yacht's sound system suddenly seemed too loud.

Curtis cleared his throat, fiddling with his martini glass. "I still think you're an orange kind of girl. The color suits you. Makes you look... warm."

Chelsie rolled her eyes, though the edge of her annoyance softened into something closer to amusement. She lifted her bloody mary and took a slow, deliberate sip. "Sure, Curtis. Whatever you say."

Curtis grinned, clearly taking her sarcasm as encouragement. He held onto that small victory—she hadn't told him to go away —as the room buzzed faintly around them. Other guests were starting to filter in from above deck now, their voices filling the parlor with renewed energy.

The game was about to begin.

Curtis took a sip of his martini, grimaced slightly—he'd probably made it wrong—and glanced at Chelsie one more time. She was looking at the orange rose again, turning it slowly in her fingers, her expression unreadable.

Maybe, Curtis thought with the eternal optimism of the

romantically deluded, this weekend wouldn't be a total disaster after all.

CHAPTER SEVEN

The yacht surged forward, cutting cleanly through the glittering sea. Its engines thrummed a low, steady roar that blended with the rhythmic lapping of waves against the hull. On deck, the festive energy was palpable. Heart-shaped balloons bobbed in the breeze, tethered to railings adorned with garlands of vibrant red roses. The vivid colors popped against the yacht's stark white exterior—the kind of over-the-top Valentine's display that managed to be both sincere and ironic.

Waiters in crisp white uniforms weaved gracefully through the mingling guests, their trays laden with champagne flutes that caught the light, chocolate-dipped strawberries glistening with a perfect sheen, and dainty hors d'oeuvres that looked almost too perfect to eat.

By the railing, Darren and Alice stood side by side, their silhouettes illuminated by golden sunlight. They looked the picture of happiness, their laughter easy and infectious as they chatted with Lacy who leaned casually against the edge of the deck. Lacy's yellow sundress caught the sunlight and billowed gently in the sea breeze.

A few steps away, Russell and Norma shared a plate of appetizers, their conversation punctuated by soft laughter and occasional eye rolls at Russell's dry humor.

Curtis lingered nearby, hovering awkwardly. He stood near Chelsie, who had her arm draped casually around Zoey's waist, her fingers resting comfortably on Zoey's hip. The subtle glances exchanged between them, the kind of looks that carried entire conversations, finally clicked something into place for Curtis.

The orange rose. The "wrong hardware" comment. It all made perfect, mortifying sense now.

Oh. Oh no.

Chelsie didn't seem to notice his discomfort—or maybe she chose not to, graciously allowing him to process his embarrassment in peace. Curtis avoided her gaze now, scanning the crowd desperately for anything that might distract him.

He didn't have to look far.

"Curtis the loser," came a cocky voice from behind him, cutting through his spiral. The drawl was unmistakable.

Shea approached, camera wrapped around his neck, with the confidence of someone who'd never met a room he couldn't work, a champagne flute in hand and a smirk firmly in place. Tattoos snaked up his wiry arms, visible beneath his rolled-up sleeves. His every move radiated mischief and self-assuredness.

"I hear there's a game room on board," Shea said, raising his glass. "Pool table, poker setup, the works. You want to check it out later? See if you've still got it?"

Curtis turned, relief flashing across his face at the perfectly timed interruption. "Sure. I'm always down for kicking your ass at something. Name your poison."

Shea smirked. "We'll see about that. Pretty sure I still remember that time you tried to bluff me with a pair of threes."

"That was one time," Curtis protested, laughing now, the awkwardness already fading. "And I maintain that you were cheating."

"Can't prove it," Shea said with a wink.

The sharp clink of a fork against glass rang out across the deck, cutting through the murmur of conversation like a bell. One by one heads turned toward the front of the yacht, conversations dying mid-sentence.

Sam stood at the bow, positioned perfectly against the backdrop of endless blue water and sky, his arms spread wide like a showman preparing for his grand reveal. He wore a confident grin, his eyes sparkling with the thrill of holding everyone's attention.

"Welcome, everyone," Sam began, his voice carrying easily over the crowd. "I trust you're all enjoying the food and drinks?"

A lively chorus of cheers and raised glasses erupted. Someone whistled. Russell shouted, "Free champagne is always good champagne!"

"Good," Sam continued, his tone dipping into something more dramatic, darker. "I'd like to thank you all for coming and, more importantly, tell you why you're really here."

The shift in his tone caught the crowd's attention immediately. Laughter faded into murmurs, and people leaned in slightly, their expressions shifting from playful to intrigued.

"You see, this was my aunt's yacht," Sam said, gesturing grandly around him. "The Red Ruby. Emilia, my aunt, named it herself. She did love rubies. And the island we're headed to? That was her island. Rose Island. *Was* being the operative word here, because, sadly, my aunt passed away a few months ago."

A hushed murmur swept through the crowd, a mix of sympathy and intrigue.

"They said it was a heart attack," Sam continued, his voice lowering just enough to make the words feel intimate, pulling everyone in closer. He paused, letting the tension build. "Or so they say."

The murmurs grew louder, whispers rippling outward. Sam raised a hand, calling for silence, his grin growing sharper. "In her will, my aunt left me a letter. A sealed letter that I was only supposed to open after her death. And in that letter, she told me something shocking—she believed her death wasn't natural. She believed someone wanted her gone."

Gasps punctuated the silence that followed. Even those who knew this was theater couldn't help but appreciate the delivery of Sam's words.

"She didn't know exactly who," Sam continued, his gaze sweeping over the crowd slowly, deliberately, making eye contact with different guests. "But Emilia, my aunt, was clever. Observant. And she narrowed it down to a list of suspects. People with motive, with opportunity, with secrets to hide."

He let the silence stretch. "And guess what?" His grin widened. "That's you."

The guests stiffened, their playful expressions giving way to a mixture of amusement, mock suspicion, and genuine curiosity. Some exchanged exaggerated glances. Others feigned shock, hands flying to their chests.

"This weekend," he said, his voice smooth as silk, "we're going to find out who the killer is. We're going to uncover secrets, follow clues, question each other's alibis. By Sunday night, there will be no more secrets. The truth will come out."

He gestured behind him with a dramatic flourish, pointing toward the horizon where a faint outline of land had begun to appear—just a dark smudge against the sky, but growing more defined by the minute.

"Straight out that way is Rose Island. And on it stands Castle De Amore, better known to those who've heard the stories as Murder Mansion."

A collective "ooh" rippled through the crowd, their excitement building.

"We'll arrive in about two hours," Sam said, his grin widening. "Until then, enjoy yourselves. Drink, eat, get to know each other—because you're going to need to figure out who you can trust. But remember—keep your eyes and ears open. This weekend, hearts will be broken."

He let the moment hang, his gaze sweeping the crowd one last time. Then he offered a slight bow and stepped back.

The murmurs and whispers returned almost instantly, guests exchanging theories, jokes, and knowing smiles. The energy had shifted, charged now with anticipation and playful suspicion.

Zoey plucked a fresh champagne flute from a passing waiter, swirling the golden liquid absentmindedly. "I hope Murder Mansion has a spa. I could really use a massage right now. And maybe a facial. Do murder mansions have facials?"

Chelsie laughed, squeezing Zoey's waist affectionately. "I don't think that's typically included in the murder package, babe."

Darren overheard and smirked, turning to Russell. "This weekend's already shaping up to be... interesting."

Russell chuckled, popping another appetizer into his mouth. "That's one word for it. I'm going with 'bizarre,' but interesting works too."

Alice laughed softly, her expression warm. "Well, at least everyone seems to be in the spirit. Look at them—they're already playing detective."

Norma, standing just a step away, nodded toward Zoey with a subtle tilt of her head, lowering her voice conspiratorially. "That's Sam's sister, isn't it? She's... a lot. Loves a drink, too, from what I've heard. Always has a glass in her hand."

Alice's smile tightened almost imperceptibly, but she brushed off the comment with practiced politeness. "She seems like she knows how to have fun. Nothing wrong with that on a weekend getaway."

Norma shrugged, the gesture carrying just a hint of judgment. "Maybe. I guess I've just never clicked with her. Different wavelengths, you know? She's very... loud."

"To each their own, right?" Darren said diplomatically, leaning down to plant a quick kiss on Alice's cheek, defusing the moment. She smiled, leaning into him, grateful for the intervention.

Around them, laughter, whispers, and champagne toasts filled the deck as the yacht pressed forward, cutting through the waves with purpose. The island grew slowly larger on the horizon, details beginning to emerge—the dark shapes of trees, the suggestion of structures.

Toward the mystery that awaited them.

CHAPTER EIGHT

The bow of the yacht pierced the ocean's surface like an arrow, cutting a perfect line through the vast, shimmering expanse of blue.

The soft breeze carried the briny scent of salt and freedom. It teased Lacy's hair as she stood near the railing, lost in thought, her fingers wrapped loosely around the cool metal. In her hand, a glass of champagne sparkled in the sunlight, the tiny bubbles rising in an endless stream like golden stars trapped in liquid.

Lacy tilted her head back and closed her eyes, letting the breeze kiss her face, feeling the warmth of the sun on her skin. It had been years since she'd been on a boat—not since that disastrous fishing trip with an ex—and the sensation of being cradled by the sea felt like a balm to her restless spirit. There was something humbling and invigorating about the ocean, its vastness making her feel wonderfully insignificant, like all her problems were just tiny specks that could be washed away by a single wave.

For the first time in a long while, Lacy felt the weight of her everyday struggles lift. No noisy cafes with broken espresso machines. No endless casting auditions ending with "We'll call you." No waiting tables for tips that barely covered rent. Just the sea, the sun, and a fleeting sense of infinite possibility.

She was so caught up in the moment that she didn't notice Sam approaching. He moved with practiced stealth, stopping just behind her. He tapped her left shoulder with a gentle touch, quickly slipping to the right. A mischievous grin spread across his face.

Lacy turned to her left, her brows furrowing in confusion when she found nothing but empty deck. She glanced the other way, only to find Sam leaning casually on the railing beside her, his grin boyish and completely unapologetic.

"Gotcha," he said, his tone light and teasing.

Lacy rolled her eyes, but couldn't suppress the smile tugging at her lips. "Very mature. What are you, twelve?"

Sam chuckled, turning his gaze toward the water. "Mentally? Probably. But it got you to smile, didn't it?"

"Barely counts if I'm smiling at how ridiculous you are," Lacy countered, but her tone was softer now, affectionate.

"Beautiful, isn't she?" Sam said, his voice quieter now, more sincere as he looked out at the endless expanse of ocean.

Lacy followed his gaze. The sunlight glinted off the waves, turning the ocean into a sea of liquid diamonds. She took a deep breath, filling her lungs with salt air. "Yeah. It's been too long since I've been out here. Years, actually. I forgot how incredible it feels. Makes you think anything's possible, doesn't it?"

Sam nodded slowly. "'Ships are the nearest things to dreams that hands have ever made,'" he quoted, his voice tinged with admiration. "Robert N. Rose. Don't know who he was, but damn if he didn't get that one right."

Lacy turned her head to look at him properly, studying his profile—the strong line of his jaw, the way the sunlight caught in his dark hair. Then, slowly, she smiled. "Yeah," she murmured, her voice soft but carrying weight.

Their eyes met, and for a fleeting moment, the rest of the world seemed to fade away. Something electric passed through the air—a recognition, a possibility.

Sam broke the silence first. "So, what have you been up to? It's been a while since I've seen you. Six months? Seven?"

"Eight, actually," Lacy said, and there was the tiniest edge to her voice—not accusation, just fact. "Since that Halloween party at Martin's place. You were dressed as Edgar Allan Poe."

"Right," Sam said, wincing slightly. "Time flies when you're drowning in paperwork and murder mystery logistics."

Lacy sighed, shifting her weight against the railing. She took a small sip of her champagne. "Oh, you know, the usual. Starving actress life. Serving mochas to people who don't know the difference between a latte and a cappuccino, hustling auditions for commercials I'll never book, living the dream." Her voice carried self-deprecating humor, but the words were tinged with weariness.

Sam chuckled, but there was sympathy in it. "The glamorous life, huh? I remember those days. Working three jobs to afford headshots, living on ramen and hope. Since taking over the company, I barely have time to write anymore."

Lacy tilted her head, her expression softening. "That's too bad. I know how much you loved writing. Your short stories were always so good—dark and twisted but with real heart. Your screenplays are wonderful. It's tough when the thing you're passionate about gets shoved to the back burner."

"It is. I find some time here and there still." Sam admitted. "But this?" He gestured to the yacht and the sea beyond. "It's worth it. I love what we're building here. Creating experiences, moments people will remember forever. I just... I don't want to give up on storytelling either. There's got to be a way to balance the two and I'm trying."

Lacy's lips curved into a small, knowing smile. "Sounds like a great whodunit script might be brewing in that head."

Sam's grin returned, wider now, the spark of ambition rekindling in his eyes. "Oh, you haven't seen anything yet. This weekend? It's just the start. I've got ideas for a whole series of these.

Different themes, different locations. Maybe even franchise it out."

"Always thinking big," Lacy said, and there was admiration in her voice.

"Why think small?" Sam replied, his eyes meeting hers. "Life's too short for small dreams."

For a while, they stood in companionable silence, the kind of quiet that only exists between people who are truly comfortable with each other. The yacht's steady rhythm carried them across the endless waves. The sound of champagne glasses clinking and distant laughter floated from the deck behind them, but neither moved to join the others.

Lacy's gaze drifted back to the horizon. The vastness of the sea was mesmerizing.

The breeze picked up slightly, catching a loose strand of her hair and sweeping it across her face. She started to reach up to fix it, but before she could, Sam was already there. Without thinking, he reached out, brushing the strand back with a gentle motion, his fingers barely grazing her cheek.

Lacy glanced at him, startled by the intimacy of the gesture. Their eyes met again, and this time, the moment lingered, stretched, neither of them pulling away. There was something unspoken in his gaze—curiosity, maybe, or admiration, or something deeper that he wasn't quite ready to name. Want, perhaps. Possibility.

Lacy felt her pulse quicken, the champagne suddenly feeling warm in her veins.

"Anything's possible," she murmured, almost as if speaking to herself, her voice barely above a whisper.

Sam didn't respond with words. But the way his gaze held hers made it clear he agreed, made it clear he'd heard her. A small smile tugged at the corners of his mouth. His hand lingered near her face for a heartbeat longer than necessary before he slowly let it fall, his fingers trailing along her jaw so lightly she almost wondered if she'd imagined it.

The yacht surged forward, cutting through the waves with purpose, carrying them closer to the island. The weight of possibilities pressed softly against the salt-swept air.

Behind them, the party continued—oblivious, cheerful, drunk on champagne and anticipation. But here, at the bow, the world had narrowed to just the two of them, to the space between, to everything they weren't saying.

And for now, that was enough.

CHAPTER NINE

The billiard room on the yacht's lower deck exuded an intimate charm, a masculine retreat that felt plucked from another era. Its dim lighting reflected off dark wood paneling—rich mahogany polished to a warm sheen—lending the space an old-world, nautical feel. Subtle details gave the room its character: brass fixtures that gleamed dully in the low light, a ship's wheel mounted on the wall like a trophy, and a compass rose embedded in the hardwood floor. The gentle sway of the boat added an unpredictable dynamic to every move, a constant reminder that they were at the mercy of the sea.

The pool table dominated the center of the room, its green felt illuminated by a low-hanging pendant light that cast a cone of brightness in the otherwise shadowy space. The felt seemed almost alive as the balls shifted slightly with the rhythm of the sea, rolling millimeters this way and that with each swell.

Curtis leaned over the table, his pool stick steady despite the gentle rocking beneath his feet, his expression focused and determined. His tongue poked slightly out of the corner of his mouth—a tell he'd never managed to break. The cue ball gleamed under the light, perfectly lined up with its striped target.

With a sharp crack, the cue ball struck home, sending the striped ball spinning across the felt and into the corner pocket with a satisfying thunk.

Curtis straightened immediately, a wide grin spreading across his face as he turned to Shea, who was slouched against the wall with his arms crossed. "Looks like it ain't your day, Mr. Shea," Curtis said, his tone dripping with playful arrogance. He clapped his opponent on the shoulder before circling the table with swagger.

Shea rolled his eyes dramatically, pushing off the wall with an exaggerated groan. "Who's shitty idea was it to put a pool table on a boat anyway? Takes the skill right out of the game. It's basically gambling at this point."

Curtis smirked, positioning himself for another shot, chalking his cue with unnecessary flair. "Oh, you mean this skill?" He struck the cue ball with precision, watching it kiss the striped ball at just the right angle and send it spinning into the side pocket.

Shea waved a hand dismissively. "Whatever, dude. The boat's doing half the work for you. Probably more than half."

Curtis shrugged, his confidence undiminished. "Guess we'll have to see if you're any better on solid ground. Though I'm not holding my breath."

That caught Shea's attention. His slouched posture straightened slightly, interest sparking in his eyes. "You think they've got a table at the mansion? At the Murder Mansion?"

Curtis leaned casually on his pool stick. "Are you kidding? Sam told me the place is stacked. Like, seriously decked out. A billiard room is basically a guarantee. Probably has one of those fancy antique tables, too."

Shea's smirk deepened. "Stacked like your mom? Because I've gotta say, that's a guarantee I wouldn't mind exploring further."

Curtis groaned, his head dropping as he shook it. "Here we go again. Seriously, why are you so obsessed with my mom's tits? It's getting weird, man."

"I'm not yet a silicon boy," Shea replied with mock sincerity, one hand over his heart. "I'm just hoping your mom will change that. You know, broaden my horizons."

Curtis burst out laughing. "You need help. Serious, professional help."

Shea shrugged, completely unbothered. "Maybe. But in the meantime, I've got you to keep me entertained. And your mom to think about."

"Oh my god," Curtis said, still laughing. "I'm telling her you said that."

"Please do," Shea replied with a wink. "Put in a good word for me. Tell her I'll give her a free photo shoot."

Curtis shook his head as he bent over the table again, his confidence at an all-time high as he lined up the eight ball for the final shot. This was it—the moment of glory. He took a breath, steadying himself, feeling the gentle sway beneath his feet, trying to time it right.

He struck the cue ball cleanly. For a moment, it seemed like the shot was doomed—the boat's subtle sway sent the cue ball wobbling slightly off course, and Curtis's face fell. But just as his confidence faltered, another shift in the yacht's motion corrected its path. The eight ball rolled steadily into the corner pocket with a satisfying clunk.

"Yes! Winner here!" Curtis declared, throwing his arms in the air like he'd just won the Olympics. His pool stick clattered onto the table, forgotten in his moment of triumph.

Shea snorted. "Pure luck. That boat did all the work. You basically just stood there."

Curtis turned with a wide grin, picking up his pool stick and twirling it in a mock fencing motion. "Luck? This is raw talent, my friend. Years of honing my craft. Maybe if you practiced more instead of thinking about my mom's—"

Before he could finish, Shea lunged forward, grabbing the stick mid-swing. With a quick yank, he pulled Curtis off balance, sending him stumbling backward until he landed awkwardly on the edge of the table, half-sitting, half-sprawled across the felt.

Shea loomed over him, triumphant. "Now those are skills. Real, physical, practical skills."

Curtis, caught off guard but not actually upset, let out a surprised laugh. "Alright, alright. Touché. You win the physical intimidation round." He pushed himself upright, brushing imaginary dust off his shirt. "But you might want to keep your distance for the rest of the weekend. With moves like that, you're definitely suspect number one."

Shea tilted his head, feigning deep thought. "Maybe. But don't worry—I'd beat you at pool before I actually murdered you. I've got priorities."

Curtis smirked. "Well, looks like I'm safe, then. At least until we get to the mansion and find that fancy table."

They both burst into laughter, the sound genuine and warm, the tension dissolving into easy camaraderie.

"I'm glad you put down that camera for a minute. This is nice. It's been awhile." Curtis said.

"It has." Shea replied. "It's going to be a lot of fun this weekend, but I definitely want to capture everything!"

He set his pool stick aside, leaning against the edge of the table. His fingers tapped idly on the wood as he glanced at Curtis, his grin fading into something more contemplative. "I wonder who the killer's going to be. Think whoever it is already knows? Or does Sam spring it on them at the last minute?"

Curtis tilted his head, considering. "Probably not. Knowing Sam, he'll drag it out for maximum drama. The guy's got more secrets than the CIA and loves every minute of it."

Shea chuckled. "Still, I wouldn't mind if it was me. I'd make a damn good killer. I've got the look, right?" He gestured at his tattoos.

Curtis raised an eyebrow. "You? Please. You'd get caught in two seconds. You can't keep a secret to save your life. Remember when you tried to surprise Martin for his bachelor party?"

"That was one time," Shea protested.

"You told him the same day we started planning it," Curtis pointed out. "The same day, Shea."

Shea's mischievous grin returned. "Maybe. But I'd have fun getting there. That's what counts, right?"

Curtis chuckled. "Well, if I'm the killer, you'll be the first to go. Curtis, in the billiard room, with the eight ball." He struck a dramatic pose, holding an imaginary weapon.

"Clue reference. Nice. Very thematic," Shea said, applauding slowly.

"Alright, alright, enough talk," Shea said, grabbing the pool stick with exaggerated flair. "Rack 'em, dick. Let's see if you can keep up the luck. Best two out of three."

"You mean three out of five?" Curtis countered, already moving to gather the balls.

"Don't push it." Shea said as he pointed the cue stick at Curtis. "It's almost murder time."

CHAPTER TEN

The yacht docked with a gentle bump against the wooden pier, the impact barely perceptible but enough to announce their arrival. Its sleek lines gleamed in the golden afternoon sunlight, the white hull reflecting the water's shimmering surface. The hum of its engines quieted to nothing, replaced by the soft lapping of waves against the hull and the distant cry of seagulls circling above.

One by one, Sam's guests began to disembark, their laughter and animated conversations cutting through the serene coastal atmosphere. Their shoes clattered against the sun-bleached planks of the dock before the path transitioned to the soft crunch of sand underfoot.

The island was a picture-perfect paradise. Turquoise waves lapped at white sand beaches that looked almost too pristine to be real, the shoreline dotted with smooth driftwood and scattered seashells that glinted like tiny treasures. Inland, a lush jungle stretched upward into rolling hills, a vibrant tapestry of greens punctuated by bursts of tropical flowers—scarlet hibiscus, brilliant orange bird of paradise, clusters of purple bougainvillea climbing toward the sky.

The air was thick and humid, heavy with the mingling scents

of saltwater, hibiscus, and sun-warmed earth. It was the kind of air that made you feel like you'd stepped into another world entirely.

The group moved in a loose, meandering cluster, each person soaking in the scenery at their own pace. Some stopped to take photos, others walked in reverent silence, and a few—like Curtis and Shea—were already making jokes about murdering someone in paradise, all while Shea snapped a thousand pictures.

Zoey lingered at the back, holding her phone aloft like a divining rod, frowning at the screen with increasing frustration. "Seriously? No signal? Of course there's no service. Why would there be service on a private island?" She sighed, lowering the phone. "Guess that Instagram post will have to wait. There goes my aesthetic beach entrance photo."

Chelsie, walking beside her with significantly less concern about the digital world, squeezed her hand sympathetically. "You'll survive a weekend without likes, babe. I promise."

"Will I though?" Zoey asked with mock despair, but she pocketed the phone and laced her fingers through Chelsie's.

A few steps ahead, Norma strolled with Alice, gesturing animatedly as she recounted what appeared to be a dramatic story. Alice listened with a warm smile, nodding at all the right moments.

Meanwhile, Russell trudged along behind them, his arms laden with more bags than seemed physically reasonable. Suitcases, tote bags, a garment bag draped over one shoulder, what looked like a cosmetics case clutched awkwardly under one arm. He huffed with each step, his face a mix of grim determination and reluctant endurance.

Lacy, walking light and carefree with a single, sensibly-sized bag slung over her shoulder, noticed Russell struggling. She slowed her pace to match his labored trudging. "Hey, looks like you packed your entire house. Need a hand? I've got two free ones going to waste."

She reached for one of the smaller bags, but Russell quickly stepped back, shaking his head. "No, no, thanks. If she sees me handing off her bags, I'm a dead man. Seriously. And you probably would be too, honestly. Collateral damage."

Lacy raised an eyebrow, her smile widening. "Ah. Got it. No interfering with the queen's luggage."

Russell chuckled, the sound tinged with weary acceptance. "Exactly. Norma doesn't mess around when it comes to her stuff. Everything has a place, everything has a purpose."

"Are different bags for different times of day or something?" Lacy asked, genuinely surprised.

"Oh, you have no idea," Russell said with a laugh.

Lacy grinned. "Hey, some girls like there options. Not all of us are like that, but nothing wrong with those who are."

Russell let out a sheepish laugh. "It's fine, really. She's... a handful. But she's my handful." He paused, then added with a self-deprecating grin, "The things we do for you girls. I mean, uh..." His voice trailed off as he realized the potential misstep. "Not all girls. Some girls. My girl, primarily."

Lacy grinned, clearly enjoying his flustered recovery. "Some girls. Not all of us demand a pack mule for a weekend trip. I believe in the one-bag philosophy myself. But, you're a good man."

They fell into an easy rhythm as they walked, their pace necessarily slower than the rest of the group. After a moment of comfortable silence, Russell glanced at her. "So, how do you know Sam? I don't think I've seen you at any of his other events."

Lacy hesitated, her smile faltering briefly before she recovered. "We dated. A couple of years ago. It was... brief but intense, you know?"

Russell raised an eyebrow, intrigued. "Really? Huh. I don't think I've ever heard about you."

Her lips twitched into a tight smile. "Well, we're not exactly close anymore. We talk occasionally. Run into each other at parties sometimes. It's friendly but... distant."

Russell's expression shifted as something clicked in his memory. His eyes widened. "Wait. Wait, wait, wait. Are you Cheeks?"

Lacy groaned audibly, but her laughter bubbled up despite herself, her cheeks flushing pink. "Yes, that's me. Oh god, he still calls me that?"

Russell laughed, nearly dropping a bag. "Sam's told me about you! Not much, but he's mentioned you. He always calls you Cheeks. I thought it was, like, a cute bartender he had a crush on or something."

"Nope, just me and my ridiculous face," Lacy said, covering her face with one hand. "It's from this face I used to make. Still make, apparently, when I'm surprised or thinking hard. It's involuntary."

"What face?" Russell asked, leaning in with genuine curiosity. "You gotta show me."

Lacy sighed, but she was smiling. She puffed out her cheeks and scrunched her nose, her eyes widening—like a confused chipmunk.

Russell burst into laughter. "Okay, that's hilarious. That's adorable. I get it now."

"It doesn't really work on demand," Lacy admitted. "It's better when it's spontaneous. But yeah, that's the face. Sam thought it was the cutest thing in the world when we were dating."

Russell's grin turned teasing. "So, ex-girlfriend invited to the romantic Valentine's Day murder mystery weekend. Sam's pulling out all the stops, huh? That's either really awkward or really strategic."

Lacy laughed softly, though her smile dimmed slightly. "I'm not really sure why he invited me, honestly. It seems like this is mostly for his close friends. People he works with, people he sees all the time. I almost feel like I'm crashing." She glanced around at the scattered group ahead. "But it should be fun. I've always loved murder mysteries. Used to read them obsessively as a kid."

Russell raised an eyebrow. "So, you don't know many people here?"

"I know a few, but not many," she admitted. "I met Shea briefly on the boat—awkward conversation about camera angles—and now you. I've met Curtis and Zoey before. That's about it. I almost didn't come, actually. Stared at the RSVP for like two weeks."

Russell laughed, nodding sympathetically. "Maybe that's why he invited you. Ulterior motives. Second chance romance. Very Valentine's Day appropriate."

Lacy shook her head firmly. "No. Definitely not. We're past that. Way past that. It's been years. He's probably seeing that Gwen woman—his assistant? They had definite chemistry on the boat."

Russell's tone shifted, growing more thoughtful. "Or maybe you're the red herring. You know, the classic mystery trope. No one here really knows you, which makes you suspicious by default. The mysterious outsider with unclear motives."

Lacy raised an eyebrow, considering the theory with genuine interest. "That would be pretty clever. Use the ex-girlfriend as a distraction while the real killer hides in plain sight. But it seems too obvious, doesn't it? My money's on someone no one would suspect."

Russell chuckled, a mischievous glint in his eye. "What if it's Sam? The ultimate twist. The mastermind pulling all the strings, orchestrating his own aunt's 'murder.' Very meta."

"That would actually be brilliant," Lacy said, laughing. "Very Agatha Christie."

They shared a laugh, their conversation carrying them along the winding path as it curved upward into the tropical hills. The air grew slightly cooler as they entered the shade of the jungle canopy, the sounds changing—less ocean, more birds and insects and rustling leaves.

Ahead, through breaks in the foliage, the mansion began to rise into view. It was massive, imposing, its towering silhouette framed by the vibrant greenery like something out of a Gothic novel. Dark stone, turrets reaching toward the sky, windows that caught the light and reflected it back like watching eyes. Its shadow stretched long and dark over the idyllic island.

Russell whistled low. "Well, that's not ominous at all."

"Murder Mansion," Lacy murmured, staring up at it. "Suddenly the name makes a lot more sense."

They quickened their pace slightly, drawn forward by curiosity and the knowledge that whatever was about to happen, whatever game Sam had constructed, it was waiting for them in that dark, beautiful building.

CHAPTER ELEVEN

The mansion loomed ahead, its silhouette rising like a dark crown against the vibrant greenery of Rose Island. The gothic architecture spoke of a bygone era, an age when buildings were meant to inspire awe and perhaps a touch of fear. Spires stretched toward the heavens like accusing fingers. Intricate stonework covered the facade—gargoyles perched at corners, their faces twisted into expressions of eternal anguish; elaborate carvings wound around windows and doorways like frozen vines.

Time had left its mark. Ivy crept along the walls, its tendrils weaving through cracks in the stone, as if the building were being slowly reclaimed by the jungle. Though modern renovations had softened some of its harsher edges—polished windows that gleamed in the sunlight, sleek exterior lights, fresh paint on the massive front doors—the juxtaposition only deepened its unsettling allure. It was a place caught between worlds, between past and present, between beauty and decay.

The guests paused at the edge of the mansion's shadow, their conversations faltering as they took in the imposing structure. Several tilted their heads back, trying to take in the full height, feeling suddenly very small. The air seemed heavier here, the distant crash of waves muted. Even the birds seemed quieter, as if the mansion commanded a certain reverence—or fear.

On the grand steps leading to the entrance, Sam stood with arms spread wide like a showman about to reveal his greatest trick. His grin was infectious, his presence commanding every eye.

"Welcome to Murder Mansion!" he declared, his voice carrying a theatrical edge, echoing slightly off the stone walls.

A wave of awe rippled through the group. Zoey and Chelsie exchanged wide-eyed glances, clutching each other's arms in giddy disbelief. Lacy, standing toward the back, let out a soft, "Wow," barely audible but heavy with genuine amazement. Even Shea simply nodded, his usual bravado giving way to genuine admiration.

Curtis whistled low. "This is insane. Like, actually insane. How did your aunt—"

"All will be revealed," Sam interrupted with a mysterious smile.

Sam stepped forward, descending one step so he was closer to his audience. His voice adopted the rich cadence of an orator well-versed in suspense. He gestured to the mansion behind him.

"She was built in 1878 by William Lovegood," he began, his words slow and deliberate. "A man of immense wealth and ambition. A shipping magnate who'd made his fortune in ways that were... let's say, morally flexible."

The guests listened intently. Norma leaned forward slightly. Russell shifted his bags to get more comfortable.

"He named it Castle De Amore for his wife, Rose," Sam continued, his hand sweeping toward the building, "and in her honor, the island became Rose Island. By all accounts, William was obsessed with her. Utterly devoted. Some said unhealthily so." He paused for effect. "But their marriage was built on a lie. According to legend—and every legend has a grain of truth, doesn't it?—Rose was no ordinary woman. She was a witch."

A ripple of murmurs passed through the group. Lacy tilted her head, her brows knitting together as she absorbed the tale.

"Rose cast a spell—a love spell meant to bind William to her forever," Sam went on, his tone growing darker. "For years, it worked perfectly. William was utterly devoted, blind to her true nature. He would have done anything she asked." He scanned the crowd, making eye contact with different guests. "But one day, he awoke, and the spell was mysteriously broken. And when he realized what she had done, when he understood that their entire marriage had been built on magical manipulation..." Sam's voice grew harder. "He was furious. Betrayed. Murderous."

The group leaned in, their anticipation palpable. Curtis's mouth hung slightly open.

"Determined to free himself completely, William searched the mansion from top to bottom. And in a hidden room behind the library, he found her spell book. An ancient tome filled with dark magic." Sam's eyes glinted. "He took it to the attic—the highest point in the house—and performed a spell of his own. A counter-spell. A truth-revealing spell meant to strip away all deception."

He paused, his voice dropping to barely above a whisper. "But when he came back downstairs... he wasn't the same. They say the house itself changed him. The spell had worked—it revealed all truths—but it had awakened something in the mansion itself. A rage. A hunger for truth that couldn't be satisfied."

Sam's voice rose suddenly. "He murdered his entire staff, one by one. The butler, the maids, the groundskeeper. Anyone who'd kept a secret, told a lie, hidden anything at all. The house demanded truth, and William became its instrument of judgment."

He lunged toward the group suddenly, his eyes wide and wild. "And just as he turned to kill his wife, knife raised above his head—SLICE!"

Several guests jumped. Alice let out a small shriek. Nervous laughter broke out.

"Rose," Sam continued, his voice lowering again, "stabbed him through the heart before he could strike. Self-defense. One thrust of a kitchen knife, right through his ribs. William Lovegood died that day—Valentine's Day, 1891. Bled out on the marble floor of the entrance hall." He gestured behind him. "Rose inherited the mansion and lived here alone until her death twelve years later. Some say she went mad with guilt. Others say the house drove her insane, whispering its demands for truth. Almost everyone says that whatever curse, whatever secrets this house holds, they are still here today. And that, my friends, is the legend of Murder Mansion."

The air felt thick with the weight of the story, the boundary between fiction and reality pleasantly blurred.

The group erupted into quiet chatter, questions and theories flying in hushed, excited voices.

Lacy stepped forward, her expression skeptical but intrigued. "Wait a second. So the house itself is... alive? That's what turned William into a killer?"

Sam turned toward her, his grin widening as though he'd been waiting for someone to step forward. "A very astute question, Lacy Lovette. A very similar name to Lovegood, I might add." He paused, letting the tension build. "That's the theory."

Sam raised a finger, his grin turning sharper. "That's the legend. William thought he was breaking Rose's spell, but he actually created something far worse. He gave the house power over everyone inside it." He let that sit before continuing. "And that's why we're here. To use the house's power to reveal the truth about my aunt's death. To see what secrets come to light when we're all trapped here together."

The group exchanged uneasy glances. The line between game and reality felt suddenly thinner.

Sam gestured dramatically toward the towering doors behind him—massive wooden things bound with iron, carved with intricate patterns. "Now, my friends, it's time to step inside. If you dare to reveal your darkest secrets. If you're brave enough to play."

With that, he turned and strode confidently into the mansion, his silhouette framed by the yawning doorway, swallowed by darkness. His footsteps echoed, then faded.

The group hesitated, exchanging nervous laughter and glances. The building seemed to wait, patient and hungry.

Zoey linked her arm through Chelsie's, whispering something that made them both giggle nervously. They moved forward together. Darren placed a reassuring hand on Alice's back, guiding her forward. Russell hung behind, still laden with bags, his eyes darting to the windows above.

Lacy lingered for a moment at the threshold, her gaze fixed on the heavy doors, on the darkness beyond. Something made her hesitate—instinct, maybe, or just the lingering effect of Sam's story.

"Come on, Cheeks!" Curtis called from just inside, his grin wide. "What's the worst that could happen? It's just a game!"

Lacy rolled her eyes but couldn't suppress her smile. Those were always the famous last words, weren't they?

With a deep breath, she stepped inside.

The air shifted as she crossed the threshold. Cooler, heavier, as though the mansion itself exhaled. The temperature dropped at least ten degrees, raising goosebumps on her arms.

The grand entrance hall stretched out before them, vast and imposing. High ceilings soared overhead, adorned with chandeliers that cast fractured light across the marble floors—the same floors where William Lovegood had allegedly bled out. The sound of their footsteps echoed ominously, multiplying, filling the space.

The group huddled closer together instinctively, their voices hushed. Above them, a grand staircase spiraled upward, its ornate railing twisting like ivy or skeletal fingers. Portraits lined the walls—stern-faced people in Victorian dress, their eyes seeming to follow the guests.

The mansion was magnificent and unsettling in equal measure, each detail hinting at secrets long buried, at stories that had played out in these rooms.

Somewhere deeper in the house, a clock began to chime, marking the hour.

CHAPTER TWELVE

The grand doors of the mansion groaned shut behind the last guest, the sound reverberating through the cavernous foyer like the final chord of a sinister symphony. The heavy thud felt final, absolute, like a coffin lid sealing or a trap springing shut.

A collective pause settled over the group as they took in their surroundings. The air inside was cool and heavy, noticeably denser than the tropical humidity outside, thick with a strange mix of romance and decay—fresh flowers and old death, perfume and dust.

Macabre paintings lined the walls in gilded frames, each depicting figures in unsettling poses. A woman in Victorian dress reaching toward something unseen, her face twisted in either ecstasy or agony. A man standing at the edge of a cliff, his back to the viewer. A child in a white nightgown holding a porcelain doll with cracked features. Their hollow eyes seemed to follow the newcomers.

Dusty tables adorned with vases of fresh red roses punctuated the gloom at regular intervals, the vivid petals a startling contrast to the faded wallpaper and dark wood paneling. The roses were perfect—too perfect, their blooms full and lush, their fragrance heavy and almost cloying.

Zoey wrinkled her nose and leaned closer to Chelsie. "It smells like Valentine's Day... and death. Like if a funeral home did themed parties."

Chelsie stifled a laugh. "Welcome to Murder Mansion. Where romance comes to die. Literally, apparently."

The guests shuffled forward tentatively, their footsteps echoing on the polished marble floor—each step multiplying into a dozen ghostly echoes. The acoustics of the space played tricks on the ear, making whispers sound louder and footsteps seem to come from multiple directions.

At the center of the foyer, a sweeping grand staircase dominated everything. Its bannister was ornately carved, polished to a deep mahogany sheen. The carvings depicted vines and roses intertwined with what might have been skulls or angels—it was hard to tell in the dim light. The staircase spiraled upward into shadows that the chandelier's light couldn't quite penetrate.

At the base of the stairs, Sam stood with his arms raised in dramatic flair, a grin of pure mischief lighting his face. Flanking him was a trio of staff, each positioned like chess pieces.

Stubby, the burly security guard, leaned lazily against the wall to Sam's left, his massive arms crossed over his chest. He had the build of someone who'd done serious time in a gym—neck thick as a tree trunk, shoulders straining against his black uniform. His expression was unreadable.

Leroy, a jovial cook whose broad smile radiated warmth, stood to Sam's right. He wore a pristine white chef's coat, his hands clasped in front of him. Everything about him suggested comfort food and laughter.

Kelly, a striking young woman whose perfectly tailored maid uniform drew more than a few lingering glances, stood at attention near the staircase. Her dark hair was pulled back in a neat bun, her posture that of someone trained in hospitality.

Standing slightly apart from the staff trio was Gwen. Poised and professional, she wore a burgundy business suit that made her look like she'd stepped out of a boardroom. Her clipboard was tucked neatly under one arm as she surveyed the group with cool assessment.

Sam clapped his hands together sharply, the sound cutting through the murmurs. "Ladies and gentlemen, welcome! Allow me to introduce your staff for the weekend."

He gestured toward Leroy first. "This is Leroy, our cook. He's the genius behind every meal you'll enjoy this weekend. Trust me, you'll want to enjoy them."

Leroy raised a hand in greeting, his grin broad and genuine. "In this house, murder's the main course," he quipped, his deep voice booming. "But don't worry—I promise the food won't kill you. That's someone else's job."

A smattering of chuckles rippled through the group.

Curtis groaned audibly, leaning toward Shea who was clicking away on his camera. "That joke's older than this mansion."

Sam continued with enthusiasm. "And this is Kelly, our server for the weekend. She'll make sure you have everything you need."

Kelly gave a playful bow. "At your service," she said, her voice carrying a slight accent.

Curtis nudged Shea. "Pretty young maid? That's like, suspect number one in every mystery ever."

Shea snorted. "Or victim number one. Fifty-fifty odds."

Kelly's eyes flicked toward them, her smile never wavering but something knowing flickering in her gaze.

"To my right," Sam said, motioning toward Stubby, "is Stubby. Security detail. He's in charge of keeping everyone safe and being your go-to guy if anything... unexpected happens."

Stubby gave a lazy thumbs-up, his expression remaining completely unreadable. His eyes, though, were sharp, constantly scanning.

"And last but certainly not least," Sam said, turning to Gwen with a smile that carried layers of meaning, "is Gwen, my right hand and the true mastermind behind all of this."

Gwen gave a slight nod, professional and controlled, her gaze sweeping the group with precision.

Curtis leaned toward Shea again. "Twenty bucks says Sam's sleeping with her. The tension is solid."

Shea smirked. "Not a chance I'm taking that bet. Too obvious."

Zoey, overhearing, turned and fixed them both with a withering glare. "You two are impossible. Do you have to sexualize every professional woman you see?"

Lacy shot them both an equally disapproving look. "Seriously? Can't you keep your juvenile commentary to yourselves?"

Curtis and Shea had the grace to look somewhat chastened.

Unperturbed, Sam pressed on. "There are maps of the mansion on the table. Your rooms are marked, as are some of the more... intriguing areas of the house. The library, the conservatory, the ballroom, the attic—places where secrets tend to hide."

He pointed toward a large window overlooking the western side of the property. "To the west, you'll find a hiking trail if you need some fresh air. It leads to a lookout point with a spectacular view." His hand shifted. "To the north, there's a private beach. White sand, calm water, very romantic."

The group murmured amongst themselves, their curiosity piqued.

Sam paced with exaggerated slowness, building anticipation. "Dinner will be served at seven sharp in the formal dining room. Until then, the house is yours to enjoy. Explore to your heart's content. But..." He paused dramatically. "One last thing you should know."

The room fell silent.

"The yacht has departed the island," he said, his tone casual but laced with unmistakable meaning. "There's no way off until Sunday afternoon. No boats, no helicopters, no convenient plot devices. Just us, this house, and whatever truth wants to reveal itself."

A ripple of unease passed through the group. Some

exchanged glances, their smiles faltering. Others chuckled nervously.

Zoey grabbed Chelsie's hand a little tighter.

Sam let the silence stretch before delivering his final line. "Enjoy your stay. Explore every corner. Trust no one." His grin turned wicked. "I'll see you at dinner. I hope."

With that, he turned on his heel and disappeared into the shadows of a nearby hallway, his footsteps echoing ominously before vanishing entirely.

For a moment, the group stood frozen, uncertain.

Zoey broke the tension with a nervous laugh. "Okay, he's definitely watched too many horror movies."

Curtis grabbed one of the maps, scanning it with exaggerated interest. "I don't know. I think he's just getting started. This is like Act One of a three-act play."

Chelsie shook her head. "He's got the drama down, I'll give him that."

Darren pulled Alice close. "It's all part of the experience. Right? This is what we signed up for."

"Right," Alice agreed, but she was gripping his hand tightly.

As the group began to disperse, breaking into smaller clusters, conversation buzzed through the room. Some clutched their maps like lifelines. Others exchanged speculative glances, already theorizing.

Shea and Curtis headed immediately for the game room. Russell was still juggling bags, looking for help.

Lacy lingered by the staircase, her gaze fixed on the shadowy corridor where Sam had vanished. Her fingers traced the edge of the banister absently.

CHAPTER THIRTEEN

The room Zoey and Chelsie had been assigned was nothing short of breathtaking, a space that seemed pulled straight from a fairytale—or at least from an interior design magazine they couldn't afford. The vaulted ceiling stretched high above, adorned with intricate crown molding. Delicate plasterwork created patterns of leaves and roses that wound around the room's perimeter.

Floor-to-ceiling windows lined one entire wall, flooding the room with golden afternoon light that danced across the dark hardwood floors—polished to such a shine you could almost see your reflection. The windows overlooked the island's western side, offering a view of jungle canopy that stretched toward distant hills.

A grand four-poster bed stood at the center like a throne, its dark wood frame carved with roses and vines. It was draped with soft, silken sheets piled high with pillows in varying shades of cream and gold. The effect was both opulent and inviting—the kind of bed you could get lost in for days.

To one side, through an arched doorway, a walk-in closet large enough to be its own room awaited, its mahogany shelving gleaming. It was a wardrobe-lover's dream, complete with a full-length mirror, a cushioned bench, and individual lighting.

Zoey stood in front of the open closet, pulling clothes from her suitcase with a mix of awe and genuine envy. "I wish I had this much closet space at home. Our entire apartment could fit in here. Just the closet. Not even the whole room."

Chelsie, meanwhile, had claimed the bed with enthusiasm. She sprawled across it dramatically, her arms flung wide. "We could just put a spell on Sam and take over the place. I'm sure there's a love spell in that book he was talking about. We could make him sign over the deed."

Zoey laughed, shaking her head as she returned to her meticulous unpacking. "Him and his stories. He's been obsessed with that kind of stuff since we were kids."

Chelsie rolled onto her side, propping her head up with one hand. "I still can't believe your brother is such a cornball. Like, he really committed to that whole performance downstairs."

"Be nice," Zoey said, mock-defensive as she folded a pair of jeans with geometric precision. "He's worked really hard on this. It means a lot to him."

Chelsie's grin turned mischievous. "It runs in the family. The cornball thing."

Zoey turned to face her, one hand on her hip, trying to look stern but failing. "Don't even start. I will whoop your little ass."

"Oh, yes, please," Chelsie teased immediately, smacking her own backside lightly. "I've been very bad. I need discipline."

Zoey rolled up a shirt that she had in her hands and snapped Chelsie right in the butt with it.

"Ouch! Oh. Mmm. Babe," Chelsie said. "That hurt and felt good all at the same time. Can I have another please?"

"Later, my little brat kitten. Later." Zoey said as she began to tickle Chelsie. Chelsie tickled back and they both started laughing.

Their laughter filled the room, echoing off the high ceilings and blending with the warm sunlight streaming through the windows.

When they settled down, Zoey gave Chelsie a soft kiss and then finished unpacking with methodical care, snapping her suitcase shut with a satisfying click and sliding it neatly into the bottom of the closet. She turned to Chelsie, whose bag sat untouched near the door.

"You're not going to unpack?"

Chelsie blinked innocently. "Later. Right now, I want to relax. We're on vacation. Murder mystery vacation, but still vacation."

Zoey rolled her eyes but couldn't help smiling. "Fine. You've got the right idea, actually. We should enjoy this while we can."

She crossed the room and flopped onto the bed beside Chelsie, sinking into the plush mattress with a contented sigh. The bed was every bit as comfortable as it looked—maybe more so.

Chelsie immediately wrapped an arm around her, pulling her close, their bodies fitting together in the comfortable way of people who'd spent many nights like this. For a moment, they lay in comfortable silence, just breathing, just being. The faint sound of waves crashing in the distance added a soothing rhythm.

Zoey turned her head slightly, a playful smile tugging at her lips. "Ever shopped in the guy department?" she asked out of nowhere.

Chelsie tilted her head, bemused. "The guy department? Once, but they were all sold out." She paused, then added with perfect timing, "Or maybe I just couldn't find anything in my size."

Zoey laughed, nudging her gently. "Figures. Your standards are too high."

Chelsie's smile softened as she absently toyed with her earring. "There was one guy, once. In college. Before I really figured things out. But it turns out he was also shopping in the guy department."

Zoey chuckled. "That explains a lot. The universe was trying to tell you something."

Chelsie shrugged, brushing the thought away with a flick of her hand. "Ancient history. Anyway, screw guys this weekend—and girls, for that matter. Other girls, I mean. This weekend is all about you, me, food, drink, and murder. In that order."

Zoey smirked, turning onto her side to face her properly. "Your little puppy dog Curtis won't like that attitude. He's probably planning his next attempt at wooing you right now."

Chelsie's grin turned wicked. "Oh, you noticed? Yeah, that orange rose thing was adorable in a completely misguided way. I think I'll mess with him a bit. It's too easy."

Zoey groaned in mock exasperation. "Poor thing. He's got the love bug bad. I saw him watching you on the boat like you were the only person there."

Chelsie shrugged. "He's harmless. Kind of sweet, actually, in that completely hopeless way. Besides," she added, her voice dropping lower, "you're lucky he's such a McLovin. Otherwise, you might have some competition."

Zoey rolled her eyes but leaned closer, her voice dropping to a sultry whisper. "I'm not worried. I'm the only one who'll be McLovin you."

Before Chelsie could respond, Zoey moved with surprising speed, straddling her with a playful grin, leaning down until their faces were inches apart.

"Now," Zoey murmured, her voice low and teasing, "let me show you what real competition looks like."

Chelsie's witty retort died on her lips as Zoey leaned in, claiming her mouth in a kiss that was equal parts playful and passionate. The giggles that had bubbled between them earlier faded, replaced by something warmer, deeper, more urgent.

Zoey's hands slid down Chelsie's sides with deliberate slowness, her touch both gentle and teasing, knowing exactly where to linger. She drew out soft gasps from her partner.

Chelsie arched into her, her fingers tangling in Zoey's hair, pulling her closer.

"Oh, now you're unpacking," she managed to murmur, her voice breathless.

Zoey chuckled against her skin. Her lips trailed from Chelsie's mouth to her jaw, down to her neck, across her collarbone, each kiss deliberate and purposeful. "Just making sure everything's in its right place," she whispered against Chelsie's throat, her hands deftly finding the button of Chelsie's jeans.

The rest of the room faded into the background—the luxurious surroundings, the golden light, the distant sound of waves, the fact that they were in someone else's house on an island with a dozen other people. All of it became irrelevant as they lost themselves in each other.

For that moment, suspended in the afternoon light, the world outside didn't exist. There was only the warmth of the bed beneath them, the weight of their shared laughter and secrets and history, and the electric connection between them.

CHAPTER FOURTEEN

The lounge was a welcome contrast to the mansion's imposing grandeur, offering a space that felt intimate and inviting. It was clearly designed as a masculine retreat—the kind of room where men of means would have retired after dinner to smoke cigars and discuss business. The dark wood paneling gleamed faintly in the low light, the flicker of the fireplace casting warm, dancing shadows. A faint smell of aged leather and smoky wood hung in the air, mixing with whiskey and something else underneath—old books, maybe, or the mustiness of a room closed up too long.

Plush armchairs upholstered in deep burgundy leather were arranged around a massive leather couch. All the furniture was centered on a glass coffee table bearing evidence of an afternoon spent unwinding: empty crystal glasses with melting ice, a half-eaten bowl of pretzels, and scattered coasters.

Russell and Darren occupied the couch, their relaxed postures mirroring the room's laid-back vibe, both having shed their jackets and rolled up their sleeves. Russell swirled his whiskey lazily, his eyes fixed on the fire. Darren leaned back, cradling a tumbler of scotch, his demeanor calm but his gaze sharp.

"So, Paris, huh?" Darren said, breaking the comfortable silence. His tone was casual, but there was genuine envy threading through it. "I'd love a job that paid me to travel. All I get is the occasional conference in Cleveland. Not exactly exotic."

Russell smirked, taking a slow sip. "It has its perks. But don't get too jealous. Most trips are just airports and boardrooms. Taxi, hotel, meeting, hotel, taxi, airport. Not exactly the Emily in Paris experience."

Darren tilted his head, curious. "Still, it must be nice to see different places, even if you're working. How do you make it work with Norma? Long distance has to be rough."

Russell let out a short laugh that didn't quite reach his eyes. "Honestly? The less we're around each other, the less we argue. Distance isn't always a bad thing. Sometimes it's the thing that keeps you together."

The bluntness hung in the air, sharp and uncomfortable.

Darren frowned slightly but chose not to press. Instead, he swirled his glass, searching for safer ground.

Russell noticed the hesitation and softened his tone. "We're not like you and Alice. You guys are perfection personified. High school sweethearts, right? Still madly in love?"

Darren chuckled, shaking his head with genuine humility. "I got lucky. Really lucky. Right place, right time, right person."

"It's sickening, really," Russell teased, though there was no real malice. "The way you two look at each other. Like you're still on your first date."

"Eleven years and counting," Darren said with obvious pride.

For a moment, they lapsed into silence, the crackle of the fire filling the gaps. They weren't close enough friends for complete ease—they'd met through these murder mystery circles, ran in the same social orbit, but didn't really know each other beyond surface pleasantries.

"So," Russell said suddenly, leaning forward to set his glass on the table, breaking the uncomfortable quiet, "who do you think's gonna bite it at dinner?"

Darren raised an eyebrow. "Bite it?"

"You know, get 'killed,'" Russell clarified, making air quotes. "It's a murder mystery, after all. Someone's bound to go first. Probably dramatically, knowing Sam."

Darren chuckled. "Who knows? Maybe no one tonight. Maybe the killer stays hidden the whole weekend and we're all just paranoid. That would be a mindfuck."

Russell snorted. "Unlikely. Way too boring. My guess is that someone 'dies' tonight—probably during or right after dinner—and the rest of us have to piece together what happened."

Darren nodded slowly, considering. "Yeah, makes sense. But it's gonna suck for whoever gets knocked out early. What do they do all weekend?"

Russell leaned back, stretching his arms along the back of the couch. "Probably. If Sam has any sense, it'll be one of the staff—like that cook, Leroy, or Stubby. They're expendable to the story." He paused, swirling his whiskey. His smirk turned sharper. "But if it's one of us? My money's on Lacy."

Darren's brow furrowed. "Lacy? The woman in the yellow dress? Why her?"

Russell shrugged, his tone matter-of-fact. "She's the odd one out. Doesn't really fit with the rest of us. Ex-girlfriend showing up to a Valentine's weekend? That's classic murder mystery victim material."

Darren's frown deepened, a defensive note creeping into his voice. "She seems nice enough. I talked to her on the boat. She's into mystery novels, actually. Knows her Agatha Christie."

"Nice doesn't mean she belongs," Russell countered, his bluntness cutting through the atmosphere. "She's... different. Quieter. Watching everyone instead of engaging. That's suspicious in a murder mystery, right? Either she's the killer or the first victim."

Darren opened his mouth to respond, to push back on the casual cruelty, but before he could, the door creaked open.

Shea strolled in, his swagger unmistakable, his energy immediately filling the room along with the flash of his camera.

"Gotta get those candids'" he said before making a beeline for the bar, grabbing a crystal tumbler and pouring himself a generous measure of bourbon.

"What's up, boys?" Shea called over his shoulder, his grin wide. "Having some quality bro time? Should I leave you to your emotional bonding?"

"Just enjoying the scenery," Darren replied, raising his glass. "And the whiskey."

Shea turned, holding up his drink in a mock toast. "To Sam's aunt, the real MVP for leaving him all this. God bless that woman and her excellent taste in real estate."

Darren chuckled, lifting his glass. "I'll drink to that. Hell of an inheritance."

Shea dropped onto the couch beside them with a contented sigh, swirling his bourbon. "To a fucking awesome weekend. Murder, mystery, and top-shelf liquor. What more could a man want?"

Russell and Darren joined the toast, raising their glasses. "To a fucking awesome weekend," they echoed, and for a moment, the tension dissipated.

As the fire crackled softly, as Shea launched into a story about some bar in Portland, Darren's thoughts lingered on Russell's earlier comment about Lacy. It didn't sit right with him —the casual dismissal, the way Russell had written her off as not belonging.

She didn't seem like someone who didn't belong. If anything, she seemed more thoughtful than most of them, more observant.

Darren glanced at Russell, who had gone back to swirling his whiskey, his expression unreadable as he half-listened to Shea's story.

Shea, oblivious to the subtle tension, stretched out on the couch, clearly in his element.

The conversation shifted to lighter topics—football predictions, travel mishaps, favorite bars. Russell told a story about a business dinner in Tokyo. Shea countered with something about Vegas that was probably fifty percent fabricated.

But underneath the easy banter, Darren couldn't shake the feeling that Russell's words carried more weight than he let on. That his comment about Lacy wasn't just speculation about the game but something else—prejudice, maybe, or jealousy, or some other emotion he couldn't quite name.

The game hadn't even officially started, but the room already felt charged with something beyond just anticipation. There were undercurrents here, tensions between people who barely knew each other, judgments being formed and alliances being considered.

The mansion's walls seemed to lean closer, listening, the wood paneling seeming to absorb their words. The firelight cast longer shadows now as afternoon waned toward evening, creating pockets of darkness the flames couldn't quite reach.

The game would begin soon.

But the men in the lounge, drinking their expensive whiskey and making their casual judgments about who would die first in a game—they had no idea what was really coming.

CHAPTER FIFTEEN

Sam's room was a blend of organized chaos and theatrical flair, a perfect reflection of its owner's personality—part creative genius, part obsessive planner, all showman. It was smaller than the guest rooms but more personal, more lived-in, with the comfortable clutter of someone who actually used their space.

A large oak desk occupied one corner, its surface buried under scattered notes in Sam's tight handwriting, hand-drawn diagrams of the mansion, and prop blueprints. The centerpiece was a detailed map of the entire property—house, grounds, beach, trails—annotated with arrows indicating movement patterns, question marks hovering over key decision points, and red Xs marking where "events" would occur. It resembled a grandmaster's chess board.

The walls were a collage of vintage murder mystery posters, each one carefully framed—The Maltese Falcon, Laura, Dial M for Murder, Rope. Between the posters, cork boards displayed photographs from past events, newspaper clippings about his aunt's company, and what looked like a timeline with strings connecting different points like a conspiracy theorist's fever dream.

The faint smell of stage makeup and latex lingered—that particular chemical scent of theatrical supplies—mingling with the musk of old wood, coffee grounds, and something else underneath: nervous energy made manifest.

A clock hung above the desk, its rhythmic ticking a steady reminder of the evening's approaching deadline. The hands were inching closer to seven—6:47 now—when the game, and the night's first "murder," would officially begin.

Curtis sat at the desk, hunched over the scattered papers with exaggerated concentration. He tapped a pen against the wood in an irregular rhythm, furrowing his brow in mock intensity. "Hmm," he muttered to himself. "Very interesting. Very suspicious indeed."

The room's stillness was abruptly shattered when a machete erupted through his chest with a dramatic thunk. Curtis's body jerked forward violently, his face smacking the desk. A splatter of fake blood—a convincing blend of corn syrup and food dye—sprayed across the papers, painting carnage across Sam's carefully annotated maps.

From behind him, Sam stepped into view, emerging from where he'd been crouched behind Curtis's chair. His expression was calm and calculating as he assessed the visual effect. He glanced at the clock—6:48—and nodded in satisfaction.

"Not bad," he said casually despite having just "murdered" his best friend. "Think you're ready? The timing looked good."

Curtis lifted his head slowly, revealing a face that wore a wide grin despite the machete protruding from his chest. "Hell yeah! Let's get slaughtered! I was born for this role."

Sam rolled his eyes but couldn't hide his amusement. He crouched down to lift the hem of Curtis's torn shirt—already pre-torn for effect—and reveal the padded vest underneath, an impressive piece of engineering. The machete's retractable ends had slid seamlessly into pre-cut slots, the illusion flawless.

"Hold still," Sam instructed, pushing the retractable blades back into place with a firm click. "This thing's trickier to reset than it looks. If you jostle it wrong, the whole mechanism jams."

Curtis craned his neck to watch. "Man, this is genius. How the hell did you make it look so real?"

Sam smirked, straightening the vest. "Trade secret. Years of obsessing over murder mysteries finally paid off. All those nights researching practical effects, watching behind-the-scenes footage, messaging prop makers at 3 AM."

With the machete reset, Sam grabbed a fresh shirt from a nearby rack and a bottle of fake blood from the desk, squeezing more crimson liquid into the vest's hollow compartments.

"Alright," Sam said, stepping back to examine his work. "Now for the final touch. We need you looking properly murdered."

Curtis peeled off the tattered shirt, revealing the vest smeared with remnants of previous rehearsals—they'd practiced this at least a dozen times. He pulled on the new shirt, crisp and white, perfect for showing blood, as Sam circled him like a fashion designer, adjusting the fabric, making sure it hung just right.

The details had to be perfect. First impressions mattered. The first murder set the tone for everything that followed.

Sam grabbed a damp cloth and wiped the sticky residue from his hands. He glanced at the clock again—6:52. The ticking seemed louder now, more insistent.

"Remember," Sam said, his voice low and serious as he leaned in close. "This is the first big moment of the night. You've got one job: make it look real. No overacting, no cheesy theatrics. Just... dead. Convincingly, disturbingly dead."

Curtis raised an eyebrow, his grin unfazed. "Relax, Sam. I've been practicing my dead face since middle school math class. Mrs. Henderson's lectures on quadratic equations? Pure death."

Sam smirked despite himself. "That's not exactly reassuring. I need commitment, not boredom."

Curtis spread his arms dramatically, striking a pose. "Come on, man. Look at me! I'm the picture of a tragic murder victim. I could be on a crime show."

Sam crossed his arms, skeptical but amused. "We'll see. Just remember—this sets the tone for the whole weekend. You screw it up, and the mystery unravels before it even starts. You're the hook."

Curtis saluted with mock solemnity. "Yes, sir. I promise to die with dignity. Future generations will speak of Curtis Garlan's performance."

Sam chuckled. "I'm counting on you. Seriously. Don't make me regret casting you."

"You won't," Curtis promised, his tone shifting to something more genuine. "I've got this. We've practiced enough. It's going to be perfect."

The clock struck seven, the chime echoing through the house.

Sam straightened, his entire demeanor changing, his expression sharpening with purpose. The director was back, the showman ready to perform.

"Alright," he said, his voice steady despite the adrenaline. "Time to kick this off. Let's go make some memories. Or at least give them a good story."

Curtis gave him a thumbs-up, his grin wide. "Or nightmares," he added with a wink.

"Why not both?"

As they left the room—Sam first, Curtis hanging back a predetermined amount, following the choreography they'd rehearsed—Sam's mind buzzed with anticipation. Every nerve felt alive, electric. This was it. The culmination of months of planning, of late nights and early mornings, of details obsessed over and contingencies planned for.

The game was about to begin, and he knew that every detail —from Curtis's "death" to the screams that would follow, to the whispers of suspicion and the accusations that would fly—would set the stage for a weekend none of them would ever forget.

His aunt would have been proud.

At least, he hoped so.

CHAPTER SIXTEEN

The dining room exuded eerie grandeur, a stage perfectly set for what was about to unfold. It was the kind of room that demanded formal dinners and hushed conversations, where generations of wealth had gathered over multiple courses and vintage wines. The elongated table stretched nearly twenty feet beneath a massive crystal chandelier, its countless prisms catching and refracting the flickering light of candles placed strategically along the polished mahogany surface. Each candle sat in an ornate silver holder, their flames dancing despite the lack of any breeze.

Shadows danced on the ornate wallpaper—deep burgundy with gold filigree patterns—and dark wood paneling that rose halfway up the walls, creating an ever-shifting backdrop. The remnants of the meal—half-eaten dishes, scattered utensils, and nearly drained wine glasses with lipstick marks—spoke of indulgence and distraction. The muted hum of conversation filled the space with the comfortable buzz of people who'd been eating and drinking for over an hour.

Russell leaned back in his chair at one end of the table, his posture relaxed, his glass of wine swirling lazily. Kelly, the maid, leaned across him to clear a plate, her movements efficient and professional, but as she reached, Russell's eyes flicked downward to her neckline before a smirk crept onto his lips, concealed by raising his glass.

Norma, seated beside him, remained oblivious, her focus locked on Lacy seated across the table. "I know!" Norma exclaimed. "They're huge! And the bathrooms? Totally ridiculous. Mine has a clawfoot tub that could fit three people."

Lacy chuckled, nodding. "This place is like something out of a storybook. There's probably hidden passages behind the walls, trap doors, secret—"

Her words were cut short as the room plunged into absolute darkness.

A collective gasp rippled through the group, sharp and startled, followed by nervous laughter that tried to mask genuine unease. Chairs scraped against the hardwood floor. Feet shuffled as the guests shifted, instinctively reaching for the table's edge, for their companions, for anything solid.

"What the—" someone started.

"Is this part of it?" Zoey's voice, uncertain.

"Must be," Darren's reply, but he didn't sound convinced.

The darkness pressed in from all sides, oppressive and absolute. The candles had gone out—all of them, simultaneously—and without the chandelier's light, the room became a void.

Then, breaking the silence, came a sound that sent a chill through the room—the unmistakable, wet slice of a blade tearing through flesh and fabric. It was visceral, raw, deeply unsettling. Not the clean swoosh of movie swords, but the horrifying schlick of metal meeting resistance.

A low, guttural groan followed, a sound of genuine pain and surprise, trailing off into a wet gurgle and then nothingness.

"Jesus," someone whispered.

Finally, a heavy thud echoed through the space as something —or someone—hit the table hard, silverware and glasses rattling with the impact. The room fell deathly silent, save for shallow, unsteady breathing.

The darkness seemed to last forever but was probably only fifteen seconds. Fifteen seconds that felt like minutes.

A soft click broke the stillness, and the chandelier's light flickered back on, first dim, then brightening, bathing the scene in its warm, golden glow.

All eyes turned immediately to Curtis's seat. His body lay slumped forward, his face pressed into the pristine white linen tablecloth, his arms splayed awkwardly. A machete jutted grotesquely from his back at an angle, the blade coming through his chest, its handle pointing toward the ceiling. The weapon gleamed faintly in the candlelight.

Blood—thick and shockingly realistic—pooled beneath him, spreading in a crimson halo that seeped into the white linen. It dripped steadily onto the floor from the tip of the blade, each drop making a soft pat sound that seemed impossibly loud in the shocked silence.

For a moment, no one spoke, no one moved. The scene was too perfectly staged to immediately process, too visceral to laugh off. Several guests had gone pale.

Then, as realization dawned that this was the game, the mystery, the thing they'd come for—the guests erupted in impressed reactions.

"Oh my God!" Zoey gasped, leaning closer with wide eyes. "That's insane. It looks so real! The blood is spreading!"

Chelsie grinned, inspecting the machete from her seat. "The blood work is amazing. Did Sam outsource this to Hollywood? That's professional-grade."

Lacy's gaze lingered on the scene, taking in every detail. Her lips curved into a small, impressed smile. "That's some serious commitment. The timing of the lights, the sound effects, the positioning. He really went all out."

Russell leaned back, his earlier discomfort evaporating. "Of course, it's Curtis. The guy lives for this kind of drama. Probably volunteered to be first."

Darren let out a low whistle, raising his glass in a mock toast toward the "corpse." "Well, that sets the tone. Bravo, Curtis. Hell of a performance."

Alice, who'd been clutching Darren's arm, finally released her grip and laughed shakily. "I actually jumped. My heart is racing."

Sam shot to his feet at the head of the table, his chair scraping back dramatically. His face was a mask of triumph and theatrical delight, eyes bright with success. He clapped his hands together once, the sharp sound commanding attention.

"Ah-HA!" he exclaimed, his voice booming. He began pacing the length of the table, his movements deliberate and predatory. "The house wastes no time! Murder Mansion demands blood, and it has claimed its first victim!"

He gestured emphatically to the table. "Curtis Garlan has fallen! Slain at dinner on Friday night, February 12th, at precisely 8:01 PM. A machete through the back—a weapon of brutality— a pool of blood, and ten suspects seated right here! One of you has done this. One of you is a murderer."

The guests exchanged amused glances, leaning into the game.

Zoey leaned closer to Chelsie, whispering, "He's having the time of his life."

Chelsie smirked. "I don't think I've ever seen him this happy. This is his element."

Sam raised his arms again. "Now," he said, his tone dropping to a conspiratorial whisper that made everyone lean in, "we must unravel this heinous crime. Who among us has blood on their hands?"

He let the question hang. "Curtis was murdered in darkness. The killer moved swiftly, silently, striking without mercy. But surely someone saw something. Heard something. Noticed something amiss."

With a flourish, he gestured toward the door. "Everyone, to the lounge! Bring your suspicions, your alibis, your accusations. The investigation begins! And remember—" his voice darkened, "—the killer walks among you."

The group rose from their seats, some moving with playful

excitement, others feigning reluctance for dramatic effect. Shea stood with exaggerated suspicion. Norma grabbed Russell's arm, playing the nervous witness. Darren helped Alice from her chair with protective gallantry.

Lacy lingered behind, her eyes fixed on Curtis's "corpse," studying the scene with genuine fascination. She tilted her head, examining the angle of the blade, the spread of the blood. A faint smirk tugged at her lips. "Do you think he's just lying there loving every second of this?"

Russell, hanging back with her, smiled as they began walking. "Knowing Curtis? He's probably grinning into the tablecloth."

Zoey, walking a few steps behind them, glanced back one more time. "The detail, though. That machete is crazy realistic. Like, I know it's fake, but my brain is having trouble accepting it."

"That's the point," Lacy replied. "Good prop work creates cognitive dissonance. Makes you doubt your own certainty."

As the guests filed out in twos and threes, their chatter and laughter filled the hallway, debating suspects, recreating the darkness, speculating about clues.

Curtis remained at the table, motionless, the centerpiece of a macabre display. The flickering candles cast long shadows across the blood-streaked tablecloth, the room steeped in eerie silence now that the audience had departed.

If anyone had stayed behind, they might have noticed his chest still rising and falling with careful, shallow breaths. They might have seen his finger twitch slightly.

But no one did stay.

The first murder was complete.

The investigation had begun.

CHAPTER SEVENTEEN

The lounge buzzed with the electric hum of curiosity and post-dinner wine, the perfect setting for the drama unfolding within its walls. The dim lighting cast flickering shadows across dark wood paneling, while the fireplace crackled softly, its flames dancing in warm contrast to the chill of mystery in the air. Plush armchairs and a large leather couch formed an inviting circle, their occupants sipping drinks as light-hearted banter filled the space. Crystal glasses clinked, and the faint aroma of whiskey and brandy mingled with the smoky scent of burning logs.

Sam paced in front of the fire like a caged tiger, his hands clasped behind his back, exuding the energy of a detective on the brink of revelation. He paused occasionally, his sharp eyes sweeping the group, lingering just long enough on each person to sow a hint of unease. His presence commanded attention, and the room fell into an expectant hush.

"Well," he began, his voice low and deliberate, "we already have so much to think about. So many questions, so few answers." He began ticking items off on his fingers. "Why Curtis? What was his secret? How did the killer do it? The lights went out for mere seconds—how did they move so quickly? Who did it?" His eyes swept over them slowly. "And the most pressing question: will they strike again? If so... when?"

The weight of his questions hung in the air, amplifying the tension despite everyone knowing this was a game. The guests exchanged glances, their expressions a mix of amusement and genuine intrigue.

The silence shattered with a loud crash—glass breaking, sudden and violent. The group collectively startled as Chelsie crumpled to the ground in a dramatic collapse. Her body went completely limp, hitting the floor with a thud. A glass rolled away from her limp hand, its shards glittering ominously on the polished floor.

Gasps rippled through the room. Darren jolted so violently that his drink spilled onto his lap. "Jesus!" he exclaimed, jumping to his feet.

Russell and Shea exchanged knowing smirks, clearly unimpressed. "Here we go," Russell muttered.

Zoey was the first to react properly, rushing to Chelsie's side with convincing urgency. She crouched down, her fingers pressing against Chelsie's wrist, then checking her neck for a pulse. The room held its collective breath.

"Wait!" Zoey exclaimed, her voice rising with shock as she felt a pulse. "She's not—"

Sam cut her off with a sharp look and subtle wink. "Breathing? No pulse? No signs of life?"

Zoey caught on quickly, straightening with a feigned grim expression. "No. She's... dead."

The word hung in the air. The room collectively tensed.

Chelsie, ever unable to resist, cracked one eye open and tugged at Zoey's pant leg. Startled genuinely this time, Zoey let out an involuntary scream, stumbling backward. "Oh my god!"

"What? What is it?" Norma asked urgently, leaning forward. "What happened?"

Zoey waved a hand dismissively, trying to recover. "Nothing.

It's just... that rigamortis thing. You know. The muscles. Twitching."

Her attempt at medical jargon—"rigamortis" instead of "rigor mortis"—drew chuckles from the group. Zoey nudged Chelsie gently with her foot. Chelsie remained perfectly still, though her faintly twitching smile didn't escape the more observant guests.

Sam stepped forward with renewed purpose, looming over Chelsie's "body" like a detective examining evidence. "She just... collapsed? In the middle of conversation? No warning? Or was it something... more sinister?"

The group buzzed with immediate speculation.

"Could be an embolism—" Alice started.

"Stroke?" Darren suggested.

Russell raised his glass, swirling its contents with exaggerated suspicion. "I think her drink was poisoned. Definitely poison."

"Look at the evidence—it's all there," Lacy agreed, pointing to the broken glass. "The timing, the sudden collapse. Classic poisoning symptoms."

Sam stroked his chin thoughtfully. "Poisoned, you say? Interesting. But we all have drinks. What was she drinking specifically?"

Lacy spoke up. "She ordered a bloody Mary at dinner and brought it with her to the lounge. The rest of us got our drinks here from the bar."

The group collectively glanced at their glasses, a subtle wave of unease rippling through them.

Sam's eyes lit up. "Interesting. Very interesting. If no one else has a bloody Mary, then it seems... intentional. Targeted. Premeditated." He paused for dramatic effect. "And here's the very intriguing thing—a bloody Mary was my aunt's favorite drink. She had one every Sunday morning without fail for thirty years."

The revelation hung in the air, adding another layer to the mystery.

Zoey, still standing near Chelsie's "body," frowned defensively. "Curtis gave her a bloody Mary earlier. On the boat, before we even got here. I saw him hand it to her."

Sam's eyebrows shot up. "Curtis gave one to her?" He turned to face the group fully. "Was Chelsie... having an affair with Curtis? A secret liaison that none of us knew about? And if the mansion revealed this truth—if the house sensed deception— perhaps its anger manifested as her untimely death. The house punishes those who hide the truth."

Zoey's jaw tightened visibly, her irritation barely concealed. "Seriously? That's where you're going with this?"

The tension was cut by Russell's dry chuckle. "If this is a soap opera, where's the dramatic close-up? Someone needs to slap someone."

A few people laughed.

Sam ignored him, addressing the room with renewed intensity. "Perhaps this was no random act. Perhaps Curtis's death and Chelsie's are connected—two parts of the same crime, the same secret. Who's next? Will the house claim another victim before dawn?"

The group shifted uneasily. Even knowing it was a game, the atmosphere had taken on a life of its own.

Shea raised his hand like a student. "Quick question—are we supposed to be solving this or just surviving until Sunday?"

"Both," Sam replied with a wicked grin. "If you can."

Before the tension could build further, Gwen appeared in the doorway, her composed figure a stark contrast to the charged atmosphere. Sam caught her eye and gave a subtle nod.

"Alright, everyone," he said, clapping his hands together to break the spell. "It's getting late, and we need to clear the room to, ah, properly dispose of the body. Can't have a corpse cluttering up the lounge all night. Bad for the ambiance." He paused, then added with perfect timing: "I suggest you lock your doors tonight. Sweet dreams... if you can sleep."

The guests began to file out, their chatter buzzing with

nervous excitement. Darren and Alice walked together, their heads bent close as they whispered theories. Russell and Shea exchanged exaggerated winks. Norma grabbed Lacy's arm. "So what do you think? Connected murders or coincidence?"

"In a mystery?" Lacy replied with a smile. "Always connected."

Zoey lingered near Chelsie's "corpse," bending down to whisper something that made Chelsie's lips twitch before stepping away, giving her girlfriend's hand a quick, hidden squeeze.

As the last of the group disappeared into the hallway, Gwen closed the door behind her with a soft click. The room, now quiet save for the crackling fire and Chelsie's careful breathing, seemed to exhale.

The performance was over—this act, at least.

On the floor, Chelsie finally opened her eyes fully and grinned. "How was I?"

Sam laughed, the tension draining from him. "Perfect. Absolutely perfect."

CHAPTER EIGHTEEN

The hallway outside the lounge pulsed with faint energy as the group dispersed, breaking into smaller clusters, their lingering chatter echoing against the high, arched ceilings. Flickering candelabras along the walls, old-fashioned gas-style fixtures converted to electric, cast warm, golden light that danced on the dark wood paneling, elongating shadows into strange shapes that seemed to move independently. The house felt alive in a way that went beyond mere architecture, its walls seemingly humming with secrets accumulated over more than a century.

Zoey lingered near the doorway, not quite ready to retire despite the late hour. Her gaze skimmed over the retreating guests before landing on Lacy, who stood a short distance away, somewhat separate from the others. Lacy's attention was fixed on one of the mansion maps, her brows furrowed in concentration as her fingers traced its lines. She looked a bit lost, a bit lonely, standing there by herself while everyone else paired off.

Zoey's lips curved into a warm smile as she approached, her movements confident and unhurried. She'd had just enough wine to make her bold but not sloppy. "Hey Lacy. How have you been?"

Lacy glanced up from the map, momentarily startled. Her

face softened into a polite smile, grateful for the interruption. "Hi Zoey. It's been awhile." Lacy gave her a hug. "I've been good. You ok? Did you know that Chelsie was getting the axe tonight?"

Zoey took a deep sigh. "No. I had no idea. I'll have to murder her again later for not telling me."

"I'm sorry." Lacy replied. "That kind of sucks on the first night."

Zoey softened her face in appreciation. "Thank you Lacy. You were always so sweet. It's ok though, Chelsie and I talked about this being a possibility. Figures that my brother would make life difficult for me. It's definitely not the first time. Probably not the last"

Lacy nodded in agreement. Zoey tilted her head, her smile widening. "So, I was thinking about hitting the hot tub on the second deck. There's supposed to be an amazing view of the stars from there, and after all that murder mystery drama, I could use some actual relaxation." She paused, her expression shifting to something more playful. "Chelsie was supposed to join me, but now that she's currently poisoned on the floor. Not the best hot tub companion."

Lacy chuckled softly, her shoulders relaxing. "Yeah. That scene was... something else. The rigamortis twitching was a nice touch."

Zoey grinned wider, leaning in conspiratorially. "Between you and me, I think Chelsie's having way too much fun being a corpse. She's going to milk this all weekend." She straightened. "Anyway, you want to come with me? Plus, it's always weird to hot tub alone. Makes you look like you're having a sad solo spa day."

Lacy hesitated, her fingers playing with the edge of the map. But Zoey's expression seemed sincere, open, uncomplicated. Her smile widened. "Sure. Sounds fun. As long as you're not planning to make me the next victim."

Zoey gasped dramatically, throwing her hands up. "Promise! Scout's honor." She held up three fingers. "Though I was never actually a scout, so I'm not sure how binding that is." She grinned, adding with a wink, "But it goes both ways. You're not going to drown me in the hot tub and claim it was an accident, right?"

They laughed, the shared humor breaking whatever tension might have lingered. Zoey gestured toward the grand staircase. "Let's get our suits on and meet back here in 15 minutes."

"Ok. Sounds good." Lacy said. They both walked off.

––––––––

THE GRAND STAIRCASE stretched upward before them. As they ascended, now in their bathing suits, the house seemed to settle into hushed stillness around them. The occasional creak of floorboards and the soft shuffle of their steps were the only immediate sounds, though distant noises filtered through—a door closing, water running through pipes, muffled voices.

"So," Zoey said, "is this your first murder mystery weekend?"

"Yeah," Lacy replied. "First one. I've read plenty of mystery novels, watched all the classic films, but never actually participated in one. You?"

Zoey nodded, her hand trailing along the smooth bannister. "Chelsie and I have done a couple before, but nothing like this. This is on a whole different level. Sam goes all out."

Lacy smiled faintly, something fond flickering across her face. "He definitely has a flair for the dramatic. Always did, even when we were dating. He'd turn grocery shopping into an adventure if you let him."

Zoey laughed. "That's one way to put it. But honestly, I think it's kind of cool. How often do you get to stay in a place like this and play detective? It's like being inside a book."

"True," Lacy agreed. "Better than sitting home alone eating Valentine's chocolate and watching Netflix."

"Amen to that," Zoey said with feeling.

Zoey slowed her pace as they reached a landing between

floors. "It's nice to have someone else to hang out with tonight. Chelsie and I usually team up for these things, but... well, with her being dead and all."

Lacy chuckled. "Yeah, I get that. And thanks for asking. I was kind of wondering how I'd fit in with everyone here. You all seem to know each other already. I'm the random ex-girlfriend crasher."

Zoey waved a dismissive hand, continuing up the stairs. "Don't worry about that. Honestly, half the fun of these weekends is teaming up with people you don't know. Keeps things interesting." She paused, then added more seriously, "Plus, you're not crashing. Sam invited you. That means you belong here just as much as anyone else."

Lacy's smile lingered, the tension in her shoulders easing as they continued upward.

Though the other guests had scattered, faint sounds of laughter and muffled conversation drifted through the walls—a reminder that despite the size of the place, they weren't entirely alone.

Zoey glanced at Lacy as they walked toward the deck access door. "So, I don't think I've ever heard the story. How did you and Sam meet?"

Lacy hesitated, her fingers brushing the corridor wall. "We met at a horror film festival, actually. We were both in line for a midnight special screening of Scream—the original—and we started talking about Kevin Williamson and it just... clicked."

Zoey raised an eyebrow. "Really? That's actually kind of perfect. Very on-brand for Sam."

Lacy gave a small shrug. "It was intense while it lasted. But after a while... it didn't end badly or anything. We just went in different directions. He got more into the business side of things after his aunt got sick, and I was trying to make it as an actress. The timing was off."

"Timing's a bitch," Zoey said with sympathetic understanding.

"Yeah." Lacy nodded. "But when he invited me to this, I figured, why not? We're still friendly. And I thought it might be fun to see what he's built."

Zoey nodded thoughtfully. "Well, I'm glad you came. You were always cool. And honestly, Sam needs more people in his life who can keep up with his weird interests."

Lacy's lips curled into a genuine smile. "Thanks. You're cool too. Definitely not what I expected when I first met you."

"What did you expect?" Zoey asked, genuinely curious.

"I don't know," Lacy admitted. "Maybe more intensity? Sam always talked about you like you were this force of nature."

Zoey laughed. "Oh, I can be. You just haven't seen that side. We never hung out much anyway. Just ask Chelsie though—I can be a nightmare when I'm stressed."

Their laughter mingled as they reached a door marked "DECK ACCESS."

Zoey paused, her hand on the handle, turning to Lacy with a playful grin. "Alright, let's see if this hot tub lives up to the hype. Sam promised me it was amazing, and if he oversold it, I'm going to be very disappointed."

As they stepped out onto the deck, the cool night air greeted them immediately—a refreshing contrast to the house's stuffiness. It carried the salt tang of the ocean, the faint sound of waves lapping against the shore, and the distant chirping of tropical insects. The deck was beautifully appointed—teak wood, tasteful lighting, comfortable loungers, and yes, in the corner, a large hot tub already bubbling invitingly. Steam rose from its surface in lazy curls.

The stars above sparkled like diamonds scattered across black velvet—more stars than either of them had seen in years. The Milky Way was visible as a cloudy band across the heavens.

For a moment, they both stood still, taking in the scene, breathing in the fresh air after hours inside. Here on the deck, under the stars, surrounded by the sounds of nature and ocean, the weight of the mystery seemed far away. The game felt distant, less real, less important.

Zoey glanced at Lacy, her smile softening into something more genuine. "This seems perfect."

Lacy nodded, her own grin growing. "Let's do this."

With that, they stepped forward and into the hot tub.

CHAPTER NINETEEN

The woods were alive with an orchestra of nocturnal sounds: the rustle of leaves in the gentle breeze, the distant hoot of an owl calling to its mate, and the occasional crack of a twig underfoot that made Curtis jump despite knowing they were alone. The moon hung high in the sky, full and luminous, casting silvery light that filtered through the dense canopy above, dappling the faint trail below in a shifting mosaic of light and shadow. A low, curling fog slithered up from the coastline, wrapping around their ankles like ghostly tendrils as they walked, cold and damp and slightly unnerving. It gave the whole scene an otherworldly quality, like they'd stepped into some Gothic fairy tale.

Gwen led the way with confidence, her strides purposeful and sure-footed despite the uncertain terrain, each step crunching softly on the gravel path that wound through the trees. She wore dark jeans and a practical jacket now instead of her earlier business suit, transformed from corporate assistant to wilderness guide. Behind her, Curtis and Chelsie followed, their footfalls slightly louder, less certain, more tentative.

Curtis glanced around nervously, his eyes flitting between the looming trees—their branches reaching overhead like skeletal fingers—and the faint glow of the moon that occasionally broke through the canopy. Every shadow seemed to move, to hide something.

Chelsie trailed just behind him, her arms crossed tightly against the chill that seeped into the air as they ventured deeper into the woods, further from the mansion's warm lights.

"This feels very Blair Witch," Curtis muttered, looking over his shoulder at the path behind them, which had already disappeared into darkness and fog. "Are we going to find stick figures hanging from trees next?"

Gwen glanced back, her sharp eyes scanning the trail they'd left behind. Her voice broke the quiet, steady and matter-of-fact. "It's about a ten-minute walk from here. Sam's aunt picked this place for a reason—perfect seclusion. Perfect murder ground."

Curtis let out a low, nervous chuckle. "Perfect murder ground. That's not ominous or anything. Just what I wanted to hear while walking through a dark forest."

Gwen's lips twitched with amusement, but she didn't break stride. "It's secluded. Quiet. No neighbors to hear anything. If you need assistance, just use the landline."

Chelsie frowned, pulling out her phone with one hand. The faint glow of the screen illuminated her face in the darkness, revealing the dreaded words: No Service. Not even a single bar.

"Yeah, about that," she muttered, waving the useless device. "There's no signal. Like, none. Not even emergency calls."

Gwen barely glanced over her shoulder, unsurprised. "Reception's garbage out here. The island's topography blocks most signals. But there's a landline in the cabin's kitchen—a direct line to Stubby at the security shack. He's monitoring it all night."

Chelsie sighed, slipping her phone back into her pocket where it was now just dead weight. "Well, that's comforting. Nothing says 'relaxing murder mystery weekend' like being completely cut off from communication."

Curtis shot her a look. "It's part of the atmosphere. Builds tension. You know Sam wouldn't pass up a chance to make this as authentic as possible."

"Yeah, well, authentic is starting to feel a lot like 'actually dangerous,'" Chelsie replied.

The path grew narrower as it snaked around a steep hill, forcing them to navigate the uneven terrain more carefully. Loose rocks shifted under their feet. Gwen moved with practiced ease, brushing aside low-hanging branches and stepping over protruding roots without even looking down.

Behind her, Curtis stumbled slightly on a root that seemed to reach up specifically to trip him, catching himself against a tree trunk. "Shit," he muttered, recovering quickly but embarrassed. "Is this hike part of the game? Because I didn't sign up for wilderness survival training."

"Consider it an adventure," Gwen replied over her shoulder. "Character building. Sam's aunt believed in earning your accommodations."

"Sam's aunt sounds like she was intense," Chelsie commented, breathing harder from the climb.

"You have no idea," Gwen said softly.

They pushed through a dense thicket of brambles and brush, the thorny branches scratching at their clothes. Curtis cursed as one scraped across his hand, drawing a thin line of blood.

But then, suddenly, the foliage parted like a curtain being drawn back, revealing a scene that stole their breath.

A secluded cabin stood perched on the edge of a jagged cliff, its weathered wood glowing softly in the moonlight like something out of a dream—or a nightmare. The structure was small but sturdy, probably decades old. Its peaked roof and stone chimney gave it a fairy tale quality, but there was something about the way it perched so close to the precipice that made it feel precarious, temporary.

Beyond it, past the cabin and the cliff's edge, the ocean stretched out endlessly, a shimmering expanse of silver and black that seemed to go on forever. Waves crashed against the rocky shoreline far below, their rhythmic roar filling the air with a raw, untamed energy that was both beautiful and threatening. The sound was constant, primordial, the heartbeat of something ancient and indifferent.

"Wow," Chelsie breathed, her voice barely above a whisper, all her earlier annoyance forgotten. Her eyes were wide with genuine awe as she took in the sight. "This is... wow."

Curtis stepped forward, his hands on his hips as he surveyed the cabin and its dramatic surroundings, turning slowly to take in the full panorama. "This'll do," he said, nodding appreciatively, trying to maintain his casual demeanor.

"It's like we're at the edge of the world," Chelsie murmured, still staring at the ocean.

"We basically are," Gwen replied.

Gwen led the way to the front door, her footsteps confident on the cabin's small porch. Her hand paused briefly on the wrought iron handle—old, heavy, handcrafted—as if absorbing the weight of the moment. She pushed the door open with a creak of old hinges, and the faint scent of salt and cedar wafted out, carried on the cool night air. The soft creak of wooden floorboards echoed in the stillness as she stepped inside, the sound lonely and isolated.

Curtis and Chelsie lingered outside for a moment longer, neither quite ready to enter, their eyes drawn back to the ocean. The waves, glinting in the moonlight, seemed to stretch forever, their vastness humbling and almost otherworldly. The cabin, nestled so precariously on the cliff's edge, felt like a dream— beautiful, remote, and tinged with an unshakable sense of foreboding.

This was the kind of place where stories happened. Dark stories.

"Ready?" Curtis asked, turning to Chelsie with a grin that was equal parts playful and genuinely nervous.

Chelsie nodded, her lips curving into a faint smile that didn't quite reach her eyes. "Let's see what Sam's aunt thought was worth the walk. Though I'm starting to understand why she picked this place."

"For murders?" Curtis asked.

"For secrets," Chelsie replied.

CHAPTER TWENTY

The cabin's interior was a blend of rustic charm and modern indulgence, its open floor plan creating an inviting space that felt far more expansive than it appeared from the outside. The living room flowed seamlessly into the dining area and kitchen, the warm glow of dim lighting casting soft golden hues across the polished hardwood floors that gleamed like honey. The walls were painted in rich, earthy tones—deep browns and forest greens—adorned with subtle nautical accents. Framed sketches of ships lined one wall, their aged paper and careful pen work suggesting they were genuine antiques. A brass anchor mounted near the stone fireplace caught the light, and an antique ship's wheel perched above the mantel, surrounded by pillar candles of varying heights.

Curtis whistled low as he stepped further inside, his earlier nervousness from the walk through the woods evaporating in the face of such unexpected luxury. He ran his fingers over the back of a plush leather couch—butter-soft, probably Italian. "This is... cozy," he said, though "cozy" seemed an understatement. "Like, seriously nice. Sam's aunt had money."

Chelsie trailed behind him, her eyes scanning the room with cautious curiosity, still on edge from everything—the fake death, the walk through the fog, the isolation. Despite the cabin's inviting atmosphere, an undercurrent of unease lingered. Her gaze drifted to the bar in the corner, an impressive setup with a granite countertop and shelves stocked with top-shelf liquor that would make any bartender jealous.

"A little too cozy," she murmured, her tone skeptical. "Like, suspiciously cozy. Who has a cabin this nice and just leaves it empty most of the time?"

Gwen stepped into the center of the room, her boots clicking softly against the polished floorboards. "It's all yours for the weekend," she announced, her voice brisk but pleasant. Reaching into her jacket pocket, she produced two small keys— old-fashioned brass ones—and tossed them onto the coffee table with a metallic clink. Beside where the keys landed lay two folded maps.

"Hiking maps," Gwen explained, gesturing toward the table. "The beach is down a path just outside—about a five-minute walk. There's also a trail that loops around the point if you're feeling adventurous." She paused, surveying the room. "The place is fully stocked—kitchen has all the basics plus some luxu- ries, bar obviously speaks for itself, there's a TV with a DVD player and movies in that cabinet, hot tub on the back deck, and a pool table in the loft upstairs. Everything you need."

Curtis's grin widened, his eyes lighting up at the mention of the hot tub. "Now we're talking. This is more like it. Way better than that stuffy mansion."

Chelsie, however, crossed her arms defensively. "Are there going to be more deaths?" she asked bluntly. "Or is it just us out here playing house?"

Gwen's lips twitched into a knowing smile. "I can't tell you that," she replied smoothly. "But if I were you, I'd think like Sam. What would he do? How would he play this?"

Chelsie groaned, rolling her eyes. "Classic Sam. Can't give a straight answer to save his life. Everything's got to be mysterious and dramatic."

Curtis leaned casually against the couch's arm, his grin widening. "Looks like it's just me and you, sugar," he said, giving Chelsie a wink. "Alone in a romantic cabin by the ocean. What could possibly happen?"

Chelsie shot him a withering look that could have frozen lava. "In your dreams. More people are definitely coming. They have to be. This is way too big a setup for just two 'victims.'"

Gwen suppressed a laugh, glancing between them with obvious amusement at their dynamic. "Well, enjoy the cabin," she said, her tone growing brisk again as she moved toward the door. "I need to get back before someone realizes I've been gone too long. Remember—landline in the kitchen if you need anything."

Without waiting for a response, she slipped out, pulling the door shut behind her. The faint sound of the latch clicking into place marked her exit, followed by the crunch of her footsteps on gravel growing fainter until they disappeared entirely.

For a moment, the cabin fell silent, the weight of being truly alone settling over them. The only sound was the faint rustle of the trees outside, their branches scraping occasionally against the cabin's exterior walls, and the distant, constant crash of waves.

Curtis pushed himself off the couch, stretching his arms above his head until his back popped. He turned to Chelsie, who had gravitated toward the bar almost immediately, surveying the selection of bottles with an appraising eye.

"Well, this is shaping up to be a real bonding experience," Curtis quipped, sauntering over to join her. "What do you say we get started on that impressive liquor collection? Seems rude not to, honestly."

Chelsie didn't look at him immediately, but her lips curved into a faint smile despite herself. "Fine," she said, reaching up to pull a bottle of whiskey off the shelf—something amber and expensive-looking. "But let's get one thing clear right now: no funny business. I'm not getting drunk enough to entertain whatever dumb ideas you've got brewing in that head of yours."

Curtis feigned offense, clutching his chest dramatically. "You wound me, Chelsie. I'm a perfect gentleman. Ask anyone."

"I did ask someone," Chelsie shot back without missing a beat, pouring herself a generous measure into a crystal tumbler. "Zoey warned me about you. Said you were harmless but persistent."

"Persistent is good, right?" Curtis asked hopefully.

"Not in this context," Chelsie replied flatly. "You'll survive," she added after taking a sip, her expression softening slightly. "Maybe."

Curtis grabbed a bottle of rum—dark, Caribbean, probably worth more than his entire wardrobe. "So," he said, pouring a generous helping into a glass, "what do you think Sam has planned for us? More murders? Creepy midnight surprises? A visit from someone in a mask?"

Chelsie shrugged, taking another sip, the whiskey burning pleasantly down her throat. "I don't know, all of the above. He loves keeping people on their toes, doesn't he? I think he loves the suspense almost as much as the reveal."

Curtis leaned beside her, close but not too close, swirling his drink. "I mean, we're already dead. Maybe we just get to relax now."

Chelsie tilted her head, considering. "I don't know. There's probably a mystery within the mystery or some crazy twist like that," she said. "He knows how to build a story, how to pace things and keep it interesting. I'll give him that."

Curtis clinked his glass against hers with a grin. "To surviving the weekend. Or, not surviving I guess."

"To surviving you," Chelsie replied, her tone dry as she took another sip, but there was warmth in it now, the beginning of camaraderie.

They fell into a comfortable rhythm, the warmth of their drinks easing some of the tension. Curtis leaned against the bar, his eyes wandering to the wide windows that framed a stunning view of the ocean beyond. The moonlight reflected off the waves in brilliant silver streaks, their rhythmic crash creating a soothing backdrop.

Chelsie, meanwhile, began rummaging through the bar's drawers, pulling out coasters, fancy cocktail napkins, bar tools, and even a small notebook labeled "Drink Recipes" in elegant cursive.

"Of course Sam's aunt had to go all out," she remarked, holding up a napkin embroidered with the words *Murder in Style* in dark red thread. "It's a little over the top. Like, who embroiders their murder mystery napkins?"

Curtis chuckled. "I think that's the whole point. Go big or go home, right? If you're going to host elaborate murder mysteries, commit to the aesthetic."

Chelsie shot him a look, her smirk softening. "You would say that. You're just like him—all drama, all the time."

Curtis shrugged, raising his glass. "What can I say? I like a little drama. Life's more interesting with production value."

As the night wore on and their glasses emptied and were refilled, the cabin settled into a quiet calm that was almost hypnotic. The sound of the waves outside grew softer, blending with the faint creak of the floorboards and the occasional groan of the wind.

Chelsie wandered toward the wide windows, drawn by the view, her drink dangling from her fingers as her gaze fixed on the moonlit ocean. "This place is... something else," she said quietly. "Like, objectively beautiful but also kind of..."

"Creepy?" Curtis suggested, joining her at the window, his hands tucked into his pockets.

"Yeah," Chelsie agreed, taking another sip. "It's beautiful, but it feels... off."

Curtis stood beside her, both of them staring out at the endless dark water. "Off how?"

Chelsie hesitated, struggling to articulate the feeling. "I don't know. Like it's too perfect. Too isolated. Like it's hiding something or waiting for something to happen." She glanced at him. "Does that sound crazy?"

Curtis studied her for a moment, reassessing her slightly. Then he turned back to the view. "It's just the game," he said, though his tone lacked conviction. "Sam's good at setting the mood. Creating atmosphere. That's all this is."

"Yeah," Chelsie said, her voice trailing off as she stared into the dark expanse. "I guess he is."

CHAPTER TWENTY-ONE

The second-story deck of the mansion offered a breathtaking view of the cliffs below, the jagged rock face plunging dramatically toward the churning water. The ocean stretched endlessly into the horizon, a vast expanse of darkness broken only by the silver path of moonlight that stretched across its surface like a road leading nowhere. The moon hung high in the star-speckled sky, casting a soft glow over the deck's polished wooden floorboards, making them gleam like they'd been freshly waxed.

The hot tub radiated inviting warmth. Steam curled into the cool night air in lazy tendrils, mingling with the light mist that hung over the ocean, creating an almost dreamlike atmosphere. The water bubbled and churned, jets providing gentle massage and creating a cocoon of warmth against the night's chill.

Zoey, Lacy, and Kelly lounged in the bubbling water, their bodies relaxed, their heads tipped back against the tub's cushioned edge, champagne glasses balanced in their hands with the careful precision of people who were pleasantly drunk but not yet sloppy. The night carried a heady mix of relaxation and mischief, their laughter floating into the darkness and dissipating like the steam around them.

Zoey reached for the open bottle—their second, or was it their third?—perched precariously on the tub's wide ledge, her movements slightly exaggerated from the champagne already warming her system. She poured herself another generous glass, her cheeks flushed pink from the heat and the alcohol, her grin wide and uninhibited.

Across from her, Kelly gestured animatedly, her hands cutting through the air for emphasis, her voice rising with excitement as she dove into her story. "We cranked it way up," Kelly said, her eyes sparkling with amusement and shamelessness. "The sauna was completely fogged over—you couldn't see your hand in front of your face—it had to be like a hundred and twenty degrees. I'm on top of him, and we're going at it like crazy, and I'm thinking we're totally alone because who else would be insane enough to use a sauna that hot?" She paused for dramatic effect, her grin widening. "Next thing I know, through all that steam, this lady walks in with her son. The kid couldn't have been more than seven. He looks right at us—and I mean right at us—and says in this perfectly innocent voice, 'Mommy, look! She's doing the cowgirl!'"

The three women burst into uncontrollable laughter, the sound carrying out into the night, echoing off the mansion's stone walls. Zoey nearly spilled her champagne as she clutched her side, tears of laughter brimming in her eyes.

"No!" Lacy gasped between laughs, her face flushed. "What did you do?"

"We scrambled off each other so fast we both almost fell," Kelly admitted, laughing at the memory. "The mom just grabbed her kid and ran out like she'd seen a crime. We got banned from that gym."

"That's my wildest," Kelly declared proudly, raising her glass as if to toast her own boldness. "Beat that."

"I'm so glad you joined us out here tonight." Zoey said as she finally started to catch her breath.

That's insane," Lacy said, shaking her head in disbelief.

"And... so much sweat. Like, physically uncomfortable amounts of sweat."

Kelly shrugged, completely unabashed, taking a long sip of her champagne. "It was worth it. The spontaneity, the risk—that's what made it hot. What about you?" She leaned forward, water sloshing slightly, her grin expectant and challenging. "What's your wildest?"

Lacy hesitated, the faintest blush creeping into her cheeks as she swirled the champagne in her glass, watching the bubbles rise. "Uh... behind a waterfall. On a hiking trip in Oregon. It's not as wild as a sauna with an audience, but it was... romantic. Private. The water was so loud we couldn't even hear each other."

Zoey tilted her head, a teasing smirk spreading across her lips. "Very Disney Princess meets Fifty Shades. I'm imaging you in a flowing dress."

"It was athletic wear, actually," Lacy said, laughing despite her embarrassment. "Very practical."

Kelly chuckled, nodding in approval, raising her glass in salute. "Not bad. Points for originality and the outdoors angle. And you, Zoey?" She pointed her glass at Zoey, champagne sloshing dangerously close to the rim. "Your number one sexcapade? Come on, don't hold out on us."

Zoey feigned reluctance, leaning back and taking a long, deliberate sip of her drink, making them wait, enjoying the attention. "Oh, I don't know. I'm a lady. Ladies don't kiss and tell."

"Since when?" Kelly shot back immediately.

"Come on," Lacy urged, leaning forward slightly, genuinely curious. "You've got to have one. You can't make us share and then hold back."

Zoey grinned, finally relenting. "Alright, fine. But this stays between us." She paused for effect. "Chelsie went down on me at a restaurant once. Fancy Italian place downtown—white table-cloths, candles, the whole romantic setup. We had a table with one of those long, draped tablecloths that went all the way to the floor." She took another sip, savoring the memory. "She pretended to drop her fork, ducked under the table, and the next thing I know, I'm trying to order dessert from the waiter—tiramisu, I think?—like nothing's happening, trying to keep my voice steady while she's... yeah."

Kelly's jaw dropped, her hand flying to her mouth. "You did not!"

Lacy covered her mouth to stifle her laughter, her eyes wide with shock and admiration.

"That is next-level bold," Kelly said, shaking her head in awe. "Respect. Serious respect. Did the waiter know?"

"I think he suspected something," Zoey admitted, grinning. "I couldn't really keep a straight face. But he was very professional about it. Got a good tip."

Kelly's grin turned devious as she leaned toward Lacy, her expression suggesting she was about to cross a line and enjoying the prospect. "Alright, your turn again. Wildest time with Sam? Come on, you can't dodge this one."

Lacy froze, her eyes widening in surprise, her glass halfway to her lips. "Um... that seems a little inappropriate," she said hesitantly, glancing quickly at Zoey for her reaction.

Zoey waved a dismissive hand, laughing, clearly unconcerned. "Oh, please. I once walked in on my brother jerking it to a Christina Aguilera poster when he was fifteen. He tried to tell me he was 'just adjusting his pants.' Nothing you say will ever top that level of scarring. I'm immune to Sam-related embarrassment at this point."

Lacy's tension broke, and the three of them dissolved into laughter, the absurdity easing her discomfort completely. The champagne helped too.

Kelly wasn't about to let up, sensing blood in the water. "So," she pressed, her grin widening, "is he good in bed? Scale of one to ten?"

Lacy blinked, taken aback. "Why would you even ask that?"

Kelly shrugged, her tone light but probing. "Not for me—for you. You still like him, don't you? It's pretty obvious."

Lacy opened her mouth to deny it automatically, but Kelly's knowing expression stopped her. The truth was written all over her face. Her eyes darted to Zoey, checking for any sign of disapproval, but Zoey's face held only an encouraging smile, warm and genuine.

Finally, Lacy sighed and splashed water playfully at Kelly. "Fine," she admitted, the words coming out in a rush. "Yes. He's cute, and I guess... I still like him. More than I thought I did. Seeing him again brought it all back."

Zoey raised her glass in a toast, her smile warm and sincere. "You know," she said, her words slightly slurred but heartfelt, "I was surprised when I saw he invited you. He doesn't usually... I mean, he keeps his personal life really separate. So the fact that you're here? I think he still likes you, too. Like, definitely."

Lacy's cheeks colored deeper, and she looked down at her glass, swirling the champagne absentmindedly. "You think so? Really?"

Zoey nodded emphatically. "Absolutely. One hundred percent. And for the record, I'm all for it. I always liked you Lacy. You're smart, funny, you get his weird horror obsession, and my brother could really use someone like you in his life. Someone who isn't intimidated by all his intensity."

Kelly grinned, raising her glass. "Looks like sparks might fly this Valentine's Day. I'm calling it now—you two are hooking up before Sunday."

Lacy shook her head and rolled her eyes, though a shy smile tugged at her lips. She took a long sip of her drink before setting the glass aside. "Okay," she said, her tone suddenly playful, emboldened by alcohol and acceptance, "you want wild? I'll give you wild." She paused for dramatic effect. "Sailboat. Middle of the ocean. Sunset. Handcuffs, blindfold, whipped cream... and a video camera."

There was a beat of stunned silence. Then Zoey and Kelly's jaws dropped in perfect synchronization.

"Sex tape!" Kelly exclaimed, laughing loudly. "I knew there was more to you! Quiet girl's got a wild side!"

Lacy's laughter joined theirs, loud and unrestrained, her earlier shyness completely replaced with easy confidence. "I've never told anyone that before. Not even my best friend. It's just been my secret with Sam."

Kelly's grin turned sly, conspiratorial. "You two are definitely hooking up this weekend. That's not even a question anymore. It's destiny. It's fate. It's—"

"It's a lot of champagne talking," Lacy interrupted, but she was smiling.

Lacy shrugged, her smile widening. "We'll see. I mean, if it happens, it happens."

Kelly popped open another bottle of champagne with practiced ease—the cork coming out with a satisfying pop—pouring fresh glasses for all three of them. As she refilled Zoey's glass, Zoey tilted her head, her expression suddenly mischievous.

"If we keep drinking," Zoey teased, leaning forward, "I bet I could get you to spill the beans. Who's the killer? Come on, you can tell us. We won't say anything."

Kelly laughed, shaking her head firmly. "Not a chance. Nice try, though. The staff plays their part—we know our roles, our scenes—but even I don't know who the actual killer is this time. Sam's being super secretive about it."

Lacy raised an eyebrow, surprised. "Seriously? You don't know? I figured the staff would have to know to coordinate things."

"Nope," Kelly replied, taking a sip. "Sam's keeping this one locked down tight. Said he wants everyone's reactions to be genuine, even ours. Could be anyone at this point—could even be me, and I wouldn't know it yet. He's probably got multiple scenarios planned depending on how things unfold."

Zoey leaned back in the bubbling water, her gaze thoughtful. "So Sam's the only one who knows the full story."

"Most likely," Kelly confirmed. "Or maybe him and Gwen. Those two are thick as thieves. But definitely no one else."

Zoey swirled her champagne, a glimmer of curiosity sparking in her eyes. Whatever secrets the weekend held, she was determined to uncover them. The champagne haze didn't dull her intrigue—if anything, it only sharpened it, made her more bold.

As the laughter continued into the night, as more champagne was poured and more secrets shared, the deck seemed to hum with the unspoken promise of what was yet to come.

CHAPTER TWENTY-TWO

Alice stood at the window of their room, her silhouette framed by the silvery glow of the full moon that hung like a luminous coin in the star-scattered sky. The mansion's vast grounds stretched out below her, a dark tapestry of shadows and moonlit patches—the manicured gardens and wild jungle borders creating strange geometric patterns in the light. Beyond, the cliffs fell sharply into the restless ocean, its surface shimmering faintly, waves catching moonbeams and throwing them back in brief, brilliant flashes.

She leaned her forehead against the cool glass, feeling the slight chill seep through her skin, grounding her. Her breath created a soft fog with every exhale, blooming and fading in rhythmic cycles. The window was slightly cracked, letting in the night air—cool and salt-tinged, carrying the distant sounds of waves and nocturnal creatures.

"It's beautiful," she murmured, her voice quiet and distant, as if speaking more to herself than anyone else. Her fingers traced the edge of the windowpane absently, her thoughts drifting to how different this was from their apartment in the city, where the view was of brick walls and fire escapes.

From the en suite bathroom, Darren emerged, towel in hand,

drying the last drops of water from his face. He paused in the doorway, taking in the sight of Alice standing there so serene. The soft moonlight caught in her hair, making it glow with an almost silver sheen, making her look almost ethereal—like something out of a painting.

Smiling to himself, feeling that familiar surge of love and gratitude, he stepped forward, his socked feet silent on the hardwood floor. Wrapping his arms around her from behind, he pulled her gently against his chest, his chin resting on the top of her head. The warmth of his embrace broke through her reverie, and she leaned back into him instinctively, fitting perfectly against his body the way she always did.

He pressed a tender kiss to the crown of her head, breathing in the scent of her shampoo—something floral and clean—mingling with the faint saltiness of the ocean breeze.

"I know," Darren said softly, his voice warm and steady. "I see it every day."

Alice turned in his arms, pivoting slowly to face him, her gaze lifting to meet his. The moonlight cast delicate highlights across her features, illuminating the warmth and love in her eyes. She wrapped her arms around him tightly, burying her face in his chest for a moment, just breathing him in, before pulling back just enough to look up at him.

"You're too good to me," she whispered, her voice tinged with gratitude and affection and a hint of wonder.

Darren chuckled, the sound rumbling through his chest, and brushed a loose strand of hair from her face with gentle fingers, tucking it behind her ear. "I may not be able to buy you a private island," he teased, his eyes crinkling at the corners, "but I can shower you with compliments all night. Unlimited compliments. A renewable resource."

Alice's smile widened, playful and genuine, her eyes sparkling with mischief. "That's all I need. Well, that and the island. Eventually. No rush. By our fortieth anniversary?"

Darren laughed, his deep chuckle filling the room. "Noted.

One private island, added to the list. Right after new car, kitchen renovation, and paying off student loans."

"Priorities," Alice agreed with mock seriousness.

Breaking free from his arms with a playful twist, Alice crossed the room with a bounce in her step, almost skipping. She jumped into the bed with childlike enthusiasm, the plush mattress cradling her as she sank into its softness with an exaggerated sigh of contentment. She pulled the thick comforter—impossibly luxurious, probably thousand-thread-count—up to her chin, burrowing into the pillows like she was building a nest.

Darren lingered by the window for a moment longer, gazing out at the moonlit grounds, watching shadows shift as clouds passed overhead. The view really was spectacular. Finally tearing himself away, he crossed to where he'd laid out his nightshirt, pulling it on, then slid into bed beside Alice.

Alice immediately snuggled into his side, seeking his warmth, resting her head on his chest in the spot that had become hers over a decade of nights together. His arm wrapped around her shoulders automatically, pulling her closer, and she draped one leg over his, tangling them together. The steady rhythm of his heartbeat under her ear brought her a sense of calm that nothing else quite could.

"You ready for more mayhem tomorrow?" Darren asked, his tone light and teasing, his free hand playing absently with her hair.

Alice traced lazy circles on his chest with her fingertip. "I was actually really impressed with today," she admitted thoughtfully. "Sam's story was spooky—that whole thing about the house revealing truths and William going crazy? That was genuinely creepy. But it was so well done, so detailed. I almost forgot it was a game for a minute. When Curtis 'died,' my heart actually raced."

Darren tightened his arm around her protectively, his voice dropping to a playful growl. "Don't worry. If any of Sam's ghosts try anything—if William Lovegood's angry spirit comes after you —I'll take care of them. I'll... I'll reason with them. Firmly."

Alice giggled, the sound soft and sweet, muffled slightly against his chest. "You're my hero. My brave protector. My knight in cotton pajamas."

Their eyes locked for a long moment, something passing between them that didn't need words—years of love and trust and shared experiences compressed into a single look. Darren leaned down, pressing a tender kiss to her lips, soft and lingering. She responded with a gentle smile against his mouth, her fingers curling into the fabric of his shirt.

"I love you," she whispered when they finally broke apart.

"I love you too," Darren replied, his voice steady and sincere. He kissed her forehead gently, then settled back against the pillows.

As the room fell quiet, as their breathing began to synchronize and slow, the sounds of the mansion began to creep in—sounds that had been there all along but became more noticeable in the silence. The faint creak of wood as the old house settled. The distant crash of waves against the cliffs. The occasional rustle of leaves in the wind, branches scraping lightly against the exterior walls.

Alice's breathing slowed, her body relaxing into Darren's warmth, going heavy with approaching sleep. For a moment, it seemed as though rest would come easily.

Then, in the stillness, in that space between waking and sleeping, Alice's voice broke the quiet.

"Babe?" she whispered, her voice small, uncertain.

Darren stirred, his voice groggy but attentive. "Yeah? What's wrong?"

She hesitated, her fingers brushing lightly against his chest, fidgeting slightly. "Can you lock the door?"

Darren chuckled, his lips curving into a sleepy smile, his eyes still closed. "Seriously? You're scared? It's just a game, sweetheart. Curtis is probably in his room eating snacks right now."

Alice tilted her head to look up at him, lifting herself slightly on one elbow. Her wide eyes shimmered in the moonlight. She bit her lip, her expression somewhere between sheepish and earnest, genuinely unsettled. "Please?" she asked softly. "I know it's silly, but... I just want it locked. I'll sleep better."

Darren opened his eyes, seeing the genuine unease in her face, and his expression softened immediately. With a resigned sigh and a teasing grin, he slid out of bed, the cool air hitting his skin and making him shiver. "Alright, scaredy cat," he said affectionately, reaching down to ruffle her hair gently. "But you owe me."

He crossed to the heavy wooden door, the floorboards creaking faintly under his weight in that way old houses do. The door itself was solid, substantial—the kind they didn't make anymore, with real heft and a vintage brass lock that looked original to the house. Twisting the lock with a firm click that echoed in the quiet room, he tested the handle to make sure it had engaged properly, then turned back to Alice, raising an eyebrow with exaggerated drama.

"There. Locked. Sealed. Fort Knox has nothing on this room. Happy now?"

Alice smiled, her expression immediately more relaxed, her shoulders dropping slightly. "Thank you. I know I'm being ridiculous."

"You're not ridiculous," Darren said, returning to bed and slipping under the covers. He pulled her close again, resuming their earlier position. "You're cautious. It's cute." He paused, then added with a grin, "You're still on your own if the bogeyman shows up though. I'm not fighting ghosts. That's where I draw the line."

Alice swatted his chest lightly, the smack barely audible, earning another laugh from him. "Good night, Darren."

"Good night, baby," he murmured, already drifting back toward sleep, his breathing evening out.

As the room fell into stillness once more, as Alice's breathing finally slowed and deepened into actual sleep, the faint glow of the moon illuminated the peaceful scene—two people wrapped together, safe in each other's arms.

CHAPTER TWENTY-THREE

The game room was a comfortable haven amidst the looming mysteries of the mansion, a masculine retreat that felt worlds away from the Gothic grandeur of the rest of the house. Warm, low lighting from strategically placed lamps high-lighted the rich wood-paneled walls—dark cherry or mahogany, polished to a subtle sheen—and the vibrant green felt of the pool table that dominated the center of the room like an altar to leisure. A hanging Tiffany-style lamp cast a steady, focused glow over the table, illuminating the scattered balls, making the colors pop against the green—reds and yellows and blues like jewels.

The room hummed with subdued camaraderie, the kind that grew naturally out of shared drinks and playful competition. Leather chairs lined one wall, a well-stocked bar occupied a corner, and various sporting memorabilia decorated the walls—signed jerseys, vintage baseball bats, framed photographs of athletes whose names had faded from memory but whose glory remained captured forever.

Shea leaned over the pool table, his stance steady and focused, his body forming that classic pool-player angle. His eyes narrowed as he lined up his shot with intense concentration, the faint clink of glass from nearby drinks punctuating the stillness. With a smooth, practiced stroke, the cue ball shot forward, cracking against a striped ball with a satisfying crack and sending it rolling smoothly into the corner pocket with a solid thunk.

"Too bad Curtis is dead," Shea quipped, straightening up with a self-satisfied smirk, chalking his cue with unnecessary flair. "Would've loved to be kicking his ass right about now. The trash talk alone would've been worth the weekend."

Leroy, the cook who'd been invited to join them after finishing his kitchen duties, rested his considerable weight on his cue stick like it was a walking staff, letting out a hearty laugh that filled the room. "Hey, man, this ain't my sport. I can cook a perfect soufflé, but I can't make these balls do what I want. It's humbling."

Russell, perched near the door on one of the leather chairs with a glass of whiskey in hand—his third, or maybe fourth—joined in the laughter, his face flushed from alcohol and camaraderie. "Well, to be fair, it ain't mine either. I peaked at beer pong in college and it's been downhill since." Turning his attention to Leroy, raising his glass in salute, Russell added, "But cooking? Now that's your sport. Killer dinner tonight. Seriously. That chicken? I don't know what you did to it, but it was incredible."

Leroy's chest puffed up with visible pride, his grin widening. "Appreciate it. Cooking's what I do best. Been doing it professionally for fifteen years. Used to work at a five-star place downtown in the city before this gig."

Shea leaned casually against the edge of the pool table, his sharp gaze shifting between his companions. "Not a bad gig, though," he said, gesturing around with his cue stick. "Cook a few meals, play some pool, hang out with cool people in a mansion on a private island. Could be worse. Could be working retail during the holidays."

Leroy lined up his next shot, squinting at the angles, nodding thoughtfully. "Yeah, it's a good setup. Been working for Sam's aunt for about three years now. But this weekend's different from the usual events. Usually, we don't mingle much with the guests. We're background, you know? Part of the set dressing. But this private party's way more relaxed. Guess it helps that most of you are Sam's friends rather than paying customers."

Shea raised an eyebrow, intrigued. "So, since it's more relaxed, think you can spill the plot for the weekend? Give us the inside scoop? Who's the killer? What's the twist?"

Leroy chuckled, shaking his head as he took his shot. The cue ball veered off course, narrowly missing its target and bouncing off the rail. "Shit," he muttered, then looked up. "Couldn't tell you that even if I wanted to. I'm as in the dark as you are. Sam's keeping this one to himself. All I know is to cook when I'm told, clean when I'm told, and play along if something happens in front of me."

Russell, lounging nearby with his legs stretched out, smirked over the rim of his glass. "So you could be the killer? The cook did it in the kitchen with the carving knife?"

Leroy shrugged, his grin widening, showing that gold tooth that caught the light. "Could be. Hell, I might end up dead, too. Sam didn't exactly give me a script. Just told me where to be and when. The rest is improvisation."

Shea laughed, pointing at Leroy with his cue stick. "If you die, we're screwed. Who's gonna feed us? Are we supposed to fend for ourselves? I can barely make toast."

"Exactly," Leroy shot back with mock seriousness. "That's why I'm staying alive. Self-preservation through culinary necessity. I'm too valuable to kill off."

Russell took a long sip of his drink, the ice cubes clinking, his mischievous grin returning as the alcohol loosened his filter. "So, Shea," he said, leaning forward with the conspiratorial air of a man about to discuss something important. "You got your eye on anyone this weekend? Any romantic prospects? How about the maid—Kelly, right?"

Shea chuckled, shaking his head as he lined up his next shot. "Nah, man. I'm here for the free booze and Leroy's cooking. That's the real romance. Me and that chicken we had? That's a love story."

"Oh, come on," Russell pressed, not willing to let it go. "She's a hot little thing. What's her deal, Leroy? She single? What's her story?"

Leroy grinned, playing along. "Single and ready to mingle, far as I know. But hands off—I've got dibs. I saw her first. Been working with her for two years."

Russell laughed, raising his glass. "You better move fast, then. Window of opportunity and all that. Weekend doesn't last forever."

Shea took his shot—another successful sink—and smirked. "Don't worry, Leroy. I'm not in the running. Not really my type anyway."

Russell feigned disappointment, his hand over his heart. "No fun, man. You're no fun. What about Lacy, then? The ex-girlfriend? She's pretty."

Shea's grin faltered for just a moment before returning, something flickering across his face. "She's cute," he admitted carefully. "But I think she's next to go. She's got that 'doomed' vibe, you know? The mysterious outsider who doesn't quite fit? Classic first victim material."

Russell frowned, his expression darkening, his tone suddenly defensive. "Nah. Sam will keep her around. He's clearly got a thing for her. You can see it in the way he looks at her. He's not gonna kill off his ex-girlfriend that easily."

Shea leaned on his cue stick, studying the table, his grin turning sly. "You think so? I bet he's actually fucking his assistant. Gwen, right? She's got 'trouble' written all over her. That whole power dynamic thing they've got going."

The remark hung in the air, sharp and unexpected. Russell's jovial expression hardened immediately. His gaze narrowed into a pointed glare, his body language shifting from relaxed to tense.

"Hey," he said sharply, his voice cutting through the room's warmth like a blade. "Watch your mouth."

Shea blinked, genuinely startled by the sudden shift. He straightened up, his playful demeanor vanishing. "Sorry," he said quickly, raising his hands in surrender. "I didn't mean anything by it. Just speculation. Part of the game, right?"

"It's not part of the game," Russell said, his voice low and controlled but carrying an edge. His knuckles were white around his glass.

Leroy, sensing the tension crackling between them, stepped in with a calming smile. "Alright, let's keep it cool," he said, moving slightly between them, his considerable presence helping to diffuse things. "We've got a long weekend ahead. No need to start a brawl over theories about fictional murders."

Russell exhaled slowly, visibly working to compose himself, his shoulders gradually relaxing though his jaw remained tight. "Fair enough," he muttered, though the edge in his voice lingered, and he looked away, taking a long drink.

The moment stretched uncomfortably, the earlier easy atmosphere shattered.

The mood gradually eased as Leroy took his next shot with exaggerated focus, trying to restart the flow of the evening. The cue ball glided smoothly across the table, missing its target but looking good doing it.

Shea focused on the game with new intensity, his movements more subdued now, clearly chastened by Russell's reaction.

Russell leaned against the wall, swirling his drink thoughtfully, staring into the amber liquid like it held answers.

"So," Leroy said after a long moment, breaking the awkward silence with determined cheerfulness, "who's winning this thing? Me or Shea?"

Russell smirked, his humor slowly returning though it didn't quite reach his eyes. "Neither of you. You're both terrible. I'm calling the next game."

"You said you weren't good at pool," Shea pointed out, grateful for the return to normalcy.

"I'm not," Russell admitted. "But I can't be worse than what I'm watching."

The three exchanged grins, the tension slowly dissipating like smoke as the banter cautiously resumed, the rhythm of their interaction trying to find its groove again.

CHAPTER TWENTY-FOUR

The bathroom was a sanctuary of heat and haze, a world unto itself, shrouded in a thick veil of steam that obscured everything beyond arm's reach.

Sam stood beneath the rainfall showerhead, his head bowed as hot water cascaded over his body, tracing every defined line of muscle across his shoulders and down his back, running in rivulets across his chest. The heat was therapeutic, almost meditative, the water pressure perfect—strong enough to massage tension from his shoulders but not so hard it felt aggressive.

His thoughts swirled as restlessly as the steam around him, refusing to settle, lingering on the events of the evening—the meticulous planning that had gone into every moment, the guests' reactions to Curtis's "death" and Chelsie's collapse, and the secrets still left to unfold. Had he paced it right? Was the tension building properly? Would they figure it out too soon or too late?

The soap in his hand glided absently across his chest, the familiar routine offering little distraction from the weight of the weekend's plot. His mind drifted from Lacy—the way she'd looked at him when they'd talked at the bow of the yacht, that old connection still there—then to Gwen, to the tangled web of truth and illusion he had so carefully constructed.

He barely registered the faint creak of a floorboard just beyond the bathroom door—old houses made noise, after all. Nothing unusual.

But then it came again—softer, slower, deliberate. Not the random settling of wood but the careful placement of weight by someone trying to be quiet.

Sam froze mid-lather, his hand stilling on his ribs, his senses sharpening instantly from relaxed to alert. He turned his head slightly, peering through the thick mist toward the white shower curtain that separated him from the rest of the bathroom.

A shadow appeared beyond the translucent barrier—faint but unmistakable, a human silhouette shifting just beyond the plastic. His pulse quickened, tension coiling in his chest like a spring winding tight. The shadow moved closer, and he could hear it now—the subtle scrape of shoes on tile, the whisper of fabric moving.

Part of his mind said this was part of the game, this was something planned that he had forgotten. But another part—the part that knew he was naked and vulnerable—wasn't so sure.

Before he could act, before he could call out or move, the shower curtain ripped open with a sharp hiss of plastic rings on metal rod.

———

Gwen's piercing gaze locked onto Sam, her expression sharp and predatory, her dark eyes glinting with something dangerous. In her hand, a gleaming knife was raised high, poised to strike, the blade catching the light and throwing it back in a wicked gleam.

For a split second—just a heartbeat—Sam's entire world contracted to that knife, his body tensing instinctively, adrenaline flooding his system.

Then came the plunge.

The blade drove toward his stomach with precision, and Sam's reflexive gasp was sharp and genuine, echoing off the tile walls. He glanced down, half expecting to see crimson streaks marring the soap and water on his skin.

But there was nothing—no pain, no tearing flesh, no wound, no blood. The knife's retractable blade had collapsed into its handle on impact, doing exactly what it was designed to do.

Sam let out a short laugh, shaking his head as relief mingled with exasperation and genuine adrenaline comedown. His heart was still racing. "Really, Gwen?" he said, his voice dry. "Really? That's how you're playing this?"

Gwen's fierce demeanor cracked immediately, her lips breaking into a wide, satisfied grin as she held up the harmless prop, admiring it like a trophy. "Gotcha. You should've seen your face. Priceless. That's genuine fear. That's the reaction we want from the guests."

Sam ran a hand through his wet hair, slicking it back from his forehead, chuckling despite himself. "You're relentless. Seriously, can I not even shower in peace? Is nothing sacred? Do I need to lock the bathroom door?"

"It's part of my charm," Gwen replied with a shrug, stepping back and twirling the knife theatrically before tossing it onto the bathroom counter with a clatter. It skittered across the marble surface, coming to rest against a bottle of cologne.

Sam was about to retort, about to say something clever about boundaries or professionalism, when Gwen took a step closer. The playfulness in her expression shifted, becoming something else—something more intentional, more dangerous.

Her hands moved to the hem of her lingerie gown—black silk, he noticed now, the kind of thing that was clearly chosen with purpose—and in one fluid, deliberate motion, she let it fall to the floor, pooling around her feet like a whisper of silk and shadow.

She stepped into the shower, completely unbothered by the

water that immediately began soaking her hair, running down her body, her skin glistening. She moved with absolute confidence, no hesitation.

"Hey," she murmured, her voice dropping to a sultry whisper that somehow cut through the sound of the water. "I thought of a way you can repay me. For all my hard work this weekend."

Sam's smirk faltered, replaced by a flicker of wariness, of recognition that this was dangerous territory they'd agreed not to revisit. "Gwen," he began, his tone cautious. "What are you doing? We talked about this."

Her fingers trailed up his chest, feather-light but insistent, leaving trails of heat despite the water. "What does it look like I'm doing?" she replied, her lips curving into a knowing smile. She pressed herself against him, her warmth undeniable, her body fitting against his with practiced familiarity.

"This isn't a good idea," Sam said, his voice trying to stay firm but tinged with obvious reluctance, with the weakness of someone whose willpower was already crumbling. "We said no more of this. After last time, we said—"

"That was months ago," Gwen interrupted, her voice soft but insistent. She tilted her head, her wet hair falling across her shoulder, her eyes gleaming with defiance and challenge. "It's just one more time. No strings, no complications. Just us. You owe me anyway—you know how hard I've worked on this weekend."

Sam studied her, the heat of the shower suddenly rivaled by the heat in her gaze, by the heat of her body pressed against his. The air felt thicker, the steam clinging to his skin. His resolve wavered visibly, his hands hovering uncertainly.

"You're impossible," he muttered, though his voice lacked any real conviction, and they both knew it.

"I know," Gwen replied, her smile widening. "That's why you keep me around."

Gwen's smile widened further, triumphant, reading his surrender before he even acknowledged it himself. She leaned in and claimed his lips in a kiss that was anything but tentative. It was urgent, demanding, a clash of need and familiarity that reignited something long buried between them—something they'd tried to forget, tried to professionalize away, but that had never really died.

Sam hesitated only for a heartbeat, some final protest dying in his throat, before surrendering completely. His hands slid to her waist, pulling her closer against him, any pretense of resistance evaporating like the steam around them. This was a bad idea—he knew it was a bad idea—but in the moment, he couldn't bring himself to care.

The kiss deepened, became more intense, the sound of the water mingling with the soft hum of their breathing. Gwen's fingers tangled in his wet hair, her touch firm yet tender, possessive yet somehow still affectionate. Sam's hands roamed, tracing the familiar curve of her back, her waist, her hips, muscle memory taking over.

The steam enveloped them like a cocoon, blurring the boundaries between past and present, between what was and what could never be, between professional and personal, between the game they were playing for the guests and the game they were playing with each other.

For a moment, the weekend faded into the background. The carefully constructed plot, the elaborate staging, the guests and their expectations—all of it dissolved into the heat and steam and the press of their bodies.

The weight of their shared history hung between them, unspoken but undeniable—all those late nights planning events, the tension that had built over months, the times before that they'd sworn would never happen again, and here they were.

They gave in to the pull of the moment, to the chemistry that had always been there, crackling beneath every professional interaction. The water streamed over them, erasing the lines of their self-imposed rules, washing away their better judgment, if only for a little while.

CHAPTER TWENTY-FIVE

The upstairs hallway stretched on like a scene from a dream —or a nightmare, depending on your state of mind and blood alcohol content. Shadows danced against the walls in strange, organic patterns, cast by the flickering glow of dim candelabras spaced unevenly along the corridor—some ornate brass fixtures that looked original to the house, others more modern replacements that didn't quite match.

Zoey's footsteps echoed faintly, a soft, irregular rhythm against the stillness, each step slightly uncertain. Her champagne-fueled buzz left her movements unsteady—not drunk exactly, but definitely not sober, that pleasant floating feeling where everything seemed slightly softer around the edges. But it wasn't enough to dull the edge of curiosity and the faint unease buzzing at the back of her mind.

The ocean breeze wafted through the hall from somewhere —a window left open, probably—carrying the faint scent of salt and something tropical, mixed with the rhythmic whisper of waves crashing far below. The sound was constant but somehow made the silence feel more profound.

Somewhere in the distance, a floorboard creaked—that particular groan of old wood settling, or someone moving through the house. The sound amplified the eerie quiet rather than breaking it, making Zoey pause mid-step, her pulse quickening. She glanced behind her down the dark corridor, seeing nothing but shadows, then pressed forward, driven by champagne-induced courage and genuine concern about where Chelsie had been taken.

She stopped in front of a door at the end of the hall—Sam's room, at least she was pretty sure, based on the layout Gwen had explained earlier. Its dark wood was slightly ajar, just a crack, enough to see that there was light inside. A faint sliver of moonlight escaped through the gap, illuminating the intricate carving along its edges—more of those roses and vines.

Raising her hand to knock, she hesitated, her knuckles hovering inches from the wood. The stillness on the other side felt heavy, almost alive, like the room itself was holding its breath.

Instead of knocking, making a split-second decision, she nudged the door open with a cautious push.

The door creaked softly as it swung open—that classic horror movie sound that was somehow worse in real life—revealing the dimly lit interior. Moonlight streamed through partially drawn curtains, casting silvery streaks across the room in geometric patterns. Zoey stepped inside, her eyes scanning the space as they adjusted.

The bed was unmade, a tangle of dark sheets spilling onto the floor like they'd been kicked off. Clothes were strewn haphazardly across a chair—jeans, a shirt, something that might have been underwear. The faint scent of steam and soap lingered in the air, mixing with cologne and something else, hinting at recent activity. The room was very Sam—organized chaos.

"Sam?" Zoey called softly, her voice barely above a whisper, suddenly aware that barging into her brother's bedroom uninvited was weird, even by their standards. "What did you do with Chelsie? Sam? Are you here?"

The room answered only with silence and the distant sound of running water.

Her gaze drifted to the bathroom door on the far side of the room, which hung slightly open, just enough to see steam escaping, billowing out into the cooler bedroom air. Through the crack, the faint sound of running water reached her ears, steady and rhythmic—a shower running full blast.

Zoey's curiosity flared, tempered by a growing unease and the nagging voice in her head that said she should probably just leave. But she'd come this far, and she needed to know where Chelsie was, what the plan was for tomorrow.

She moved closer, each step hesitant but deliberate, her bare feet soundless on the plush carpet—she'd kicked off her shoes somewhere, couldn't remember where. She pressed her palm against the bathroom door, feeling the moisture-swollen wood, pushing it open just enough to peer inside.

The room was a haze of steam, thick and almost impenetrable, the air heavy with heat and moisture that immediately made her skin feel damp. Zoey's gaze landed on the shower—one of those large, modern walk-in types with glass walls that were currently completely fogged—where two shadowy figures stood locked in a passionate embrace.

The water cascaded over them, glinting off their intertwined forms, and even through the steam and fog, the intimacy of what she was seeing was unmistakable. Bodies pressed together, hands moving, the kind of kissing that was definitely going somewhere.

For a moment, Zoey's brain struggled to process the scene, to reconcile what she was seeing with what she'd expected to find. Her breath hitched audibly—a small gasp she couldn't quite suppress—and she instinctively stepped back, nearly stumbling over her own feet. Her heart pounded in her chest, adrenaline mixing with embarrassment and champagne.

The intimacy of the moment—the raw vulnerability of the figures before her—made her feel like an intruder, a voyeur, though she hadn't intended to be.

Her eyes flicked downward, desperate to look anywhere else, landing on a neatly folded pile of clothes resting on a teak bench beside the shower. Atop the stack sat a sleek black planner, its cover glinting faintly in the low light—expensive leather, the kind that cost real money, with gold edging.

Zoey froze, recognition hitting her like a jolt of electricity. She'd seen that planner before. Gwen carried it everywhere, consulted it constantly, treated it like the nuclear codes.

"Gwen," she murmured under her breath, the pieces snapping together with sudden clarity. Not Lacy. Not some random hookup. Gwen. Sam's assistant. His right hand. His... apparently more than assistant.

She let out a short, disbelieving laugh—quiet, more of a huff of air—shaking her head at the absurdity, at the cliché of it all. "Well, at least someone's getting some," she whispered to herself, finding humor in it despite the awkwardness.

That explained so much, actually. The way they worked together, the late nights, the tension she'd sometimes sensed between them that she'd attributed to work stress.

Zoey backed out of the bathroom as quietly as she'd entered, moving carefully, her hand finding the doorframe as she steadied herself. Her thoughts raced—should she say something to Sam? Pretend she didn't see? Tell Chelsie? Keep it to herself?

She slipped out of the bedroom, closing the door behind her with a soft click that seemed impossibly loud in the quiet hallway. The latch engaging sounded like a gunshot to her hypersensitive ears.

The hallway stretched before her, dim and endless, the shadows seeming darker now, deeper. The candelabras flickered —just the bulbs being old, probably, but it felt ominous in the moment.

Her pace quickened as she moved down the corridor, her footsteps light against the hardwood but faster now, almost hurrying. A part of her wanted to laugh off what she'd seen, chalking it up to Sam's usual intensity—he did everything passionately, why would relationships be different?—and Gwen's boldness.

But another part of her couldn't shake the odd feeling that had settled in her chest—a mix of unease and intrigue and something she couldn't quite name. It wasn't judgment exactly. More like... concern? Worry about what happened when the weekend ended, when they had to go back to working together professionally. This seemed like the kind of thing that complicated everything.

"Just a little harmless fun," she muttered to herself, though the words rang hollow even as she said them, bouncing off the walls and coming back sounding false.

Was it harmless? Probably. Sam was an adult, Gwen was an adult, they could do what they wanted. But something about it felt... off. Not wrong exactly, just not quite right. Like a piece of the puzzle that didn't fit the way it should. Maybe it was just her rooting for Lacy over Gwen.

As she descended the grand staircase, her hand trailing along the smooth bannister, the mansion seemed to shift around her. Or maybe it was just the champagne wearing off. The shadows deepened, seeming to pulse slightly with her heartbeat. The house's secrets thickened in the night, becoming almost tangible.

Zoey couldn't shake the feeling that what she'd stumbled upon was just one thread in a much larger, much darker tapestry. Sam and Gwen's love affair was just one secret among many in this house.

And whether she wanted to or not, she was already tangled in it. She'd seen something she wasn't supposed to see, knew something she wasn't supposed to know, and that changed things. That made her part of the web. Or did it? Was she supposed to see that? Was it part of the game? Her mind wandered.

At the bottom of the stairs, she paused, looking back up into the darkness of the second floor. Should she go back? Confront Sam? Forget the whole thing?

No. She'd leave it alone. For now.

She needed to find her room or find Chelsie—wherever they'd taken her for the "body disposal"—and sleep off the champagne. Tomorrow would be complicated enough without adding this to it.

But as she walked through the mansion's ground floor, heading toward her room, she couldn't help but wonder what other secrets were lurking in the shadows. What other intimate moments were happening behind closed doors or perhaps behind open doors waiting to be found.

And most pressingly—where the hell was Chelsie, and when could they compare notes about this increasingly weird weekend?

CHAPTER TWENTY-SIX

Chelsie's eyes fluttered open, consciousness returning in slow, uncomfortable waves. Her head pounded with the dull, insistent rhythm of a lingering headache—the kind that pressed behind her eyes and made her skull feel too small. The whiskey and the late hour were both conspiring against her now.

The silence in the cabin room was thick, almost physical, broken only by the faint rustle of the curtains as a gentle breeze nudged them through the window she'd left cracked open.

She groaned softly, her hand groping blindly across the unfamiliar nightstand for the lamp she knew had to be there somewhere. Her fingers found the switch, and warm, amber light spilled over the room, chasing away the shadows that had been clinging to the edges like living things.

She sat up slowly, wincing at the movement, her fingers pressing into her temples as she tried to ease the ache with pressure. Her thoughts were sluggish, weighed down by the lingering effects of the evening's indulgence, too much whiskey. Her mouth felt dry, cottony, and she needed water. And the bathroom.

With a quiet sigh, she swung her legs over the side of the bed, her bare feet brushing against the cool, worn floorboards.

The chill sent a shiver up her spine, jolting her slightly more awake, goosebumps rising on her skin. She was dressed only in a tank top and a pair of cheeky underwear—the cabin had been warm when she'd gone to sleep, but now the night air felt cooler, almost cold.

She stood and stretched, her muscles protesting with little aches and pains. Her back popped.

The room was simple, sparsely furnished compared to the mansion—just a bed, a single nightstand, and a small dresser pushed against the far wall. No luxury here, just the basics.

Chelsie cast a brief glance around, the faint glow of the lamp catching the edges of the furniture and creating deep shadows in the corners. Something about the stillness of the night felt heavier than it should, more oppressive. The cabin felt more isolated than it had when Gwen had left them here. More alone.

She padded toward the door, her steps soft against the floor, trying not to wake Curtis in the other room. The wood creaked faintly as she eased it open, revealing the dimly lit hallway beyond—just a short stretch connecting the two bedrooms to the bathroom and main living area.

Moonlight trickled in through a narrow window at the far end, casting pale, silvery streaks across the walls that seemed to shift and move as clouds passed overhead. The silence was almost oppressive, every sound amplified—her breathing, her heartbeat, the settling of the old cabin's boards.

Chelsie moved carefully, her fingertips grazing the wall for reassurance, for orientation in the dim light. She passed Curtis's closed door, pausing briefly to listen. The quiet from within was absolute—just the faint sound of snoring, barely audible. Satisfied, she continued toward the bathroom, her gaze darting nervously to the shadows that seemed to stretch and shift with every step.

It was just the moonlight playing tricks, she told herself. Just an unfamiliar place at night. Nothing to worry about.

Reaching the bathroom door, she grasped the handle—cold

metal against her palm—and pushed it open, stepping inside. The faint scent of damp tiles greeted her, that particular bathroom smell of moisture and soap. She reached for the light switch, her hand fumbling on the wall before finding it.

The fluorescent bulb flickered uncertainly—once, twice—before buzzing to life with that harsh, electric sound, casting a stark, clinical glow over the small space. The light was too bright after the darkness, making her squint.

Chelsie shut the door behind her and leaned momentarily against it, the cool wood soothing against her back, grounding her. She took a breath, trying to shake off the weird feeling of unease that had settled over her. It was just the whiskey, the unfamiliar location, the lateness of the hour. Nothing more.

She moved to the toilet, lowering herself with a weary sigh. The whiskey from earlier was definitely catching up to her—she'd lost count of how many glasses they'd gone through.

As she finished and flushed, the sound impossibly loud in the small space, she shuffled to the sink, turning on the tap and letting the cool water cascade over her fingers. She splashed some onto her face, gasping slightly at the shock of the temperature. The cold chased away the last remnants of sleep fog, made her feel more alert, more present.

She did it again, cupping water in her hands and pressing it against her closed eyes, feeling it run down her cheeks and drip from her chin.

Her reflection stared back at her from the mirror when she opened her eyes—tired, disheveled, makeup smeared slightly under her eyes. She ran her fingers through her tousled hair, attempting to smooth it into some semblance of order, but the action felt futile. She looked like she'd been through something.

"Get it together, Chelsie," she murmured to herself, her voice barely audible over the hum of the fluorescent light and the drip of the faucet. "It's just a weekend. Just a game."

She turned off the faucet and reached for the towel hanging nearby—rough, cheap, not like the plush ones at the mansion.

Drying her hands and face, she let out a slow breath and moved to the door, feeling slightly more human.

She flicked off the light, plunging herself back into darkness for a moment before opening the door.

As she opened the door, the hallway greeted her with its dark, silent embrace. The moonlight seemed dimmer now, or maybe her eyes just hadn't adjusted yet after the bright bathroom light. She stepped forward, her bare feet brushing against the cool wood, leaving the bathroom behind.

The shadows seemed to ripple—just her imagination, surely, just her eyes playing tricks in the darkness.

But before she could fully process the motion, before she could even register that something was wrong, two pink-gloved hands shot out of the darkness beside her.

The grip was instant and unyielding, professional. One hand clamped over her mouth, smothering the scream that tried to break free, that tried to warn Curtis, to call for help. The other gripped her head with a force that sent panic surging through her veins like ice water.

Chelsie's eyes widened in terror, her body thrashing instinctively, trying to break free, to fight back, to do something. Her hands clawed at the arm across her face, her nails digging in, but the grip was too strong, too practiced.

Her muffled cries were frantic, desperate, her breaths shallow and quick through her nose, her heart hammering so hard she could hear it in her ears.

This wasn't the game.

This wasn't part of the mystery.

This was real.

The gloved hand over her mouth silenced every plea, every gasp. The cold leather pressed against her skin, smelling of something chemical, something wrong. It was the last sensation she truly registered before her head twisted sharply, violently, far beyond any natural range of motion.

SNAP!

The sickening sound echoed through the empty hallway, impossibly loud in the oppressive silence—the sound of vertebrae separating, of a neck breaking, of life ending in an instant. It was a sound that couldn't be mistaken for anything else.

Final.

Absolute.

Her body went instantly limp, crumpling to the floor in a heap, lifeless. The fight left her all at once, like strings being cut. She fell awkwardly, one leg folded under her, one arm twisted at an unnatural angle. Her wide eyes stared blankly ahead, frozen in an expression of terror and confusion, pupils dilated, seeing nothing now.

Seeing nothing ever again.

The figure in the shadows lingered for a moment, standing over her still form, breathing quietly, calmly, completely unaffected by what they'd just done. Gloved hands flexed once, twice, as if working out tension. The pink gloves were pristine—no blood, no evidence, nothing.

Then, with deliberate, unhurried steps—the confidence of someone who knew they had time, who knew they wouldn't be discovered—they slowly picked up Chelsie's lifeless body and melted back into the darkness, disappearing as silently as they'd appeared.

CHAPTER TWENTY-SEVEN

Curtis jolted awake, a sharp intake of breath filling his lungs as his heart thundered in his chest like a drum. The transition from sleep to waking was violent, disorienting—that horrible sensation of falling that yanks you back to consciousness.

For a moment, he lay frozen, staring at the unfamiliar ceiling, trying to remember where he was. The cabin. Right. The isolated cabin on the cliff.

The quiet seemed to press in around him, oppressive and thick, the stillness amplifying every tiny sound—the faint rustling of the wind outside testing the cabin's walls, the distant crash of waves far below, the settling creaks of old wood.

His mind raced, grasping for the threads of a dream that dissolved too quickly to remember, leaving only impressions— running, fear, something chasing him. A creeping unease settled over him, the kind that lingered long after waking, that made your skin crawl for reasons you couldn't quite articulate.

Something felt wrong, but he couldn't say what.

He rubbed his face roughly, his palms cool against his damp skin—he'd been sweating in his sleep, the sheets slightly damp beneath him. "Just a dream," he muttered to himself, though the words did little to reassure him. "Just your brain being stupid."

Shifting, trying to get comfortable again, he pushed aside the hiking map that had slipped onto his chest during the night—he must have fallen asleep looking at it. He swung his legs over the edge of the bed, his bare feet brushing against the cold, uneven floorboards. The chill shot up his legs, fully waking him.

He wasn't going to get back to sleep. Not with this feeling.

Turning on the small lamp beside the bed, he watched as its warm, yellowish glow spilled across the room, chasing away the oppressive shadows. The light helped, made things feel more normal, more real.

Stretching, working the stiffness from his back, Curtis stood, running a hand through his disheveled hair. He slowly made his way to the door.

The hallway beyond his room was dim, with just the faint silver light from the moon streaming through that small window at the far end. Curtis stepped carefully into the corridor, his steps muffled against the worn wood, trying not to make noise. The air was cool—cooler than he expected—and carried a faint, salty tang mixed with something else he couldn't quite identify.

He stopped in front of Chelsie's door, which was slightly ajar —just a crack, enough to see darkness beyond. Had she left it open? Was she up?

Hesitating, feeling vaguely creepy about this but unable to shake his unease, he nudged it open wider with his fingertips, leaning his head inside cautiously.

"Chelsie?" he whispered. "You awake?"

The bed was there, visible in the moonlight from her window. Neatly made—or maybe just undisturbed—with a lump visible beneath the blankets. She must be asleep, buried under the covers.

For a brief moment, his mind wandered, a fleeting thought tempting him to step closer. She'd looked beautiful in that pink dress on the yacht. But he shook it off, feeling immediately foolish, chuckling softly at himself. She'd made her position crystal clear. And she was with Zoey anyway.

"Good night, Chelsie," he murmured, more to himself than to the figure under the covers, his voice barely audible. "Sweet dreams."

Pulling the door shut gently, hearing the soft click of the latch, he turned away, feeling a little foolish for giving Chelsie the orange rose on the yacht earlier.

Curtis made his way down the hall toward the bathroom, his bladder reminding him why he'd probably woken up in the first place. The drinks from dinner and the rum he'd had before bed were demanding to be processed.

Reaching the bathroom door, he pushed it open—it swung easily, hinges silent—and flipped up the light switch.

Nothing. Darkness.

He tried again, flipping the switch back and forth several times—up, down, up, down—but the darkness remained unbroken.

"Figures," he muttered under his breath, exasperation mingling with growing unease. "This place has to be ancient. Probably hasn't been updated since the seventies."

He considered going back for his phone to use as a flashlight, but that seemed excessive for just taking a piss. He could see well enough.

He stepped inside, and pull the door shut leaving it slightly ajar to let in a sliver of moonlight from the hallway. The dim light illuminated the edges of the small space, casting long, uneven shadows that seemed to shift and dance with the faint breeze coming through the cracked bathroom window—had that been open before? The temperature was noticeably cooler in here.

Positioning himself by the toilet, Curtis let out a quiet sigh as he began to relieve himself, the sound seeming impossibly loud in the silence. The tension in his shoulders eased slightly as his body relaxed.

He glanced over his shoulder nervously, his eyes darting toward the hallway visible through the cracked door, paranoid that Chelsie would see him and his *hardware.*

The silence stretched unnervingly, broken only by his own breathing and the distant ocean. Then—the faint creak of a floorboard. The cabin settling. Or was it?

He flinched, his stream interrupting for a moment. "Get a grip, man," he muttered, shaking his head at his own paranoia. "It's just an old cabin. Old places make noise."

He turned his gaze back forward, focusing on the mundane task at hand, trying to think about anything else. Tomorrow they'd explore the island, maybe swim at that beach Gwen had mentioned.

SLICE!

THUMP.

Curtis looked down to see his penis sinking to the bottom of the toilet bowl. The strike was sudden, vicious, and blindingly painful beyond anything Curtis had ever experienced. The blade —something sharp, surgical, precisely aimed—sliced through flesh and nerve with clinical efficiency.

Curtis's scream tore through the quiet cabin, raw and primal, echoing down the hall and probably carrying into the night beyond. A sound of pure agony, of violation, of horror.

He stumbled forward, his body moving on instinct, slamming into the wall for support as his legs threatened to give out. His gaze dropped backed to the toilet, where blood swirled in the water—vivid crimson blooming from him like a grotesque flower.

Trembling, shaking violently, his hands shot to his groin, clutching desperately at the gaping wound, trying to hold himself together, trying to stop the bleeding. Hot, sticky blood spilled through his fingers, over his hands, down his legs. Warm. Too warm.

His breaths came in short, panicked gasps, hyperventilating, his mind unable to accept the reality. The shock was overwhelming, his vision already starting to blur at the edges, his body going into crisis.

Before he could fully comprehend the scope of his injury, before he could scream again or try to run or do anything, a shadowy figure loomed behind him. The glint of a blade caught his eye in the moonlight, slick now with his blood, and he barely had time to react—his hands moving weakly to defend himself—before the knife plunged into his stomach.

The pain was sharp and all-encompassing, different from the first wound—deeper, more visceral, stealing the breath from his lungs completely. He tried to scream but couldn't, just a wet gasp escaping.

His body convulsed, muscles spasming as he crumpled to the floor, his legs finally giving out entirely. He landed hard on the cold tiles, the impact jarring but distant, his body going into shock.

Blood pooled beneath him rapidly, spreading across the tiles in a dark, spreading stain, warm against his cooling skin. So much blood. He didn't know a person had so much blood.

His vision blurred further, the world around him dimming, going gray at the edges and then darker. Through the haze, through eyes that wouldn't quite focus anymore, he caught a glimpse of the figure standing over him, looking down at him.

Their features were obscured by the shadows, or maybe his vision was just failing. He couldn't tell. But he could see the knife, slick with blood—his blood—gleaming faintly in the pale moonlight.

The figure didn't move, didn't speak. Just stood there. Watching him die.

Curtis tried to speak, to ask why, to beg for help, to say something, but his mouth wouldn't work right. Blood was in his throat. His lungs weren't working. Nothing was working.

As darkness consumed him, pulling him down like deep water, Curtis's final thought was a desperate, unspoken question that he would never get answer to:

Why?

CHAPTER TWENTY-EIGHT

The golden-orange hues of dawn stretched across the lush landscape, painting the island in a tranquil glow that promised another beautiful day in paradise, despite the horrors that had unfolded in the night. Waves crashed rhythmically against the jagged cliffs far below, their salty mist catching the early sunlight like thousands of diamonds suspended in the air, creating momentary rainbows that vanished as quickly as they appeared. The sky was clear, the temperature already warming, the morning mist beginning to burn off the grounds.

Within the mansion, the serenity of the morning clashed with the faint hum of human life stirring—the old building creaking as people moved through it, plumbing groaning as showers started, the distant clatter of someone in the kitchen beginning breakfast preparations.

No one yet knew that two people who'd gone to sleep last night would never wake up, except the killer of course.

In Russell and Norma's guest room—a spacious suite on the mansion's second floor with a view of the eastern gardens—Russell sat hunched over a small antique desk he'd repurposed as a workspace, already dressed in khakis and a polo shirt, deep into his morning routine as if he'd never left the office.

The pale glow of his laptop cast shadows on his face in the pre-dawn dimness, the screen a portal to the world he had ostensibly left behind for the weekend. His fingers moved swiftly across the keyboard, the clatter of keys forming a rhythm, occasionally punctuated by aggressive clicking when something frustrated him.

Next to him, positioned carefully on a leather coaster, a steaming mug of coffee rested within reach—black, no sugar, the way he always took it. The occasional sip fueled his focus, though the coffee was going cold as he got absorbed in spreadsheets and emails that couldn't possibly be as urgent as he was treating them.

Behind him, the bed shifted as Norma began to stir, the expensive sheets rustling. A soft groan escaped her lips, her hand reaching instinctively toward the empty side of the bed where Russell should have been, finding only cool sheets and a pillow that had been abandoned hours ago.

Her eyes fluttered open, squinting against the faint light streaming through the partially drawn curtains—Russell must have opened them when he woke up, always an early riser, unable to sleep past six even on vacation.

She propped herself up on one elbow, her blonde hair messy from sleep, her gaze settling on Russell's back with a mixture of affection and exasperation. This was so typical.

"Morning," she murmured, her voice still heavy with sleep.

Russell glanced over his shoulder, offering a brief smile that didn't quite reach his eyes. "Good morning," he replied, his tone pleasant enough though distracted. His attention quickly returned to the glowing screen.

Norma stretched languidly, her arms reaching wide as a contented sigh escaped her. "You're already working?" she asked, disbelief in her tone though she shouldn't have been surprised. This was Russell. This was what he did. "We're on an island. At a murder mystery weekend. And you're working."

"Just trying to stay ahead of the game," Russell replied,

shrugging without looking away from his screen. "You know how it is. The Paris office doesn't care that I'm out of the country. And Mitchell's been screwing up the Henderson account."

Norma rolled her eyes, swinging her legs over the edge of the bed, her bare feet touching the plush rug beneath. "Brought work to the party," she muttered under her breath, more to herself than to him, though loud enough that he could probably hear.

She padded across the room toward him.

Leaning over him from behind, Norma placed a quick kiss on Russell's cheek, her lips brushing against the faint stubble on his jawline. "You need to take a break," she said softly, her words carrying both a suggestion and a plea. "Remember what the therapist said? About work-life balance?"

"Yeah, yeah," Russell replied, barely looking up, not really hearing her. His fingers continued to dance across the keyboard, his attention anchored to numbers and projections and problems that felt more manageable than actual human connection. "Just need to finish this one thing."

It was never just one thing. They both knew it.

Norma sighed, shaking her head as she moved toward the bathroom, giving up for now. "I'm taking a shower," she announced, her voice light but firm.

"Okay," Russell muttered, his focus unbroken, probably not even registering what she'd said.

She paused at the bathroom door, turning back toward him, trying one more time. "Is there coffee left?"

Russell's hand froze mid-type, the question finally penetrating his work-focused haze. He glanced at the empty glass pot on the small coffee station they'd set up on the dresser—he'd finished it an hour ago, hadn't he? Guilt flickered across his features.

"Uh, no," he admitted sheepishly, finally making actual eye contact with her. "I'll make more. Sorry."

"Thanks," Norma said, flashing him a faint smile that suggested forgiveness, or at least acceptance. "Two sugars. You remember?"

"Two sugars," Russell confirmed, nodding. "I got it."

As the bathroom door clicked shut behind her, Russell let out a long sigh, running a hand through his hair. He leaned back in his chair, the tension in his shoulders easing momentarily as he allowed himself a brief break. He stared at the laptop screen —the words and numbers blurring slightly.

What was he doing? Why couldn't he just shut it off?

After a moment, he stood, stretching his back which protested with a series of small pops, and made his way to the corner where the coffee station waited.

The coffee machine gurgled softly as Russell set it to brew, going through the familiar motions—fresh filter, measured grounds, water to the line. The aroma of freshly ground beans began filling the room, rich and earthy, one of his favorite smells.

He leaned against the counter, his arms crossed as he stared out the small window overlooking the mansion's grounds. The morning sunlight highlighted the dew still clinging to the grass of the formal gardens below, each droplet catching the light like a tiny prism. It was beautiful, he had to admit. Norma had been right to push for this trip.

His mind wandered as he waited, the low hum of the machine blending with his thoughts. The weekend was meant to be a distraction, a playful escape from the grind. A chance to reconnect with Norma, to show her he could be present, could be fun.

Yet, despite the elaborate games and picturesque setting, he couldn't fully shake the weight of his responsibilities. Guilt about checking email when he'd promised not to started to creep in.

The coffee pot sputtered as it finished brewing, breaking through his reverie. He poured two mugs—matching ceramic ones that had been provided with the room—adding two sugars to one, stirring carefully, before setting it aside for Norma. Taking a sip of his own—still too hot, burning his tongue slightly—he let the warmth spread through him, a small comfort in the stillness of the morning.

The faint sound of running water stopped, the shower shutting off with a squeak of old pipes. A few moments later, the bathroom door creaked open, steam billowing out. Norma emerged, wrapped in a fluffy white towel—one of the mansion's luxury touches—her damp hair clinging to her shoulders and back. Her skin was flushed pink from the heat.

She smiled when she saw the mug waiting for her on the counter, the gesture small but appreciated. Russell was trying, at least.

"Thanks," she said, taking the mug carefully, testing its temperature before taking a sip. The sweetness of the sugar balanced the coffee's bitterness perfectly. "Perfect," she added, her smile widening genuinely. "You remembered."

Russell returned her smile, watching as she leaned against the counter beside him, her shoulder touching his. For a moment, they stood in companionable silence, both looking out the window, the weight of the day ahead momentarily forgotten. Just two people, married fifteen years, still finding small moments of connection.

"You know," Norma said, breaking the quiet, her voice gentle rather than accusatory, "you could put the laptop away for a few hours. Enjoy the island. Enjoy me." She bumped her hip against his playfully. "I'm much more interesting than spreadsheets."

Russell chuckled, his gaze softening as he looked at her—really looked at her—seeing the woman he'd married rather than just a fixture of his life. "Maybe you're right," he admitted, though his tone carried the slightest hesitation. "I could probably step away for a bit."

Norma nudged him playfully with her elbow, sloshing her

coffee slightly. "No maybe about it," she said, her voice light but firm, the kind of firmness that came from years of dealing with his workaholic tendencies. "Now finish your coffee. We've got a mansion full of mysteries waiting. And I want to explore that beach Gwen mentioned."

CHAPTER TWENTY-NINE

The kitchen hummed with the quiet rhythm of morning activity, the heart of the mansion stirring to life while most of its occupants still slept or were just beginning to wake. Gleaming pots and pans hung from overhead racks in organized rows, catching the soft glow of the fluorescent lights and throwing back reflections like copper mirrors. The air was thick with the aroma of sizzling bacon—that unmistakable smell of Saturday morning—buttery toast browning under the broiler, and freshly brewed coffee, creating a comforting cocoon.

The steady crackle of frying eggs underscored the scene, each sound blending seamlessly into the symphony of a busy kitchen. It was a familiar music to Leroy, as natural as breathing. The hiss of butter in a hot pan, the scrape of a spatula against cast iron, the bubble and pop of something simmering on a back burner.

Leroy stood at the center of it all in his pristine white chef's coat, his movements efficient and practiced despite his large size. He'd been up since five-thirty, the way he always was when there was a full breakfast to prepare. He worked with a calm focus that came from years of professional cooking, flipping pancakes on the griddle with a deft flick of his wrist, each one landing perfectly centered on the warming plate. His soft whistling filled the room—some old Motown tune, probably the Temptations—dancing lightly over the clinking of utensils and the occasional hiss of steam.

The door swung open with a quiet creak, and Sam stepped in, his footsteps deliberate but unhurried, still in sleep clothes—sweatpants and a t-shirt, his hair slightly damp from a shower. The moment the warm, savory scents hit him, he inhaled deeply, closing his eyes briefly, his face lighting up with a genuine smile.

"Morning, Leroy," he greeted, his tone easy and cheerful. "The best-smelling room in the house. Hell, best-smelling room on the island."

Leroy glanced up from the griddle, his wide grin spreading instantly across his face, his gold tooth catching the light. "Morning, boss. You ready to fuel up? I've got enough food here to feed an army—or at least a mansion full of misfits playing detective."

Sam chuckled, crossing the room with easy strides to peek at the platters lined up on the counter. His eyes widened at the spread—scrambled eggs, crispy bacon, sausage links, pancakes stacked high, toast arranged in neat rows, hash browns golden and perfect, fresh fruit cut and arranged artfully.

"Looks amazing, as always," he said, reaching out to snag a piece of bacon from a plate, unable to resist. He bit into it with a satisfying crunch, nodding appreciatively. "Perfect. How do you make bacon this good?"

Leroy shook his head, a laugh rumbling in his broad chest. "Trade secret," he said, then added with a teasing tone, "Careful, now. Keep sneaking bites, and the rest of 'em are gonna riot when they find out breakfast's short."

Sam raised his hands in mock surrender, the bacon still clutched in one like evidence. "Alright, alright. I'll leave the masterpiece intact. For now. But I'm not making any promises about lunch."

Sam leaned casually against the counter, settling in, watching as Leroy poured a fresh batch of scrambled eggs from a large bowl into a serving dish with practiced care. Steam rose in delicate swirls, catching the morning light streaming through the kitchen window.

"You're really outdoing yourself this weekend," Sam said, his tone shifting to something more sincere. "Everyone's raving about the food. I heard Norma say that chicken last night was the best thing she'd ever tasted. And you know Norma—she's not easy to impress."

Leroy shrugged, a faint blush creeping onto his dark cheeks, clearly pleased but trying to play it cool. "Just doin' my job," he said modestly, though his grin betrayed his pride. "You know me —if you're gonna kill a guy, at least make sure his last meal's a good one. Can't send 'em to their doom on an empty stomach."

Sam laughed, shaking his head at the dark humor. "I don't think they're taking 'Murder Mansion' that literally. At least, I hope not."

Leroy winked, his tone playful. "Not yet, anyway. Weekend's still young."

There was something in the way he said it—just a joke, clearly, but Sam felt a small, inexplicable chill run down his spine. He shook it off. Just the early hour, the lingering effects of last night with Gwen, his mind still processing the weekend's elaborate setup.

As Sam pushed off the counter, stretching his back, preparing to head out and start the day's activities, he paused briefly at the door, his hand on the frame. He turned back, his expression more serious now.

"Seriously, Leroy," he said, making eye contact. "Thanks for everything. You're the glue that holds this whole crazy weekend together. I couldn't do this without you."

Leroy waved him off with a laugh, though his expression softened, clearly touched. "Go on, get outta here. Let me do my thing. You got guests to entertain, mysteries to orchestrate. I got eggs that need tending before they get rubbery."

Sam nodded, his grin still in place as he slipped out the door, pulling it closed behind him.

The room fell quiet for a moment, save for the soft crackle of bacon continuing to crisp and Leroy's whistling, which picked up again as soon as the door clicked shut—the same Motown tune, cycling through verses he'd known since childhood.

With the bustle of guests yet to descend, it was still early, Leroy allowed himself a rare moment of peace. He leaned against the counter, wiping his hands on a towel tucked into his apron strings as he surveyed his work with a critical eye.

Platters of food sat ready and waiting, each one a testament to his skill and dedication. Everything was arranged just so, colors balanced, portions generous but not wasteful. It was art, really, even if most people just shoveled it down without thinking about the care that went into it.

His gaze drifted toward the small kitchen window above the sink, where the first rays of proper sunlight filtered through, casting warm streaks across the tiled floor and stainless steel surfaces. The golden light caught the steam rising from the food,

Leroy's thoughts wandered briefly to the weekend ahead, to what remained of it. They were already one day in, and so far things seemed to be going smoothly. The guests were a colorful bunch, their personalities as varied as the breakfast dishes he'd prepared. He couldn't help but wonder how today would unfold —what twists Sam had planned, whether anyone would figure out the mystery, and whether the game would bring out the best or the worst in the group.

He'd seen both over the years. Some people loved these events, got really into the spirit, worked together. Others got competitive, paranoid, let their uglier sides show. You never knew which way it would go.

Shrugging off the thought, Leroy returned to his work, adjusting the presentation with meticulous care. A piece of bacon that was slightly crooked got straightened. A pancake that wasn't perfectly stacked got repositioned. The fruit needed to be fanned out just a bit more.

The kitchen was his domain, a space where he found purpose and pride, where he had control and expertise. Even amidst the chaos of a murder mystery weekend, even surrounded by people playing at fake death and danger, this was real. This was what he knew.

As the sunlight grew brighter, shifting from golden to white as the sun climbed higher, and the hum of distant voices signaled the mansion's awakening—footsteps on stairs, doors opening and closing—Leroy's soft whistle filled the room once more.

A calm melody in a morning poised on the edge of intrigue.

CHAPTER THIRTY

The hallway stretched before Lacy, illuminated faded portraits lining the walls in ornate, tarnished frames. The subjects were mostly Victorian-era figures in formal dress, frozen in time with haunting gazes that seemed to track her movements. One woman in particular, with severe features and dark eyes, appeared to follow her with particular intensity.

A shiver ran down her spine, raising goosebumps on her arms, though she told herself it was just the chill of the mansion's old bones, the draft that seemed to seep through every crack.

Her fingers tightened around the map she held, the paper slightly crumpling under her grip. She'd found it in her room this morning—slipped under her door during the night, presumably by Sam or one of the staff. She suspected that everyone had gotten one. Her eyes darted to the bold label marking her destination, written in what looked like red marker: *Creepy Attic*.

She exhaled sharply, steeling her nerves as she reached the base of a narrow staircase that disappeared into darkness above, the steps worn smooth by countless feet over the decades. A single rope served as a bannister, and she could see cobwebs stretching between the railings.

"This is a bad idea," she muttered to herself, her voice sounding small and uncertain in the empty hallway. "A really, really bad idea."

But her feet betrayed her doubt, her curiosity and her love of mystery stronger than her common sense. She began ascending the creaking steps one cautious tread at a time, each one groaning under her weight as if protesting her presence.

The attic greeted her with a wave of musty, stale air that clung to her skin and filled her lungs—the smell of dust and old fabric and something vaguely organic, like decay. It was stuffy despite the cold, the air feeling thick and used. Shadows pooled in every corner, deep and impenetrable.

Her hand fumbled along the wall just inside the entrance, her fingers brushing rough wood and something that felt disturbingly like cobwebs—she yanked her hand back instinctively—until she finally found what she was searching for. A dangling cord, its fabric covering frayed and rough against her palm.

She tugged it gently, and a single bulb flickered to life overhead with a buzzing sound, casting a weak, uneven glow across the room that somehow made the shadows seem deeper by contrast.

Her gasp escaped before she could suppress it, sharp and genuine.

Slumped against a nearby wooden beam, only a few feet from where she stood, was a human figure—legs sprawled, head lolled to one side, arms hanging limp. Her heart thundered in her chest as she froze, her entire body going rigid, her mind racing.

Then, as the swinging light settled and illuminated the figure more clearly, the lifeless sheen of its glassy eyes caught her attention—too glassy, too reflective, clearly plastic—and she let out a breathless laugh that was part relief, part self-deprecation.

"A damn prop," she muttered, shaking her head, pressing a hand to her racing heart. "This place is going to give me a heart attack. Jesus."

She took a few cautious steps deeper into the attic, her boots kicking up small clouds of dust that swirled in the beam of weak light. The room was a chaotic collection of eerie memorabilia that seemed to go back decades. Shelves groaned under the weight of faded books with cracked spines, theatrical masks with grotesque expressions, and old props that looked like they'd seen better days. Piles of fake skeletons, bloodied costumes on hangers, empty vials labeled with things like "POISON" and "DEADLY NIGHTSHADE," and various weapons both fake and possibly real littered the floor and every surface.

A bottle of fake blood caught her eye, sitting on a shelf at eye level. Its deep red liquid swirled as she lifted it carefully, the consistency visible through the glass—corn syrup based, probably. She set it back down with a soft clink, suppressing the urge to laugh at her growing paranoia.

Everything here was designed to unsettle, to create atmosphere. Sam's aunt had been thorough in her dedication to the macabre.

In the far corner of the attic, partially obscured by a blood-stained wedding gown, a faint flicker of light drew her attention. A small desk sat beneath its own dim bulb, its surface cluttered with scattered papers, aged books with leather bindings, and withered roses in a cracked vase, their petals dried and brittle.

Her curiosity pulled her forward, her mystery-loving instincts overriding any remaining caution. This had to be a clue, had to be part of Sam's elaborate game. The map had led her here specifically.

As she approached, carefully stepping over a pile of what looked like Victorian funeral clothes, her gaze locked onto a single sheet of paper atop the stack of books. Its title, written in bold red ink that looked disturbingly like blood, stopped her breath.

The Will of Emilia White

Emilia. Sam's aunt. This was her will—or at least, a prop version of it for the game.

Her fingers trembled slightly as she picked up the document, the paper old and slightly brittle, yellowed at the edges. The weight of its potential significance pressed heavily on her chest. Her eyes skimmed the ornate text, written in formal legal language, her pulse quickening with every name she read:

ROSE ISLAND, CASTLE DE AMORE, AND ALL OTHER ASSETS OF MURDER INC., INCLUDING THE COMPANY ITSELF, SHALL BE ENTRUSTED TO, IN ORDER OF HEIRS:

1. Samuel Scury

2. Curtis Garlan

3. Chelsie Turner

4. Darren Sarper

5. Alice Sarper

Her brow furrowed deeply as she reached the end of the list, confusion mixing with intrigue. The abruptness left her hungry for more, questions multiplying. Why only five names? Why these specific people? Where was Zoey—Sam's own sister? Where was she herself, or Russell and Norma, or any of the staff?

Flipping the page over with growing urgency, she found nothing but blank paper, slightly foxed with age. Frustration bubbled inside her as she rifled through the pile of books and papers on the desk, searching for context, for the rest of the document, for anything that would explain.

Why were these specific people named? What did it mean for the game? Were Darren and Alice next to die?

Curtis and Chelsie were listed as second and third in line. But they were already "dead"—in the game. Did that mean something? Was this the motive Sam had constructed? A fight over inheritance?

A faint creak broke her concentration, cutting right through her thoughts like a sharp blade. The sound of deliberate, measured footsteps echoed from the staircase she had just climbed—slow, heavy, purposeful. Not the casual steps of someone exploring, but something more intentional.

The hair on the back of her neck stood on end, her body's instinctive alarm system triggering.

Someone was coming. Someone knew she was here.

Her mind raced. Was it one of the guests? Sam checking on her progress? Or someone—or something—else entirely?

The game suddenly felt less like a game. The isolation of the attic, the distance from anyone else, pressed in on her awareness.

Panic gripped her as she glanced around the cluttered room with new urgency. The attic offered little in the way of hiding spots that wouldn't leave her exposed. The prop corpse? Too obvious. Behind the shelves? Not enough space.

Her eyes landed on a second door tucked behind a stack of old costumes and what looked like a coffin leaning against the wall—she hadn't noticed it before, it was so shadowed.

Without hesitation, driven by pure instinct, she grabbed the will, folding it quickly and stuffing it into her back pocket, and darted toward the hidden door. Her movements were as swift as she could make them while still trying to be quiet. The floorboards betrayed her with a faint creak that seemed impossibly loud, but she didn't stop.

Her heart hammered in her chest so hard she could feel it in her throat as she reached the door, turned the handle—thank god it wasn't locked—slipped through the narrow opening, and eased it shut behind her with excruciating slowness, trying not to let it click.

The adjacent hallway—or maybe it was more of a passage— was dark and narrow, its air even colder than the attic's. No windows, no light at all except what leaked through the crack beneath the door. Lacy pressed her back against the wall, the wood rough and cold through her shirt, her breaths shallow as she clutched her chest, trying to calm her racing heart.

She strained to listen, her ears picking up the faintest sounds from the attic beyond the door. The footsteps had reached the top of the stairs—she could hear them clearly now, the creak of that first attic floorboard.

They stopped, followed by a long, eerie silence that was somehow worse than the sound of approach.

Were they looking around? Searching for her? Had they seen the will was missing?

She bit her lip hard enough to taste copper, her mind whirling with questions, scenarios, fears. Who had been up there? Had they seen her? Were they still there, waiting for her to emerge?

And why did this will, with its ominous list of names—Curtis and Chelsie who were "dead," Sam who stood to inherit everything, Darren and Alice who seemed like such innocent bystanders—feel like just a thread that would connect to a larger puzzle piece that would reveal something much darker?

Her fingers found the folded paper in her pocket, touching it for reassurance, for proof this was real. The will felt important, vital even. But was it part of Sam's elaborate fiction, or just a red herring placed to trick her?

Her journalist instincts were screaming that this was a story, that something wasn't adding up.

She needed to find Sam. Or maybe she needed to avoid Sam. She wasn't sure which.

As the silence stretched on, oppressive and absolute, Lacy resolved to find answers. If there was one thing she knew from her years of reading mysteries, from her own aborted journalism career, from her actress nights studying scripts, it was that secrets didn't stay buried forever—not anywhere, and especially not this weekend on this island.

Every mystery had a solution. Every secret eventually came to light.

She just hoped she'd survive long enough to find out what this one meant.

Taking a deep, steadying breath, she began to feel her way down the dark passage, one hand on the wall, moving away from the attic and whoever—or whatever—had followed her there.

Behind her, through the door, she heard a single sound: the creak of a floorboard, moving in her direction.

They knew where she'd gone.

And they were coming.

CHAPTER THIRTY-ONE

The cart of table settings rattled down the hallway, pushed by Kelly in her perfectly pressed French maid uniform. She hummed softly to herself, mentally running through the breakfast setup—silverware, napkins, water glasses. Another day, another elaborate scene in Sam's theatrical world.

She turned the corner into the dining room, looked up, and screamed.

Dangling from the chandelier, necks in nooses, faces dead white, were Darren and Alice. Their bodies swayed slightly with the momentum of Kelly's entrance, the chandelier chain creaking ominously under the weight.

Within seconds, footsteps thundered through the mansion.

Shea and Lacy sprinted down the stairs first, followed closely by Russell and Norma.

"More murder. How fun," Norma remarked dryly as they descended.

Russell grinned despite himself. "Let's see who kicked the can this time."

Zoey appeared last, in no rush whatsoever, slugging down the stairs while yawning. "It is so too early for this," she muttered, still in her pajamas, hair disheveled from sleep.

The group gathered around Kelly just inside the dining room doorway, all eyes drawn upward to the hanged couple.

"Wow," Shea said, tilting his head as he studied the scene with professional appreciation. "That looks pretty real."

A side door slammed open with a bang. Everyone jumped.

Leroy and Gwen entered from the kitchen.

"Sorry. Damn door," Leroy said, flexing his biceps with a grin. "Guess it can't handle these guns."

Then he spotted the scene above and his grin widened. "Uh-oh, and the body count rises."

"Two more already," came Sam's voice from behind them.

Everyone jumped again, several people letting out startled yelps. The group spun around to see Sam standing in the main doorway, directly behind them, looking entirely too pleased with himself.

Norma grabbed her heart. "Jesus," she muttered under her breath. "Is that everyone?"

Sam stepped forward, his gaze sweeping over the chandelier with satisfaction. "Looks like someone is mighty desperate this Valentine's Day."

Shea laughed—he was the only one. "Sorry," he added quickly when everyone stared at him.

Russell crossed his arms, his analytical mind already working. "I don't get it. What's the connection?"

"What do you mean?" Sam asked innocently.

"Curtis, Chelsie, now these two," Russell explained. "There has to be a connection, right? Is this when we look for a mysterious clue or something?"

Sam smiled politely, clearly about to humor him with some theatrical explanation. "Well, it seems to me as though—"

"Actually, I already found a clue," Lacy interrupted, stepping forward.

She held up a yellowed piece of paper—the will from the attic.

Zoey sighed deeply, wanting nothing more than to go back to

bed, but figuring she might as well go through the motions. "What's that?"

"I was doing a little snooping in the creepy attic," Lacy explained, "and I found this. It looks like a copy of your aunt's will. That is, if her name is Emilia White."

She studied Sam for a response, watching his face carefully.

He gazed at her for a moment, looking very impressed—even a little turned on. He gave her a ferocious smile. She returned it.

Then Sam snapped back to business. "Yes. That's her. I don't see why her will would be significant though."

"It's very significant," Lacy said. "Listen."

She began to read aloud: "Rose Island, Castle De Amore, and all other assets of Murder Inc., including the company itself, shall be entrusted to, in order of heirs: Samuel Scury, Curtis Garlan, Chelsie Turner, Darren Sarper, Alice Sarper..."

Faces looked on in anticipation. Leroy grabbed Gwen's arm, ready for the next name.

"And?" Sam prompted.

"That's it," Lacy said, lowering the paper. "That's the end of the page. There were no more."

"Well," Sam said thoughtfully. "It looks like we might have a motive."

Zoey continued playing along, half into it now that things were getting interesting. "Wait a minute. You already knew about her will. You had to have. In fact, you're the only one here who knew."

"Good point," Shea added, pointing at Sam. "And your name is first on that list. You're not dead yet. So far every name below you is."

"Yeah," Norma agreed, her eyes narrowing.

Sam raised his hands, perhaps a bit too quickly. Everything was going just as he'd planned.

"Hold on now," he said. "Before you all pull the trigger, you should know that I have not seen a copy of the will. My aunt's lawyer is the only one who has, and unless he's got a helicopter or a private yacht, I would conclude that he's not the killer."

He paused, letting that sink in. "Furthermore, yes, I am at the top of the list, but I already inherited the company. There is no reason for me to kill anyone. I would say that whoever is at the bottom of that list is someone to worry about."

Russell wasn't convinced. "Unless you plan on killing everyone on the list before they kill you."

"Greed," Leroy added sagely. "It's a bitch."

Lacy held up the paper again. "Maybe the list is a fake. Nobody here has seen the real will, right?"

Shea spotted his opportunity to mix things up, his eyes glinting with mischief. "True. And you happen to be the one who found it."

Sam laughed, the sound genuine and amused. Everyone's focus snapped back to him.

"Look," he said, his tone becoming more serious. "Anyone here could be the killer, including myself. I would just suggest, since we have another night together, not to judge so quickly. Study the facts. Look at the details. And definitely..." he paused for emphasis, "watch your backs."

He let that hang in the air for a moment before adding, "Now, under the circumstances, breakfast will be served in the ballroom today."

Sam turned on his heel and exited.

The room stood still as eyes scanned one another for clues, for tells, for guilt.

Above them, Darren and Alice continued to sway from the chandelier, their "corpses" perfectly still.

Zoey simply headed directly through the tension and out the door, apparently over the whole thing. Others slowly followed, murmuring amongst themselves, theories already forming.

The group dispersed slowly, some heading toward the ball-room where the promise of Leroy's cooking awaited, others grav-itating toward their rooms for a moment to process what they'd just seen. The mansion seemed to absorb their nervous energy, the old walls holding secrets and whispers.

Lacy lingered in the hallway, the will still clutched in her hand, her mind working through the implications. The paper felt too authentic, the language too precise. Was it real? Was it planted? And if it was real, what did that mean for everyone on that list?

She glanced back toward the dining room, where Darren and Alice had hung from the chandelier. They were already gone. Their performance was flawless even in stillness. Sam's commitment to the craft was undeniable. Every detail, every scene, choreographed to perfection.

Lacy was sure that more clues would be presented soon. She told herself that she was going to figure this mystery out. Until then, it was time to eat. She folded the will and tucked it into her pocket, then headed toward the ballroom. The smell of bacon and coffee drifted through the hallways, a comforting contrast to the macabre theatrics of the morning.

CHAPTER THIRTY-TWO

The sun poured through the floor-to-ceiling windows of the cabin, bathing the interior in a golden glow that made everything look softer, warmer, more alive. The light danced across the polished wood floors and rustic furniture, creating moving patterns as clouds passed overhead. Outside, the gentle murmur of the ocean blended with the occasional rustle of leaves from the surrounding jungle, creating a serene backdrop—the kind of peaceful soundtrack you'd pay money to listen to while trying to sleep in the city.

Darren stood by the window, his hands in his pockets, his posture relaxed as he admired the view. The cliffs below were shrouded in morning mist that was just beginning to burn off, the waves crashing against the rocks in a rhythmic lullaby. He'd been standing there for several minutes, just breathing, just being, feeling more relaxed than he had in months.

Behind him, Alice wandered the room with the unhurried curiosity of someone on vacation, running her fingers along the smooth surface of the coffee table, examining the artwork on the walls, glancing at the array of maps left on various surfaces.

"It's gorgeous here," she said, her voice soft with genuine

awe. "Hard to believe something so peaceful could be part of a murder mystery. It feels wrong, almost. Too beautiful."

Darren turned from the window, his lips curving into an affectionate grin. "Perfect setting for a little drama, though. Think about it—Gothic mansion, isolated island, beautiful views. Sam's probably thrilled with himself. This is his dream scenario."

At the bar in the corner, Gwen twisted the cap off a bottle of water, taking a long sip before leaning back against the counter. Her relaxed posture and easy smile stood in sharp contrast to the tension probably simmering back at the mansion.

"Pretty cool spot, right?" she said, breaking the comfortable silence, her voice carrying a note of pride. "This cabin's one of my favorite places on the island. Found it on my first scouting trip."

Darren nodded appreciatively. "Yeah. Definitely beats the chaos back at the mansion. Don't get me wrong, the mansion is impressive, but it's a lot. This feels more... human-sized."

Alice joined him by the window, leaning against the arm of the couch. "Speaking of chaos, where are Curtis and Chelsie? I thought they'd be here. Weren't they supposed to stay at the cabin?"

Gwen shrugged casually, gesturing toward the coffee table where a single folded map lay abandoned, its edges worn from handling. "Looks like they grabbed one of the maps and took off early. Maybe they're exploring the beach trail. Or, knowing Curtis, they're probably trying to out-sass each other on a hike."

Alice chuckled, shaking her head fondly. "Sounds about right. Curtis can't help himself. Did you hear about the orange rose?"

"Classic," Gwen agreed with a grin. She reached into her messenger bag, pulling out two more maps and handing them to the couple. "Here. Just in case you decide to go all outdoorsy. There's a really beautiful lookout about two miles up the north trail. Worth the walk if you're into that sort of thing."

Alice accepted the map but immediately set it down on the table with a definitive thunk. "Oh, I think we're staying in today," she said with a knowing smirk, glancing at Darren. "You mentioned a hot tub?"

Gwen pointed upstairs, her grin widening. "On the deck. Best spot on the island. Perfect temperature, incredible view, total privacy. You can see the sunset from there—it's magical."

Alice's eyes lit up with enthusiasm, and she turned to Darren with a playful smile that promised relaxation. "Hot tub it is, then. No hiking, no maps, no murder mysteries. Just us and some bubbles and maybe a bottle of wine."

Darren laughed, shaking his head in mock defeat. "Sounds like a perfect plan to me. Who needs exercise when you can have jets and champagne?"

Gwen capped her water bottle and slung her bag over her shoulder, preparing to leave them to their morning. "Well, I'll leave you two lovebirds to it," she said, her tone light and teasing. "I've got my own mysteries to handle back at the mansion—places to be, people to 'murder.'" She made air quotes around the word.

Alice snorted, her laugh genuine. "Very on-brand. Don't work too hard."

With a wink and a mock sinister grin, Gwen headed for the door, her footsteps echoing on the wooden floor. "Have fun!" she called over her shoulder. "Don't do anything I wouldn't do— which leaves you with a lot of options!"

"See you later," Darren replied, watching her disappear through the door.

The cabin fell into comfortable silence, the faint hum of nature outside the only sound now. The moment felt private, intimate, as if the island had temporarily paused its eerie games to offer them a reprieve.

Darren turned to Alice, his expression softening as he closed the distance between them. "Finally, some quiet," he said, slipping an arm around her waist and pulling her close. "Just us. No murder, no games, no audience."

Alice leaned into him naturally, resting her hands on his chest, feeling his heartbeat. "It's nice," she agreed quietly. "Almost makes me forget we're part of some elaborate murder mystery. Almost makes me forget about real life waiting back home."

Darren chuckled, brushing a strand of hair from her face with gentle fingers. "Almost. But let's not think about that right now. Not about the mystery, not about Monday morning, not about anything except this."

Alice tilted her head, her smile playful and inviting. "Oh? And what should we think about instead?"

Darren's grin widened. "Well," he said, drawing her closer, "there's a very cozy couch over there that hasn't been properly broken in. And we have the whole cabin to ourselves. And it would be a shame to waste that."

Alice rolled her eyes but couldn't suppress her laugh. "You're impossible."

"And you love it," Darren teased, catching her hand and pulling her back when she made a half-hearted attempt to step away. He kissed her cheek, his lips brushing against her skin as he whispered, "Let's take advantage of this place while we can. Who knows when we'll get another chance like this?"

Alice shook her head, though her smile betrayed her, her eyes shining with affection and desire. "Fine," she said, her tone mock-defeated. "But only because we're alone and because I love you, but let's head upstairs. I don't want Curtis and Chelsie barging in."

They shared a lingering kiss, unhurried and sweet, the warmth of the morning light enveloping them like a cocoon. For a brief moment—their last peaceful moment—the cabin felt like a world apart from the mysteries and dangers lurking on the island. It was just the two of them, wrapped in each other's presence and the peaceful glow of the morning.

"Hot tub after?" Alice asked, her voice soft against his lips.

"Hot tub after," Darren agreed, his grin widening as he led her toward the stairs.

CHAPTER THIRTY-THREE

The grand room, illuminated by the soft amber glow of an ornate chandelier, felt both majestic and ominous—like dining in a gilded cage. Crystal pendants cast fractured light across the cream-colored walls, dancing shadows that seemed to move with a life of their own. The sound of silverware clinking against fine china punctuated the air, accompanied by the occasional murmur of conversation that never quite rose above a whisper.

Despite the outward calm, the lingering tension from the weekend's unfolding events created an undercurrent that was impossible to ignore. It pressed against everyone's chest like an invisible weight, making even the simple act of eating feel performative.

At a small table near the western windows, Sam leaned forward across the polished wood, speaking quietly with Russell. Their heads were bent close together, expressions carved with seriousness that made Sam's usually animated features look almost foreign. Every few seconds, Sam's gaze flitted to the rest of the room, his sharp eyes scanning the other guests. His fingers drummed absently against his coffee cup, a nervous tell he probably didn't realize he had.

At the main table, Norma and Shea shared a laugh as they finished their meals, their camaraderie a bright spot in an otherwise muted morning. Shea leaned back in his chair, patting his stomach with exaggerated satisfaction.

"Man, Leroy outdid himself," Shea declared, his voice carrying across the room with easy confidence. Kelly swooped in to clear his plate with practiced efficiency. "That breakfast was almost worth the risk of getting murdered."

Norma smirked, shaking her head as she set down her napkin. "You're impossible."

"Hey, if I'm going out, I'm going out with a full stomach," Shea replied with a wink. "Priorities."

By the doorway, Lacy spotted Zoey making her way out, moving with the slow shuffle of someone operating on three hours of sleep and pure stubbornness. Lacy stepped forward, her voice warm but laced with curiosity.

"Hey, Zoey."

Zoey turned, her expression brightening slightly despite the tiredness etched across her face. Dark circles shadowed her eyes, and her usual careful composure had given way to something more raw and genuine. "Hey, Lace. Is it okay if I call you that?"

"Sure," Lacy replied with a shrug, her lips curving into a small smile. She liked Zoey—there was something refreshingly honest about her exhaustion. "I was thinking about snooping around some more later. Want to join me? I figure two sets of eyes are better than one, especially when we're looking for... whatever the hell we're looking for."

Zoey let out a loud yawn, covering her mouth with one hand as she shook her head. "Oh, thanks, but I think I'm gonna head back to bed. This whole breakfast-at-8-AM thing? Not my vibe." She gestured vaguely toward the windows where morning light streamed in with offensive brightness. "I'd rather not sleepwalk through the next murder, you know? Need to be alert if I'm going to dodge whatever fresh hell this place has planned."

Her disheveled hair—still bearing the imprint of her pillow

on one side—and slightly smudged mascara painted the picture of someone far too exhausted to entertain morning adventures. "See what I mean? I look like I've already been murdered and poorly reanimated."

Lacy chuckled, crossing her arms as she leaned against the doorframe. "Fair enough. Just be careful, though." Her voice dropped, losing its playful edge. "You never know what's lurking around here. Go to sleep, and you might not wake up."

The words hung between them for a moment, heavier than Lacy had intended.

Zoey rolled her eyes playfully, though something flickered in her expression. "Please, I'll take my chances. Worst-case scenario? I join Chelsie in the afterlife. Might be the best sleep-over ever." Her grin lingered, brittle at the edges. "At least she'd have good gossip by now."

Her steps were slow and deliberate as she shuffled out of the ballroom, one hand trailing along the wall for balance, disappearing into the hallway's shadows.

Lacy watched her go, a flicker of amusement mixed with unease crossing her face. She wondered if Zoey's casual attitude was genuine or just another mask.

As Lacy turned back toward the room, she passed Russell, who was rising from his chair with a tired stretch that made his spine crack audibly. She offered him a brief smile before continuing on.

Russell glanced at his watch, muttering under his breath about deadlines that seemed absurd given their circumstances.

From across the room, Norma approached him, her steps purposeful, her voice bright and teasing in a way that was clearly forced but appreciated. "Hey, babe," she said, looping an arm around his waist. "Shea wants to go for a hike. Want to join us? Get some fresh air, clear our heads?"

Russell hesitated, his jaw working as he considered. His expression turned apologetic. "I'd love to, but I've got to finish those stupid reports. I know, I know—vacation and all that. But

I figure if I knock them out now, I can actually relax later. Maybe even enjoy what's left of this disaster."

Norma frowned slightly, her brow creasing. "Okay," she said, though her tone carried a note of concern. "You're sure? It's probably safer in pairs. Or threes, actually."

Shea chimed in, having wandered over to join them, leaning casually against a chair with his arms crossed. "Yeah, man, don't you watch horror movies? Lone wolf equals dead wolf. It's like, rule number one."

Russell grinned, unable to help himself. He straightened, adopting a mock-serious tone that mimicked Sam's flair for the dramatic. "At Murder Mansion, if you're going to die, you're going to die."

The trio laughed, the sound genuine and warm, momentarily breaking through the tension.

Norma reached up, giving Russell a quick peck on the lips. Her hand lingered on his chest, fingers splaying against the soft cotton of his shirt. "Well, try not to be dead when I get back," she teased lightly, though her eyes searched his face and lingered on him for a moment longer than usual.

Russell chuckled, squeezing her hand and bringing it briefly to his lips. "I'll be here, alive and kicking—or typing, I guess. Mostly typing."

"Promise?" Norma's voice was softer now, the joke fading.

"Promise," Russell said, and meant it.

Norma turned to Shea, nudging him toward the door with her elbow. "Come on, let's get moving before I change my mind and chain myself to Russell's laptop."

"Dead or alive, Russ, see you in a bit." Shea quipped over his shoulder as they left, his hand raised in a casual salute.

Russell watched them go, his easy smile fading into something more contemplative as their voices disappeared down the corridor. He returned to his table, pulling out the chair with a soft scrape against the marble floor.

The room had begun to quiet, the other guests dispersing

into their own corners of the mansion. The echo of footsteps and the soft rustle of fabric faded into the distance, leaving Russell momentarily alone with his thoughts—thoughts that were growing darker and more circular with each passing hour.

He sat back down, picking up his laptop with a sigh that came from somewhere deep in his chest. The screen blinked to life, casting his face in pale blue light. The tapping of keys soon filled the room, a solitary sound amidst the sprawling silence.

CHAPTER THIRTY-FOUR

The backyard of the mansion basked in the soft, golden light of mid-morning, the kind of light that made everything look like it belonged in a dream. The sun cast playful ripples across the crystal-clear pool, each wave catching the light and tossing it back in shimmering fragments. Gentle waves lapped at the pool's edge under a light breeze that carried the salt-sweet scent of the ocean, the sound of distant seagulls adding to the idyllic scene.

It was almost enough to make someone forget about murder. Almost.

Sam and Lacy lounged on plush poolside chairs, the surrounding gardens a riot of vibrant greens and pops of blooming color—fuchsia bougainvillea, bright orange birds of paradise, deep purple jacaranda blossoms that had fallen like confetti across the manicured lawn. The setting was absurdly romantic, which made the tension coiling in Sam's stomach feel even more pronounced.

In Lacy's lap rested a small, elegantly wrapped gift, the silver paper catching the sunlight. She stared at it like it might disappear if she blinked, her expression a blend of surprise and disbelief.

"I can't believe you got me a present," she said, her voice soft and tinged with wonder. Her fingers traced the perfect edges of the bow. "I don't know what to say. Thank you."

Sam leaned forward slightly, resting his elbows on his knees. His grin was easy and mischievous. "You can start by opening it," he said, gesturing toward the box. "The suspense is killing me"

Lacy gave him a cute smile and carefully peeled back the wrapping paper. She took her time, treating it with reverence. Beneath it lay a simple box. She opened it to find a small collection of chocolates nestled inside, each one individually wrapped in foil that gleamed like tiny jewels.

She held them up, tilting her head as she looked at Sam with a teasing smile. "Chocolates?"

"You told me you usually spend Valentine's Day alone with a box of chocolates," Sam said, leaning back and crossing his arms, trying to appear casual even though his heart was hammering. "This way, you're sticking to tradition—just with better company. Significant upgrade, if I do say so myself."

Lacy laughed, shaking her head as color rose to her cheeks. "Okay, that's sweet. Really sweet, actually. Thank you." She popped one of the chocolates into her mouth, her eyes closing briefly in appreciation. "Oh, these are good. Like, really good."

But before she could close the box, her fingers brushed against something else inside, something that rustled. She reached in and pulled out an envelope, cream-colored and elegant. Her brow furrowed with curiosity as she opened it. Her eyes widened.

"Are these...?"

Sam nodded, his grin widening into something almost boyish. "Season tickets to the theater. I know how much you love going, and Les Mis is playing this season. Isn't that your favorite?"

Lacy's face lit up like someone had turned on a switch. "It is! Oh my gosh, you remembered that?" Her voice cracked slightly. "Sam, this is amazing. You really didn't have to do this."

Sam shrugged nonchalantly, though his playful grin betrayed

how pleased he was. "Don't start with the 'you shouldn't have' stuff. I own a whole damn island now—it's the least I could do. Plus, I figured you'd need something to look forward to after we get off this death trap."

Lacy gave him a mock scolding look, pointing a chocolate at him like a weapon, but couldn't hide her smile. "Well, thank you. This is... wow. I'm actually speechless."

"There's more," Sam said, his tone light but carrying a hint of excitement.

Curious, Lacy reached into the box again, pulling out a neatly bound stack of papers. She froze as she realized what she was holding—a screenplay. The title page was replaced by a simple piece of paper that read "For Lacy."

"What is this?" she asked, her voice laced with intrigue.

Sam leaned forward, his expression turning serious but warm. "Hopefully my next feature film. I'd like to start production early next year. Been working on it for months."

Lacy flipped through a few pages, her gaze darting over the opening lines. Even from just the first scene, she could tell it was good—the kind of good that got attention, won awards. "This looks incredible," she murmured, clearly impressed. "The dialogue is so sharp. You're letting me read it?"

"Not just read it," Sam said, his grin returning with full force. He took a breath. "I want you to be my leading lady."

Lacy's head shot up, her eyes wide. "Wait—me?" she asked, her voice rising in disbelief. The script nearly slipped from her fingers. "Seriously? Sam, I'm not—I mean, I've done indie films and theater, but this is..."

Sam shrugged again, though his grin betrayed his excitement and certainty. "I think you'd be perfect. You've got the talent— more talent than half the people getting leading roles these days. And you're a starving actress, right? This could change every- thing for you."

Lacy laughed, though there was a tremor of emotion beneath it, tears threatening at the corners of her eyes. "Sam, I—thank you. I'd love to. God, I'd love to." She pressed a hand to her mouth, overwhelmed.

"Well," Sam said, smirking as he leaned back, "you should probably read the whole script first. Make sure you actually like it. Maybe you'll hate the character. She's complicated—kind of messy, actually."

Lacy nodded, clutching the script against her chest like it was made of gold. "You're amazing," she said softly. "You know that?"

"I try," Sam said with a wink.

Lacy hesitated before speaking again, her tone quieter now, more uncertain. She set the script carefully on the table between them. "You know, this whole trip, I kept wondering why you invited me." She looked down at her hands. "I thought maybe it was some elaborate way to ask me to be your valentine or something. Then I thought I was being stupid and reading too much into it."

Sam's expression softened, the playful gleam in his eyes giving way to something deeper, more sincere. The mask he usually wore slipped away. He reached into his pocket and pulled out a single sheet of paper, handing it to her without a word.

Lacy took it, her fingers trembling slightly as she unfolded it. Her breath caught audibly as she read the bold, handwritten title at the top:

BE MY VALENTINE?

For a moment, the world seemed to still. Even the waves seemed to quiet.

Lacy stared at the words, reading them again and again as if they might rearrange themselves. Her lips parted in surprise, and Sam watched a dozen emotions flicker across her face—shock, joy, disbelief, hope.

Then, a radiant smile broke across her face, lighting up her features in a way that made Sam's heart skip a beat. "I'd love to," she said, her voice filled with emotion. "Yes. Absolutely yes."

Sam stood, holding out a hand to her. Lacy rose, slipping her hand into his as he pulled her close. They stood by the edge of the pool, the soft sound of rippling water and the distant crash of waves filling the air around them.

"I've missed you," Lacy said, her voice barely above a whisper as she rested her head against his chest, feeling the steady thump of his heartbeat. "So much. More than I let myself admit."

Sam's arms tightened around her. "I've missed you too, cheeks." The old nickname hung between them, familiar and warm.

Lacy laughed, the sound slightly watery, and pulled back just enough to puff out her cheeks and scrunch her nose at him—a playful gesture that made Sam chuckle and transported them both back to their dating days.

Slowly, Sam leaned in, his hand coming up to cup her face, thumb brushing across her cheekbone. His lips brushed against hers in a kiss that was both tender and charged with unspoken feelings, with years of almost and what if and maybe someday.

Lacy responded instantly, her arms winding around his neck as the world around them seemed to fade away. For that moment, there was no mansion, no mystery, no murder—only two hearts finding their way back to each other.

When they finally pulled apart, foreheads touching, both breathless, Lacy smiled. "Best Valentine's Day ever," she whispered.

"Even with the murders?" Sam asked, unable to help himself.

"Even with the murders," she confirmed, laughing. "Though let's try to avoid making this a tradition."

CHAPTER THIRTY-FIVE

The wildflower clearing a few miles from the mansion basked under the golden mid-morning sun, its vibrant blooms swaying gently in the breeze like nature's own celebration. Purple lupines mixed with bright yellow daisies, wild roses climbed between the trees, and delicate baby's breath dotted the landscape like snow that had forgotten to melt.

Norma straddled Shea on the heart-patterned blanket they'd brought from the mansion, her long, wavy hair catching the light as it tumbled over her bare shoulders in honey-blonde waves. The sun warmed her skin, making her feel alive in a way she hadn't in years—not with Russell, not in their meticulously planned life back home. Here, in this moment, she was free.

Her laughter—genuine and unguarded in a way it hadn't been since they'd arrived on this cursed island—mixed with Shea's low, appreciative chuckle. For this moment, at least, they'd forgotten about murder and mystery and death. There was only heat and want and the electric connection that had been building between them since the yacht.

Shea's hands roamed up her sides, leaving trails of fire in their wake, his calloused fingers finding every curve, every sensitive spot that made her breath catch. When his hands tangled in her hair, pulling her down with just enough force to make her gasp, she surrendered to it completely. Their lips met in a heated kiss that tasted like morning coffee and the chocolate croissants they'd stolen from breakfast, sweet and forbidden in equal measure.

The connection between them was electric, each touch igniting sparks that made the rest of the world disappear. Norma's body moved against his with a fluid rhythm, her hips rolling in a dance as old as time itself. Shea's grip tightened on her waist, his fingers digging into her flesh with an urgency that matched her own, guiding her movements, deepening the connection between them.

She leaned back slightly, arching her spine, letting the sun kiss her exposed skin while Shea's mouth found the sensitive hollow of her throat. His teeth grazed her pulse point, and she let out a soft moan that was swallowed by the rustling leaves and distant ocean waves. This was reckless, dangerous even—Russell could finish his work early, someone could wander by—but that edge of risk only made everything more intense.

Their movements grew more urgent, more desperate. Shea's hands were everywhere—her back, her hips, tangling in her hair again as he pulled her mouth back to his for another searing kiss. She could feel his heart hammering against her chest, matching the wild pace of her own. The wildflowers around them seemed to pulse with the same rhythm, the clearing itself becoming part of their private world.

When the tension finally broke, it was like a wave crashing over both of them—overwhelming, all-consuming, leaving them breathless and trembling. Norma's fingers dug into Shea's shoulders as she rode out the sensation, her head thrown back, golden hair cascading down her spine like a waterfall. Shea's grip on her was almost bruising, holding her to him like she might disappear if he let go.

Finally, their breathing slowed, chests heaving in synchronization, bodies still pressed together as the aftershocks subsided. The world gradually came back into focus—the warmth of the sun, the soft blanket beneath them, the chirping of birds that had witnessed their stolen moment.

Shea rolled to his side, reaching for his clothes scattered across the blanket like evidence of their passion. Norma collapsed onto the blanket beside him, her skin flushed and glistening with a sheen of sweat that made her glow in the dappled sunlight. Her lips curved in a satisfied, almost feline smile—the kind of smile that came from feeling wanted, desired, alive.

For a few perfect seconds, she allowed herself to float in that post-orgasmic haze where nothing else mattered, where Russell and responsibilities and real life didn't exist.

"I'm going to go pee," Shea announced nonchalantly as he pulled his shirt over his head.

Norma tilted her head, giving him a bemused look. "Right now? Seriously?" She propped herself up on one elbow. "What, were you holding it in the whole time?"

Shea shrugged, grinning that boyish grin as he grabbed his pack. "They say it's good to go afterward. Prevents UTIs or something. I don't make the rules."

Norma raised an eyebrow. "Who's 'they?' Name one source."

"I don't know—doctors or something. Medical professionals." He waved her off dismissively. "I read it in a magazine once. Men's Health, maybe? Or was it Cosmo?"

Norma rolled her eyes but couldn't hold back a small laugh. "Fine, whatever. Just hurry up. Russell's probably done with his work by now and out there sniffing around for us like a bloodhound. Last thing I need is him catching us in post-coital bliss."

Shea winked, already moving toward the tree line. "Don't miss me too much," he said, sauntering off toward a cluster of bushes with exaggerated swagger.

Norma shook her head, watching him leave with affection warming her chest. "Guys are so weird," she muttered to herself as she began gathering her scattered belongings—bra hanging from a low branch, socks somehow ten feet apart.

Shea wandered deeper into the bushes, humming under his breath—some pop song he'd heard on the radio during the boat ride. He unzipped his pants, glancing around idly as he relieved himself against a tree trunk. The rustling leaves and chirping birds created a natural symphony that would've been soothing under different circumstances.

But a faint sound beneath it all made him pause mid-stream.

A soft crunch of footsteps on dead leaves. Too deliberate to be an animal.

Shea turned his head, squinting into the trees where shadows pooled thick and dark. "Hello?" he called out, his voice steady but tinged with curiosity and unease. When no reply came, he forced a laugh that sounded hollow even to his own ears. "Alright, nature, chill out. You're freaking me out here."

He finished quickly, suddenly eager to get back to Norma and the safety of numbers, zipped up, and started back toward the blanket.

As Shea stepped into the clearing, pushing aside the last branch, Norma was just finishing packing up.

"Alright. Let's go." Shea said.

She looked at him with a concerned look.

"What?" He asked.

"Now I feel like I should go," she replied while giving him a puppy dog look.

Shea rolled his eyes. "Oh my gosh. Go ahead."

She pointed to the other side of the clearing. "Go pick me some flowers over there." she said before starting off to the bushes.

"As you wish princess," Shea replied turning and walking past a tree on the edge of the clearing. He looked up at the leaves gently blowing in the wind. He continued and as he passed the second tree the blow struck without warning.

SLICE!

A sharp, searing pain ripped through his abdomen like fire, stealing his breath in one brutal instant. He stumbled forward, his hand flying to his stomach as warm blood—his blood, so much of it—seeped through his fingers, sticky and terrifying.

"What—" he gasped, trying to form words that wouldn't come.

Turning, his wide eyes locked onto a grotesque figure. The killer wore a hideous Cupid mask, its cherubic face twisted into something obscene—lifeless eyes staring out from painted sockets, a smile stretched too wide across pink plastic cheeks. Tiny wings jutted from the sides of the mask.

In the figure's gloved hand gleamed a bloodied knife, the blade catching sunlight as crimson dripped onto the wildflowers below.

Shea opened his mouth to scream, to call for Norma, to do anything, but only a wet gurgle emerged. He watched the blade rise, arc through the air in terrible slow motion, then plunge down into his body again.

And again.

And again.

Each strike was swift, deliberate, and brutal—mechanical almost, like the killer was following a recipe. His knees buckled as the strength bled out of him along with his life. He collapsed onto the ground, the flowers splotched with blood around him.

Pain gave way to numbness. The world tilted, colors bleeding together.

His last thought was of Norma, of wanting to warn her.

As the light faded from his eyes, the figure stood over him, tilting its head as though admiring its handiwork. The plastic Cupid face stared down at him, eternally smiling.

Without a word, without hesitation, the killer turned and disappeared into the trees like smoke, leaving only silence and death in their wake.

———

Norma returned moments later.

"Alright, I'm ready," she called out, her voice carrying playful impatience."Let's get back before someone starts a betting pool on what we were really doing out here—"

She stopped mid-step, mid-word, mid-breath.

Her words died on her lips as her gaze fell on the blood-soaked scene before her.

Shea's body lay sprawled on the ground, twisted at an unnatural angle, his lifeless eyes staring blankly at the sky above. The wildflowers around him were splattered with blood, their vibrant petals stained deep crimson. So much blood. She'd never seen so much blood.

"Shea? Are you okay? Is this part of the mystery? This is not cool." Norma said, so confused.

As she walked closer it was apparent that this was not part of the weekend. She had never seen a dead body, but she knew nonetheless.

Norma's stomach churned violently, bile rising sharp and acidic in her throat. She stumbled backward, her hands flying to her mouth to contain the scream building there.

"Oh my God," she whispered, her voice trembling. "Shea?"

It came out as a question, as if asking might change the answer.

She took a hesitant step forward, her instincts warring with the primal urge to run. Kneeling beside him, she reached out with shaking hands, her fingers brushing against his cooling skin. Still warm, but not warm enough. Wrong. All wrong.

The reality of his death hit her like a tidal wave, stealing the air from her lungs. Her gaze fell to the deep wounds that marred his torso—too many to count, overlapping, the knife marks precise and unrelenting. A metallic tang filled the air, coating her tongue, and the nausea rose sharply.

She turned her head and retched, gasping.

"No, no, no," she whispered, shaking her head violently as if denying the scene could undo it. "This can't be real. This isn't real. Wake up, Norma. Wake up."

But she didn't wake up, because she wasn't asleep.

A sudden rustle in the bushes—from the same direction the killer must have fled—snapped Norma out of her daze. Her head jerked up, her eyes scanning the trees with wild desperation, pupils dilated with terror.

"Who's there?" she shouted, her voice breaking into a raw scream. "Show yourself! SHOW YOURSELF!"

Silence answered. The kind of silence that's worse than any sound.

Panic clawed at her chest like a living thing, and she scrambled to her feet, nearly tripping over Shea's body. Her hand touched his blood-soaked shirt, and she jerked back with a sob.

The killer could still be here. Watching. Waiting.

Norma turned and ran, abandoning everything—the bag, the blanket, Shea's body, their stolen moment of happiness. Her feet pounded against the ground as she sprinted toward the mansion, branches whipping at her face and arms, leaving scratches she didn't feel. Her breath came in ragged gasps, her mind racing with terror and disbelief and the image of those dead eyes staring at nothing.

CHAPTER THIRTY-SIX

Sam moved purposefully through the cluttered attic, his steps muffled on the creaky wooden floor that threatened to give way beneath him. Around him, the eerie stillness seemed alive—breathing, watching—the muted air filled with the scent of aged wood, mothballs, and something faintly metallic.

Cobwebs stretched between rafters like silky, sheer curtains, and dust motes danced in the weak light. The attic was larger than he'd remembered from his childhood visits, stretching back into shadows that the single bulb couldn't quite penetrate. Every surface was covered—old furniture draped in sheets, boxes stacked haphazardly, props from decades of his aunt's theatrical productions piled like discarded dreams. He had only been up here once since his aunt past and hadn't fully explored the large area.

He passed a grotesque severed hand perched on a stack of crumbling books, its silicone fingers frozen mid-curl in what might have been a wave or a warning. The detail was impressive—complete with painted fingernails and realistic knuckle wrinkles. Sam had to admit, Aunt Emilia had excellent taste in props.

He paused briefly to inspect a mannequin that appeared to

be standing guard. The figure was dressed in a blood-splattered shirt, the crimson stains artfully applied, and wore a retractable knife vest, similar to the vest Curtis had donned for his theatrical "death." Sam ran his hand over the vest, feeling the mechanism that would allow a blade to seemingly penetrate flesh while actually retracting safely into the handle.

A smirk tugged at the corner of his lips. "Curtis always loved the dramatic," he muttered, shaking his head.

A glint of silver caught Sam's eye, and he turned to see a machete headband resting on a nearby shelf between a rubber chicken and what appeared to be a jar of preserved eyeballs. Fake ones, he hoped.

He picked up the headband, examining its gory illusion—the blade appeared to be embedded directly into the skull cap, complete with painted blood and bits of what was supposed to be brain matter. The craftsmanship was disturbingly good.

With a mischievous grin, he slid it onto his head, adjusting it until it sat properly, and stepped toward a cracked mirror propped against the wall. His reflection stared back, his head appearing gruesomely split down the middle, the machete blade bisecting his face in a way that should have been fatal but instead looked almost comical.

He chuckled softly at the absurdity, tilting his head to inspect the effect from different angles. "Genius," he murmured, before pulling the headband off and tossing it onto a pile of props that included a witch's hat, several wigs, and what looked like a realistic snake.

The humor of the moment lingered, softening the tension that had been etched into his features. He'd needed that laugh more than he'd realized.

As he moved deeper into the attic, navigating between a steamer trunk and a coat rack draped with period costumes, his gaze landed on the desk in the far corner. It was an antique roll-top, the kind his aunt had always preferred, surrounded by wilted roses in crystal vases whose petals had blackened and curled with age. The roses released a faint, sickly-sweet smell of decay.

The sight brought an unbidden memory of Lacy holding up the will earlier, her sharp wit slicing through the room's tension, her eyes flashing with that particular brand of cleverness he'd always admired.

Sam's grin widened as he approached the desk, running his fingers along its worn surface. "Didn't think you had it in you, Lacy," he muttered, the words tinged with admiration. "Full of surprises."

He opened the drawer to the desk revealing a vile that read "poison." Sam grabbed it from the drawer. "Except, you missed this one Lacy," he said to himself before putting the small tube in his pocket. "I guess we'll have to hide you somewhere more obvious."

Sam, continuing to explore, reached for a prop gun wedged between a pile of ancient books on the desk—leather-bound things that looked like they hadn't been opened in decades. The gun was heavier than he'd expected, realistic enough to pass for real at a distance.

As he pulled it free, the precarious stack toppled with a cascade of dust, one of the heavier tomes hitting the floor with a dull thud that echoed through the attic. A small photograph fluttered from between the pages like a falling leaf, spinning through the air before landing face-up near his feet.

Curious, Sam bent down and picked it up, brushing off the dust. The image was old but vivid, the colors slightly faded but still clear: a younger Sam—maybe ten years old, gap-toothed and grinning—stood smiling between his Aunt Emilia and Zoey. His aunt looked vibrant and alive, her hair darker then, her smile genuine and warm. Zoey was about eight, her face round with baby fat, wearing a ridiculous frilly dress that he remembered her complaining about for the entire visit.

All three of them were framed by the ornate backdrop of this very mansion, standing on the front steps beneath the stone archway. The laughter frozen in their expressions seemed to echo faintly in the attic's stillness, a haunting reminder of a simpler time.

Sam's brow furrowed slightly as he stared at the photo, his jaw tightening. The edges were worn, as though it had been handled many times—loved, maybe, or at least frequently revisited—yet its placement in the book suggested it had been deliberately hidden.

Why would Aunt Emilia hide this? Why not display it with all the other family photos downstairs?

He ran his thumb over the surface, feeling the slight texture of the photographic paper, a faint smile flickering on his lips. "Forgot about this one," he murmured, his voice softer now, almost tender. That had been a good summer. One of the last before everything got complicated.

He flicked the photo lightly with his finger, the sound barely audible. Turning it over, he found no notes or dates—just the blank, faded backing, slightly yellowed with age. No explanation for why it had been hidden.

His mind worked quickly, piecing together a plan as connections formed like puzzle pieces clicking into place. He folded the image carefully and slipped it into his pocket where it rested against his chest like a secret.

"Too good to stay buried," he said under his breath, his tone conspiratorial. A spark of excitement lit his eyes as he scanned the attic, his director's mind already staging the scene, planning the reveal.

This photograph was going to be a new piece of the puzzle, and he knew exactly how to use it.

Sam straightened, casting a final glance at the scattered mess of props and papers, the mannequins that seemed to watch him with blank faces, the shadows that pooled in the corners. His steps were deliberate as he moved toward the door, weaving between the cluttered artifacts, his hand brushing the photograph in his pocket like a talisman.

"We'll just have to hide you somewhere someone will find you also," he whispered to himself, a sly grin playing on his lips. "Somewhere interesting. Somewhere that'll make them think."

He descended carefully, the steps groaning beneath his weight, and disappeared into the darker hallway below.

CHAPTER THIRTY-SEVEN

The cool breeze brushed against Lacy's skin as she moved cautiously along the mansion's side, hugging the stone wall like it might offer protection. Her map crinkled softly in her hands, the edges already worn from constant folding and unfolding. She glanced over her shoulder, her heart thudding in her chest, ensuring no one was following her. The air was still, almost unnaturally so, but she couldn't shake the feeling that eyes might be watching from the mansion's countless windows—dark squares that stared down like accusing faces.

The afternoon sun filtered through the trees, dappling the path with light and shadow. Every rustling leaf could be footsteps. Every bird call could be a signal.

Her gaze landed on a small, nearly concealed set of stairs she'd noticed on the map but hadn't been able to find until now. They led downward, partially hidden by overgrown ivy clinging to the stone facade like nature was trying to reclaim what had been built. The steps seemed to beckon her, whispering promises of secrets.

Taking a steadying breath, she descended, her footsteps echoing faintly against the stone walls. The temperature dropped with each step, the coolness seeping through her clothes. The cool, earthy scent of the lower levels wrapped around her as she reached the base, where a heavy wooden door stood waiting.

Its iron handle was cold under her touch as she tested it, half-expecting it to be locked. To her surprise, it gave way easily with a click, the door creaking open on protesting hinges to reveal a pitch-black void.

Lacy fumbled for a switch near the doorframe, searching blindly until she found the toggle. With a faint click, dim bulbs flickered to life, buzzing slightly. They cast a muted yellow glow over the space that did more to create shadows than eliminate them.

The wine cellar stretched out before her like a cathedral dedicated to forgotten vintages, rows of dusty oak shelves disappearing into the shadows. Bottles of all shapes and sizes lined the shelves in surprising organization—someone had once cared deeply about this collection. Their faded labels hinted at years, perhaps decades, of history.

Her boots clicked softly against the stone floor as she ventured deeper. The air was heavy with the mingling scents of aged wood, damp stone, and the sharp, earthy tang of wine—some of which had probably seeped from broken bottles over the years.

She ran her fingers over the smooth curve of a bottle, lifting it carefully to inspect the label. A port, the year etched into the paper—1963—stood out clearly despite the dust.

"Fancy," Lacy muttered with a soft laugh that felt too loud. She blew the dust from the glass, watching the motes dance. "Aunt Emilia definitely had taste. This bottle's probably worth more than my car."

Her exploration continued, her steps measured and deliberate as she trailed her fingers along the shelves. Each corner held a new curiosity—barrels thick with cobwebs, an ancient corkscrew mounted on the wall with an ornate handle, and a small table cluttered with tasting notes written in faded ink.

She paused to read one, squinting: "1982 Bordeaux - notes of tobacco and dried fruit, excellent structure." The handwriting was elegant, looping.

As she turned down another aisle, distracted by reading labels, her foot snagged on something uneven—a piece of stone jutting up from the floor, different from the rest. She stumbled forward, her hand darting out to steady herself against the wall. The sudden impact dislodged a brick, sending it tumbling to the floor with a resounding clunk that echoed through the cellar like a gunshot.

Lacy winced at the noise, freezing as she glanced over her shoulder. Her heart hammered as she waited, but no footsteps came.

Kneeling, she reached for the brick with shaking hands, intending to slot it back into place. But as she crouched, a glint of metal caught her eye in the hollow space the brick had left behind.

The gap in the wall held something unusual—a small, inconspicuous lever tucked neatly into the darkness, its presence clearly intentional, clearly hidden.

"What the hell?" Lacy whispered, her breath hitching as her fingers hovered over the lever. Her mind raced. Was this part of the game? Another one of Emilia's elaborate theatrical touches? Or something else entirely?

She hesitated, her eyes scanning the wall around the gap. It seemed like any other part of the cellar. But the lever's deliberate placement, the specific brick that concealed it, told a different story. This wasn't accidental. Someone had built this. Hidden it. Wanted it found only by those who were looking closely enough.

Her curiosity flared hot and insistent, overriding any lingering caution. She grasped the lever, its metal cold and slightly rough against her palm, and gave it a firm pull downward.

The sound of grinding stone filled the cellar, mechanical and ancient, the vibrations reverberating through the walls. Dust and small bits of debris rained down from above, catching the faint light as they fell like snow.

A section of the stone wall to her right shifted outward with grinding reluctance, moving on some hidden mechanism that must have been decades old. The gap was just wide enough to squeeze through, its edges rough and uneven.

Lacy scrambled to her feet, stepping back as she took in the hidden passage with wide eyes. The darkness beyond seemed alive, an impenetrable void that beckoned with quiet menace. A faint draft wafted out carrying with it the musty, stale scent of air long trapped.

"Seriously?" Lacy muttered, her voice tinged with awe and disbelief. "This place is unreal. Who builds secret passages in their wine cellar? Actually, scratch that—of course Emilia did."

She peered into the passage, straining to make out any details in the oppressive darkness. The faint light from the cellar barely penetrated the shadows, dying just a few feet in. Her heart raced at the thought of what might lie beyond—more rooms? Treasure? Bodies?

Was this part of the game? Or had she stumbled onto something the others weren't meant to find?

Her fingers tightened around the map until it crumpled, and she took a tentative step forward. The passage seemed to stretch endlessly, its walls narrowing slightly as they disappeared into the gloom. She could make out rough stone walls, different from the finished stones of the cellar—these were natural, cave-like.

Lacy hesitated at the threshold, a war raging between self-preservation and insatiable curiosity. Finally, with a determined nod that was mostly for herself, she straightened her shoulders.

"You've come this far," she whispered to herself. "Might as well see where it leads. Besides, Sam said we should explore, right? This definitely counts as exploring."

With a deep breath, she stepped into the passageway, the darkness swallowing her whole. The temperature dropped immediately, and she could hear the sound of water dripping some-where in the distance—slow, rhythmic, ominous.

The hidden door shifted closed behind her with a soft thud, the mechanism operating automatically, leaving the cellar silent once more.

In the darkness, Lacy fumbled for her phone, her fingers slippery with nervous sweat, and activated the flashlight. The beam cut through the black, revealing a narrow tunnel that stretched ahead, its walls glistening with moisture.

"Okay," she breathed, forcing her feet to move forward. "Okay. You can do this."

CHAPTER THIRTY-EIGHT

The kitchen was alive with steam, music, and the heady aroma of good food that could make even the most anxious stomach growl. Leroy was like a maestro conducting a symphony of flavors, his apron—emblazoned with "Kiss the Cook"—flapping as he spun to the beat of the music blaring from the small speaker on the counter.

The tune was jazzy and infectious, something with horns and a walking bassline that made it impossible to stand still, and Leroy belted out the lyrics with unbridled enthusiasm, his baritone rich and smooth as honey.

Steam curled up from simmering pots on the stove, rising in white tendrils that caught the afternoon light. The scent of garlic, rosemary, and fresh bread mingled in the air, creating an olfactory masterpiece that spoke of comfort and home despite the mansion's dark undercurrents.

He stirred a pot of marinara with one hand—the sauce bubbling gently—while tossing a loaf of bread from hand to hand like a hot potato, his movements surprisingly graceful for his six-foot-three frame.

"Baby, I'm a star!" he declared, twirling with the bread in one hand and a spatula in the other, completely lost in his element.

His eyes were closed, head tilted back, utterly transported. "Ain't nobody gonna dim my light!"

The kitchen was his domain, the one place in this increasingly terrifying mansion where he felt completely in control, where death and mystery couldn't touch him. Here, he was king.

The kitchen door creaked open slowly. Kelly stepped inside, her polished maid uniform looking almost too pristine for the rustic space. She leaned casually against the doorframe, arms crossed, her lips curled into an amused smirk as she watched Leroy's one-man show. Her dark eyes sparkled with mischief.

He hadn't noticed her yet, too engrossed in hitting a particularly dramatic high note that made his voice crack slightly. When he spun around mid-chorus, spatula pointed at the ceiling like a microphone, his eyes locked onto hers.

He froze mid-performance, spatula still airborne, one foot lifted in what had been the beginning of another twirl.

For a beat, silence hung between them.

Then he broke into a broad grin that transformed his entire face. "Well, well, well," he said, his voice dropping to a deep, dramatic tone. "If it isn't the queen of sass herself." He swept into an exaggerated bow. "Kelly, you look like you just stepped out of a Hollywood picture. Grace Kelly ain't got nothing on you."

Kelly raised an eyebrow, tilting her head as she pushed off from the doorframe and sauntered further into the room. "And you look like you just stepped on a banana peel in a cartoon. What are you doing, Leroy? Auditioning for a cooking show or having some kind of breakdown?"

"Entertaining myself," he replied, tossing the spatula onto the counter with a flourish. "What's life without a little showbiz? A little pizzazz?" He snapped his fingers. "Especially in a place like this, where people keep dropping like flies. Gotta keep the spirits up—the living spirits, that is."

Kelly walked farther into the kitchen, the playful glint in her eyes never fading. "I'm here for the cart," she said, glancing around at the organized chaos—cutting boards covered in diced vegetables, pans waiting to be washed, fresh herbs bundled on the counter. "Is this it?" She gestured to a serving cart loaded with covered dishes near the industrial refrigerator.

Leroy shook his head, waving a hand dismissively as he turned back to his marinara, adding a pinch of salt and tasting it from a wooden spoon. "Nah, Sam took care of the table settings already. Said he wanted to help us out, as if this job isn't already a cakewalk." He made a face at his own lie. "Well, okay, maybe not a cakewalk, but you know what I mean."

Kelly blinked, genuinely surprised. Her eyebrows rose nearly to her hairline. "Really? He did the settings himself? Sam personally set the table?"

"Yup," Leroy confirmed, stirring the marinara with practiced ease. "Even helped me with the pasta earlier—rolled it out and everything. The guy's got some skills I didn't expect from a Hollywood director. If he ever gets tired of running this whole murder mansion thing, I might have to hire him as my sous chef."

Kelly chuckled, the sound warm and genuine as she leaned against the counter. "Best boss ever," she said, her voice softening with real affection. "Seriously. Where else are you going to find someone who owns an island, invites you for a mystery weekend, and then still rolls up his sleeves to help with dinner while people are dying?"

Leroy glanced at her, his grin widening into something more sincere. "See? That's why you and me get along, Kelly. We recognize greatness when we see it." He pointed the wooden spoon at her for emphasis. "Also, we both have impeccable taste in music, excellent work ethic, and devastatingly good looks."

She rolled her eyes but couldn't hide her smile. "Alright, Casanova. I'll go check on his work and make sure it's actually great. Knowing Sam, he probably arranged everything all artistic and impractical."

"Hey now," Leroy protested with mock indignation. "The man's an artist. Give him some credit."

As Kelly turned to leave, adjusting her apron and smoothing down her uniform, Leroy called after her, his voice playful but tinged with mock seriousness. "Hold up, Miss Kelly! When you get back, I have a very important question to ask you. Life or death level important."

Kelly paused in the doorway, one hand on the frame, glancing back over her shoulder with an arched brow. "Let me guess. Something about being your valentine?"

"Bingo," Leroy replied with a wink, pointing finger guns at her that he immediately regretted but committed to anyway. "You know me too well. We're like two peas in a pod. Two beans in a burrito. Two—"

"Two idiots in a murder mansion?" Kelly suggested, cutting him off.

"Exactly!" Leroy beamed. "See? We finish each other's sentences. That's true love right there."

Kelly shook her head, laughing softly—a sound that rang like bells in the warm kitchen. "You're ridiculous, Leroy. Absolutely ridiculous. But hey, keep cooking like that," she gestured to the pots simmering on the stove, "and I might just consider it. Maybe."

With a final smirk, she pushed the door open and disappeared into the hallway, her laughter trailing behind her like perfume, fading as her footsteps echoed away.

Leroy stood still for a moment, staring at the closed door with a contented smile that softened his usually animated features. His chest felt warm in a way that had nothing to do with the heat from the stove.

The music on the speaker shifted to an upbeat number—something with a strong backbeat and bright piano chords—and he snapped back to reality. Grabbing a dish towel from where it hung on the oven handle, he swung it over his shoulder, resuming his dance moves as he returned to the stove. His feet moved in a little shuffle-step, hips swaying as he checked the bread in the oven, the golden-brown crust perfect.

"Still got it," he murmured to himself, grinning.

The kitchen remained a haven of warmth, humor, and creativity—an oasis of joy amid the growing tension within the mansion. Copper pots gleamed on their hooks, herbs dried in bunches near the window, and the steady rhythm of cooking continued unabated.

For Leroy, it was more than just a workspace; it was his stage, his sanctuary, and his little piece of happiness in a house steeped in mystery and danger.

He turned up the music, letting the brass section wash over him, and got back to work. There were mouths to feed, even in a murder mansion. Especially in a murder mansion. People needed comfort food when death was knocking at the door.

"Baby, I'm a star," he sang again, softer this time, more to himself than anyone else.

And in his kitchen, at least, it was absolutely true.

CHAPTER THIRTY-NINE

Kelly's hand trailed along the hallway's cool, smooth wall as she moved, her steps light and rhythmic, as though she were dancing through her own private music video. Her fingers brushed against the raised pattern of the wallpaper—subtle embossed roses she'd dusted a hundred times but never really noticed until now. Her mind floated elsewhere, far from the confines of the grand mansion and its dark intrigue, drifting to thoughts of Leroy's ridiculous grin and the way his eyes had sparkled when he'd mentioned his "important question."

The faint sound of distant conversation and the muffled clinking of dishes barely registered as she hummed a soft tune under her breath—the same jazz number that had been playing in the kitchen. Her maid uniform, immaculate as always despite a long day's work, swished softly with her movements.

Kelly's lips curved into a faint, dreamy smile, the kind reserved for someone who had momentarily found peace in an otherwise chaotic world. For just these few moments, walking through the mansion's elegant corridors, she wasn't thinking about murder or mystery or death. She was thinking about possibility. About maybe.

The sunlight streaming through a nearby window caught the

small silver pendant at her throat—a gift from her grandmother —making it flash like a tiny star. She touched it briefly, unconsciously, a nervous habit she'd had since childhood.

As she turned a corner, the grand ballroom came into view, its polished floor gleaming under the cascade of sunlight streaming through towering windows that stretched nearly floor to ceiling. The room, with its empty tables and chairs arranged neatly for the next gathering, exuded an air of calm. The space was so serene it felt almost sacred.

Everything was perfect. Sam had done an excellent job with the table settings. The silverware gleamed, the napkins were folded into elegant swans, and fresh flowers—white roses and baby's breath—adorned each table.

Maybe I will say yes, Kelly thought, her smile widening slightly. *Why not? Life's too short.*

Her thought was cut short. Her peace shattered in a heartbeat.

A flash of steel caught Kelly's attention just as it sliced through the air behind her—a glint in her peripheral vision, sunlight reflecting off metal. The blade glinted cruelly in the golden afternoon light, its edge impossibly sharp.

She barely had time to react, barely had time to turn her head, before it found its mark with surgical precision.

The knife plunged into her throat with horrifying efficiency.

Her body jerked back violently, and her eyes went wide with shock—pupils dilating as her brain struggled to process what had just happened. Her hands flew to her neck instinctively, clutching at the wound, feeling the foreign object embedded there, but the warm rush of blood spilling between her fingers, pulsing with each rapid heartbeat, told her it was too late.

So much blood. Too much blood.

She tried to scream, but only a wet gurgle emerged, bubbles of air and blood mixing at her lips. The world around her blurred at the edges, vision tunneling. The golden sunlight that had seemed so beautiful moments before now felt harsh, blinding.

A choked gasp escaped her lips as she stumbled backward, her heels catching on the edge of a Persian rug. Her heart pounded violently against her ribs, her instincts screaming at her to move, to escape, to fight back, but her strength was fading fast, draining away with the blood that now soaked the front of her pristine uniform.

No, she thought desperately. *Not like this. Not now.*

Kelly's body collided with the edge of a nearby table, the impact jarring her spine and rattling the carefully arranged plates and glasses. Crystal water goblets trembled, catching the light. They teetered for a moment before crashing to the floor in a violent cascade.

The sharp sound of shattering china and glass echoed through the empty ballroom like a scream she couldn't voice, a violent contrast to the eerie silence that followed—broken only by her wet, labored breathing.

Her knees buckled, but she managed to cling to the table's edge, her trembling hands leaving bloody streaks on the pristine white tablecloth like abstract art—crimson fingers grasping for purchase, for life, for one more moment.

Her lips moved as if to speak, trying to form a name— Leroy's name, maybe, or a plea for help—but no words came. Only wet, rasping gasps as the life ebbed from her.

Her vision flickered. Darkness crept in from the sides, eating away at the world.

In a final, desperate attempt, Kelly extended one shaking hand behind her, as if to point toward her unseen assailant, to leave some clue, some evidence of who had done this. Her fingers stretched toward the space where the killer must be standing, watching.

Her other hand slipped from the table, nerveless now, sending the cloth cascading down along with its contents. Plates and cutlery clattered to the floor in a roar of metal and porcelain. The swan napkins fell among the wreckage, their elegant folds now meaningless.

She dropped to her knees, her body swaying unsteadily as if drunk, as if she might somehow catch her balance and stand again.

But she wouldn't.

With one last, shuddering gasp—a final inhale that never became an exhale—Kelly collapsed, her cheek pressing against the cold floor, her wide eyes still open, still seeing but no longer processing.

Blood pooled around her, dark and stark against the ballroom's polished wood, spreading in an ever-widening circle that reflected the sunlight like a terrible mirror.

Her vision narrowed to a pinpoint, the sunlight dimming as her consciousness faded. Her last thought was of the kitchen, of warmth and laughter and jazz music. Of Leroy's smile.

Then nothing.

The ballroom, once a place of grandeur and life and celebration, now bore the marks of unspeakable violence. Blood streaked across the fallen tablecloth and scattered shards of broken glass that glittered like diamonds in the sunlight.

Kelly's lifeless body lay amid the wreckage, her maid uniform —the one she'd pressed so carefully that morning—soaked through with red that was already beginning to darken as it dried. Her hand was still extended behind her, pointing, accusing, though at what or whom only the killer knew.

Her eyes stared at nothing, glazed and empty, the light gone from them permanently. The small silver pendant at her throat— or what remained visible of her throat—was now stained crimson.

The sunlight that streamed through the windows felt cruel in its indifference, casting a golden glow over the macabre scene like a spotlight on a stage. Curtains swayed gently in the breeze from a cracked window, their soft rustle the only sound in the now-silent room.

A single white rose from one of the centerpieces had fallen near Kelly's head, its petals already spotted with her blood.

Death had claimed another victim within the walls of the mansion, but this time it was for good. There would be no after death march to the cabin. There would be no Valentine's Day with Leroy. The once-vibrant Kelly—who had hummed jazz tunes and laughed at Leroy's jokes and made this place feel a little less lonely—was now a haunting reminder of the dark game unfolding around them.

And somewhere in the mansion, a killer walked free, their blade still wet with Kelly's blood.

CHAPTER FORTY

Zoey descended the staircase with a bounce in her step, her earlier grogginess completely gone after a solid nap and a splash of cold water on her face. Her lively energy had returned in full force, her sharp wit sharpened and ready for whatever the day ahead might bring. The sunlight filtering through the foyer windows caught the highlights in her hair and made her skin seem to radiate warmth. Her expression was bright and carefree —the look of someone who'd successfully recharged and was ready to tackle the world.

She'd even taken the time to fix her makeup, covering those dark circles and adding a swipe of lip gloss. If she was going to be trapped on a murder mystery island, she might as well look good doing it.

As she reached the base of the stairs, her hand trailing along the polished bannister, Russell suddenly lunged from a doorway, his arms wide in a mock attack, fingers curled like claws.

"Boo!" he exclaimed, his voice echoing in the open space.

Zoey yelped, a sound more surprised than scared, leaping back with her hand clutching her chest. Her heart hammered against her ribs. "What the hell, Russell!" she snapped, her glare cutting through his immediate burst of laughter. "Are you trying to give me a heart attack? Because that's how you give someone a heart attack!"

Russell grinned unapologetically, clearly pleased with himself. His eyes sparkled with mischief. "Just making sure you're awake. You said you were going back to sleep. Wanted to verify you didn't turn into a zombie or something."

Zoey smacked his shoulder with mock annoyance, though there was real force behind it. "You're such a child. Seriously, what are you, twelve? Do you still put whoopee cushions on chairs?"

"Only on special occasions," Russell replied with a wink.

"Come on," Zoey said, shaking her head but unable to completely suppress her smile. "Let's get moving. I'm starving, and Leroy promised there'd be leftovers from breakfast. If you made me miss the good stuff with your stupid jump scare, I'm going to be very annoyed."

Russell gestured dramatically down the hall, sweeping his arm in an exaggerated bow. "After you, oh queen of sass."

"Queen of sass and common sense," Zoey corrected, walking past him. "You should try the latter sometime."

As they turned the corner and stepped through the wide double doors into the grand ballroom the sight before them stopped them dead in their tracks.

Kelly's lifeless body lay sprawled on the polished floor near an overturned table, her throat slashed in a gruesome arc. Blood pooled beneath her, dark and stark against the light wood, spreading in a shape that reminded Zoey horribly of wings. The delicate white of her maid uniform was soaked through with crimson. The bright morning sun streaming through the towering windows only intensified the horror, illuminating every terrible detail with cruel clarity—the shattered plates, the scattered silverware, the tablecloth pulled to the floor.

Zoey froze completely, every muscle in her body locking up.

Her playful smirk vanished, replaced by an expression of pure shock.

"Oh my god," she muttered, her voice barely audible, coming out choked and small. Her gaze was locked on Kelly's pale face, on those open eyes that stared at nothing.

This looks real, her mind screamed. *This looks actually real.*

Russell stepped forward cautiously, his usual swagger completely gone. His expression had gone grim, all the humor drained away. "Shit," he said, his voice low and rough. "This one looks very real, doesn't it?"

Even as he asked, he knew the answer. It looked too real and the smell, metallic and wrong, told him something was off. Or maybe Sam just went above and beyond for this one.

Zoey shook her head, finding her voice though it came out strangled. "It's too real. So gross," she whispered. Then, louder, with more urgency, "We've got another one!" Her voice cracked a bit on the last word.

Zoey's call echoed down the corridor, bouncing off walls and disappearing into the depths of the mansion. She stepped back toward the doorway on shaking legs, her eyes darting nervously around the room. The killer could still be here. Could still be watching. Should she look for clues or for protection. Her mind was utterly confused.

Russell leaned into the hallway, cupping his hands around his mouth. "Body in the ballroom! Come on, people!" he called, his tone attempting to mask his unease with humor, but it rang hollow now.

The mansion remained eerily quiet. No rushing footsteps. No voices calling back. Just silence, heavy and oppressive.

Zoey frowned, glancing at Russell with wide eyes. "Where is everyone?" Her voice had taken on a slightly hysterical edge. "Where the hell is everyone?"

Russell shrugged, his usual confidence dimmed to a flicker. He ran a hand through his hair, making it stick up at odd angles. "Norma and Shea went hiking. They could be anywhere on the island by now. Kelly's..." He gestured helplessly at the body. "Not coming. Obviously. Sam's probably running around somewhere playing director."

Before Zoey could reply, movement at the end of the hall caught her eye. Sam appeared, striding toward them with purpose, with Gwen close behind looking concerned. Relief flooded through Zoey so suddenly it almost made her dizzy.

"There you are," Zoey said, her tone sharp with exasperation and barely controlled panic. "We found the next victim. This one looks super real Sam."

The ballroom side door opened and Leroy stepped in followed by Lacy. "What going on?" Leroy said as he spotted Kelly on the ground. "Damn. Does this mean I'm serving too?"

Sam quickened his pace, his sharp eyes narrowing as he spotted Kelly's body through the doorway. He froze for a moment, just a beat, the color draining from his face like someone had pulled a plug. All the easy confidence, the director's control, drained away.

Gwen gasped softly behind him, her hand flying to her mouth as she stepped closer, peering around Sam's shoulder. Her face went white.

Sam moved forward almost mechanically, like his body was operating on autopilot while his mind tried to catch up. He knelt by Kelly's side, his hands hovering over her as though unsure whether to touch her. His fingers trembled.

"This isn't planned," he murmured, his voice barely audible, the words more for himself than anyone else. "This wasn't supposed to happen. This isn't part of it."

Russell crossed his arms, his signature smirk creeping back as a defense mechanism. "Right. Real convincing," he said, but his voice lacked its usual bite. "What's the next clue, maestro? Who do we vote off the island?"

Sam's head snapped up, his expression fierce—more intense than any of them had ever seen. His eyes blazed. "This isn't part of the game, Russell," he growled, his voice cold and cutting. "She's dead. Actually dead."

The words hung in the air like a heavy cloud, pressing down on them, making it hard to breathe. The group exchanged uncertain glances, the tension in the room palpable.

Russell opened his mouth to retort, but Sam was on his feet in an instant, grabbing him by the front of his shirt with both fists. The sudden movement shocked everyone, and Russell stumbled as Sam pulled him forward, their faces inches apart.

"She's dead!" Sam roared, his voice filled with raw anger and fear and something that sounded like grief. "This isn't a goddamn performance! She's really dead! Do you understand me? Kelly is dead!"

Russell's cocky demeanor crumbled completely as Sam released him with a shove that sent him staggering backward. He caught himself against the doorframe, his wide eyes betraying the first flicker of genuine fear. His hands shook.

The room was silent except for Sam's heavy breathing and the quiet sounds of shock and fear.

Sam turned to the others, his chest heaving as he fought to steady his breathing. "Listen to me," he said, his tone firm but quieter now, more measured. "This is real. The game is over. Someone in this mansion is a murderer. An actual murderer." He looked at each of them in turn. "One of us did this."

The group stood frozen, the reality sinking in like ice water in their veins. Gwen's hands shook as she crossed her arms, her gaze darting to Kelly's lifeless form before looking away quickly. Zoey's face was pale, her earlier energy replaced by a volatile mix of fear and determination.

Leroy muttered a curse under his breath, his jaw working as he fought to keep control. His hands clenched into fists. "Who did this?" he asked quietly. "Who the fuck did this?"

Lacy clutched her arms, her face pale as she took a step back from the doorway, unable to look at the body anymore. Her eyes were glassy with unshed tears.

Zoey spoke, her voice steady despite the tremor in her hands. "So what do we do now?"

Sam straightened, squaring his shoulders, his resolve hardening. He had to take control. Had to be the leader they needed. "We get help. We try to find out who's behind this," he said. "And we survive." He paused, looking at each of them, knowing that one of them could be a killer.

CHAPTER FORTY-ONE

Norma burst through the ballroom doorway like a wild animal fleeing a predator, her wild eyes darting frantically around the room, taking in the gathered group, the overturned table, Kelly's body. Her breaths came in heaving gasps that sounded painful, her chest rising and falling rapidly. Her hair clung to her sweat-drenched face in dark, tangled strands, and dirt smudged her cheeks and forearms. Her trembling hands gripped the doorframe for support, knuckles white.

"Sam! Sam!... Shea!... He's..." she choked, the words tumbling out between ragged breaths. "He's... dead. Really... really dead. Not fake dead. There was so much blood—"

Her voice cut through the air like a blade, sharp and desperate. The tension in the room snapped taut, everyone turning to her in stunned silence.

Sam groaned, clutching his head with both hands as if to stave off the chaos threatening to overwhelm him. "Jesus Christ," he muttered, his voice low and strained. "Are you sure? Norma, are you absolutely sure?"

Norma nodded frantically, her tear-streaked face pale with horror, her eyes red-rimmed and unfocused. "I saw him," she whispered, but the whisper somehow carried through the entire ballroom. Her voice cracked like breaking glass. "It was—it was awful. His eyes... they were just... staring..."

Russell moved toward her immediately, wrapping his arms around her as her knees threatened to give out. She collapsed against him, her body shaking with suppressed sobs.

Lacy crouched beside Kelly's lifeless body, her trembling fingers pressing lightly against the woman's neck, searching for a pulse she knew wouldn't be there. The skin was already cooling. She withdrew her hand slowly, wiping her fingers on her jeans as if she could wipe away the memory of that coldness. Her face was grim.

"She's dead," Lacy confirmed softly, her tone devoid of hope. "I think she's been dead for a while."

Zoey's composure began to unravel like a sweater caught on a nail, her usually sharp demeanor replaced by raw, naked fear that made her look younger, more vulnerable. "Please," she begged, her voice trembling as she turned to Sam, her hands clasped together. "Tell me this is some elaborate joke. Tell me this is part of the weekend, that you're all just really committed to the bit."

Sam's haunted eyes met hers, and his silence said everything his words couldn't. The weight of his expression—the guilt, the fear, the overwhelming responsibility—crushed the last shred of denial in the room.

Leroy, usually the first to crack a joke, balled his fists tightly until his nails bit into his palms. His voice rose with rage that vibrated through his entire body. "Who the fuck is this sick bastard?!" he shouted, the words echoing off the high ceilings. "Who does this? Who kills Kelly?" His voice broke on her name. "I swear, I'll cut him up myself if I find him. I'll make him pay for what he did to her."

Russell pulled Norma into his arms as she shuddered against him, her face buried in his chest. His voice, though steady, carried an edge of fear. "We need to call the police. Now. Right now."

A flurry of motion followed as everyone pulled out their

phones, desperation written across their faces. Hands fumbled with devices, thumbs swiping frantically across screens.

Gwen was the first to speak, holding her phone up as if offering evidence. "I don't have a signal," she said, her voice laced with frustration and the beginning of panic. "Nothing. Not even one bar."

"Me neither," Lacy added, holding her phone aloft, moving it in different directions like a divining rod searching for water. "It's like the service just... died."

Sam slammed his phone onto the table with enough force that the screen cracked slightly, the loud clatter making everyone jump. "Dammit!" he growled, staring at his ruined phone. "No reception. Nothing."

Russell stepped forward, his phone held high above his head, moving toward the windows. "I had one earlier," he said, his voice tinged with desperate hope. "When I was working. Maybe..." He tapped at the screen, moving closer to the light. His expression lit up suddenly. "Got it! I've got a bar! One bar!"

Relief swept through the room like a physical wave, people exhaling breath they hadn't realized they'd been holding.

Russell quickly dialed 911, his fingers shaking slightly. The line connected—they could all hear the ringing—and he spoke with urgency that bordered on manic. "Yes, we need help. Two people are dead—murdered—on Rose Island, Castle de Amore. Yes, Rose Island. Can you—hello? Hello?"

His face twisted with frustration as the line crackled and popped with static. "Hello?! Can you hear me? We need help! People are dying!"

The call abruptly dropped, the line going dead with a flatline beep that sounded too much like a heart monitor. Russell cursed, gripping the phone, trying again, then again.

"They said they'd send help, but I couldn't get all the details. The connection was shit. They're contacting the Coast Guard, I think. They said something about a boat. We're supposed to stay put and wait."

"Stay put?!" Zoey's voice cracked with panic, rising nearly to a shriek. "Are you kidding me? We're sitting ducks! We're targets in a shooting gallery!"

Lacy's voice broke through the noise, sharp and cutting through the chaos. "Wait a second. Why don't we just use the landline? Isn't that what it's for?" She looked at Sam pointedly. "This mansion has to have a landline. I saw one in the study."

The room fell silent as everyone turned to Sam, their eyes boring into him with varying degrees of suspicion and accusation. He hesitated, his face tightening as though bracing for a blow.

"The landline's down," he admitted, his voice low, almost ashamed. "It's been down since yesterday."

"What?!" Russell stepped closer, his expression incredulous, anger flashing in his eyes. "And you're just now telling us this? You knew the phones were down and you didn't say anything?"

Sam held up his hands defensively, backing up a step. "It wasn't a big deal until now! I didn't think—I mean, we all had our cell phones. I was going to get it fixed when we got back to the mainland. How was I supposed to know someone would actually start killing people?"

"You didn't think?! That's your excuse?!" Zoey's voice rose, her fear turning to anger that needed a target. "People are dead, Sam! Kelly's dead! Shea's dead! And you didn't think the phones being down was worth mentioning?"

Sam's patience frayed like old rope under tension, snapping with an almost audible crack. "Listen to me!" he barked, his voice slicing through the growing chaos. "The emergency line and radio at the security shack still work. That's our best shot. That's why we have backup systems. We can use those."

"What about the security guard?" Lacy asked, her suspicion clear, her eyes narrowing. "We haven't seen him once this entire weekend. Where the hell is he? What's his name again?"

Russell nodded, his tone harsh, accusatory. "Yeah, what if

Stubby's our killer? He'd know this place inside and out. He'd have access to everything."

Sam's jaw tightened, a muscle jumping in his cheek. "That's why I'm going to the shack," he said, his voice firm. "I'll use the emergency line, grab the radio, and bring back Stubby. If he's not there, I'll know something's up. If the equipment's been sabotaged, I'll know."

Russell crossed his arms, his stance aggressive. "And if he is there? What if he comes at you with a knife?"

Sam's eyes darkened, his expression hardening. "Then we'll know for sure. I'll be ready."

"I'm coming with you," Leroy said, stepping forward without hesitation, his voice leaving no room for debate. His jaw was set, his eyes still filled with rage over Kelly's death. "You're not going alone. Two sets of eyes are better than one, and if we run into trouble, you'll need backup."

Sam looked at him for a long moment, seemed about to argue, then nodded once. "Fine. But we move fast, we stay together, and we don't take any chances." He turned to the others. "The rest of you stay in the lounge and don't leave. Lock the doors if you have to. Push furniture in front of them. Don't open up for anyone except me or Leroy."

"What about the others?" Zoey asked, her voice shaking, her eyes wide. "Curtis and Chelsie? Darren and Alice.? What if they're already..." Her words trailed off, but the implication hung in the air like smoke.

The room grew heavier, the atmosphere thick with dread as the group exchanged uneasy glances. What if the killer had been busy? What if there were more bodies they didn't know about yet?

Sam placed a hand on Zoey's shoulder, his grip firm but gentle, his tone softer now. "We'll get Stubby first. Then we'll check on the cabin. I promise we'll figure this out."

Reluctantly, she nodded, though her eyes said she didn't believe him.

The group began to shuffle toward the lounge, their movements sluggish with fear, feet dragging. Every shadow seemed threatening now. Every corner could hide a killer.

Sam and Leroy exchanged a final glance—a moment of understanding passing between them—before heading toward the mansion's front entrance, toward the security shack somewhere on the grounds.

Their footsteps echoed through the mansion's empty halls, each footfall sounding too loud, too exposed.

As the others gathered in the lounge, herding together like frightened sheep, the mansion's oppressive silence closed in around them like a fist. The shadows seemed darker than they should be, the air heavier, harder to breathe.

Tension crackled like a live wire, each person acutely aware of their vulnerability, of the fact that the killer could be anyone. Could be one of them.

They arranged themselves throughout the room—some on the sofas, some in chairs, Russell and Norma together near the fireplace. No one sat with their back to a door. Everyone kept their eyes moving, watching.

Gwen whispered, her voice barely audible. "Do you think they'll make it back?"

It was the question they were all thinking but hadn't wanted to voice.

Lacy didn't answer immediately, her gaze fixed on the door they'd locked behind Sam and Leroy. Her fingers tightened around the armrest of her chair, her knuckles white.

Finally, she spoke. "They have to."

Zoey finally spoke, her voice grim but determined. "They have to. Because if they don't..." She didn't finish the sentence. Didn't need to.

The group sat in silence, the weight of their situation pressing down on them like a physical force.

Time dragged on with agonizing slowness, every creak of the

mansion amplifying their unease, making them jump. Was that a footstep? A door opening? Or just the house settling?

The waiting had begun, and with it came the harrowing realization that none of them were truly safe.

Not really.

Not until they knew who was behind this.

And maybe not even then.

CHAPTER FORTY-TWO

The thick canopy overhead blocked much of the sunlight, leaving the woods in a perpetual state of dimness that made it difficult to judge the time of day. The narrow, uneven trail forced Sam and Leroy to tread carefully, watching their footing on roots that twisted across the path like grasping fingers. Their boots crunched over fallen twigs and leaves, each snap and rustle seeming too loud in the oppressive quiet.

Every step felt heavier than the last, as if the oppressive atmosphere of the forest weighed them down physically. The air was damp and cool, carrying the earthy smell of decomposing leaves and moss. Somewhere in the distance, a bird called out—a harsh, grating sound that made them both flinch.

Leroy cast a sidelong glance at Sam, his usual playful demeanor completely absent, replaced by something harder, more focused. "Sam, what the hell is going on?" he asked, his voice low but tense, barely above a whisper. "I need you to level with me, man."

Sam sighed, his breath visible in the crisp air. "I don't know, Leroy," he replied, frustration lacing his tone. "I wish I did. I wish I had answers, but I'm as lost as you are."

"These people are your friends," Leroy pressed, his voice

rising slightly. His hands clenched at his sides. "You've known them for years. Who do you think's behind this? Someone's got to have a motive. People don't just start killing for no reason."

Sam shook his head, his face set in a grim expression. "I can't imagine any of them doing this," he said, his voice hollow with disbelief. "Curtis wouldn't. Russell's too pragmatic. Norma's too... normal. Of course not Zoey. Lacy..." His voice caught slightly. "No. None of them."

They walked in silence for a while, the only sound the occasional snap of a twig or rustle of leaves. The woods felt like they were closing in, the trees growing closer together, the shadows deeper.

Leroy finally broke the quiet. "What about Stubby? You think it could be him?"

Sam hesitated, his brow furrowing. "Stubby's a good guy," he said finally, though he sounded less certain than he wanted to. "Known him for three years. He's ex-military, takes his job seriously. But..." He gestured ahead. "We'll know soon enough. The shack's got monitors, cameras covering most of the island. If someone else is here—someone who's not supposed to be—he'll have seen them."

Leroy squinted through the trees, spotting the weathered structure in the distance. "And if he hasn't seen anything? If he's not there?" he asked, his steps slowing.

Sam stopped and turned to face him, his expression dark. "Then we've got a real murder mystery on our hands," he said, his voice flat. "And either him or one of our friends is a killer."

"Your friends." Leroy said before exhaling sharply through his nose. "Well, this is just fucking great," he muttered, his tone dripping with sarcasm that barely masked the fear underneath. "I came here to cook, man. To make good food and maybe flirt with Kelly." His voice broke slightly on her name. "Not to play detective in a horror movie."

Sam placed a hand on his shoulder, his grip firm, grounding. "We'll figure it out, Leroy. One way or another. I promise you, we're getting off this island alive, and we're going to make whoever did this pay."

Leroy looked at him for a long moment, then nodded. "Damn right we are."

The small building came into view as they broke through a particularly dense section of undergrowth, its weathered walls blending into the forest around it. The structure was modest—maybe twelve by twelve feet—with peeling paint and a roof that had seen better days.

The air seemed colder here, somehow, the silence even more oppressive. No birds sang. No insects buzzed. Nothing.

Sam paused at the door, his hand hovering over the handle, suddenly reluctant. Something felt wrong.

"Ready?" he asked, glancing at Leroy, his voice barely a whisper.

Leroy nodded, his jaw tightening. "Let's get this over with."

Sam pushed the door open cautiously, the creak of the hinges echoing eerily in the stillness. Inside, the dim light barely illuminated the room—a single window covered with grime filtering weak sunlight.

Both men froze as the gruesome scene came into focus.

Stubby's torso was propped grotesquely against the desk, positioned like some macabre puppet. Candy Valentine hearts—the cheap kind with messages like "BE MINE" and "TRUE LOVE"—spilled from his mouth and the hollowed cavities where his eyes had been, cascading down his chest in a horrifying parody of abundance. His severed arm had been rigged with wire to hold a gun aimed directly at the door, the fingers positioned around the trigger.

The rest of his body was a mangled mess, blood pooling beneath the desk in a dark, congealing puddle. The metallic smell hit them like a wall.

Before either man could react, before they could process the full horror—

POP!

The gun fired with a sound that seemed impossibly loud in the confined space.

Sam and Leroy dove in opposite directions on pure instinct. Leroy crashed to the floor hard, gasping for breath as he scrambled to his knees. Sam pressed himself against the wall beside the door, his heart pounding so hard he could feel it in his throat.

For several seconds, neither of them moved, both waiting for something else to happen.

When the smoke cleared—thin wisps curling toward the ceiling—their eyes fell on the gun, still clutched in Stubby's severed hand. Dangling from the barrel was a small paper sign, swaying gently from the recoil.

In bold red letters that looked like they'd been drawn with marker, it read: HAPPY V-DAY GOTCHA!

"Jesus Christ," Leroy muttered, pulling himself to his feet on shaking legs. He turned to Stubby's mutilated remains, his stomach churning violently. He had to look away, had to swallow hard against the bile rising. "Whoever did this is one sick bastard. This is... this is beyond sick. This is evil."

Sam stood slowly, his eyes scanning the room with a mix of horror and determination, forcing himself to look past Stubby's body. "No kidding," he said, his voice rough. He stepped carefully over the bloodstained floor. "This took time. This took planning. Whoever did this wanted us to find him like this."

Sam reached for the red telephone mounted on the desk, carefully avoiding touching anything else. He pressed it to his ear, hoping against hope.

Silence. Not even a dial tone.

He jiggled the receiver, pressed the cradle button repeatedly. "The line's cut," he said finally, slamming the phone down hard enough to crack the plastic casing.

"Of course it is," Leroy muttered, his voice bitter, hollow. He glanced at the bank of monitors mounted on the wall—five screens that should have shown various views of the island. Most displayed nothing but static. The others showed darkness. "Let me guess—the cameras are out too?"

Sam nodded, his jaw clenching. He moved to the control panel, pressing buttons, toggling switches. Nothing. "Guest house cameras are cut. Completely dead. And the radio's gone." He gestured to an empty bracket on the wall where equipment should have been. "Ripped right out. They took the whole unit."

Leroy's fists balled at his sides, his knuckles cracking. "So, what now?" he demanded, his voice rising with barely controlled panic. "We just sit here and wait for this psycho to pick us off one by one? Hide in the lounge until we starve or until the killer decides to finish the job?"

Sam didn't answer immediately. Instead, his gaze shifted to the wall behind Leroy, focusing on something that made a faint grin tug at his lips despite the horror. "Not exactly," he said, motioning toward a poster of a bikini-clad woman—incongruous and tacky in this blood-soaked space.

Leroy frowned, following his gaze. "Really, Sam? Now? You're thinking about pin-ups at a time like this?"

Sam grabbed a nearby fire extinguisher from its wall mount and, without ceremony, smashed it into the wall behind the poster. The drywall crumbled easily, revealing a hidden metal case mounted in a hollow space between the studs.

"Stubby was ex-military," Sam explained as he carefully retrieved the case. "He liked to be prepared."

He opened it to reveal two handguns—Glock 19s, standard issue—and several loaded magazines. He checked one to make sure it was loaded, then handed the other to Leroy.

"Now we even the odds."

Leroy examined the weapon, his grip steady despite the tension. The weight of it was comforting, solid. Real. "Well," he said, checking the chamber and cocking the gun with practiced ease, "this is a little more my style. This I can work with."

Before leaving, Leroy turned back to Stubby's remains, looking at what was left of the man who'd greeted them at the dock just days ago with a friendly wave and a bad joke. He hesitated, his expression softening, the anger giving way to something sadder.

"Sorry, man," he said quietly, his voice thick. "You deserved better than this. You deserved a hell of a lot better than this."

Sam placed a hand on Leroy's shoulder, squeezing once. His voice was firm. "Let's go. We've got a killer to stop. And people to protect."

The two men stepped out of the shack, pulling the door closed behind them, their weapons at the ready, held low but prepared. The forest seemed darker now than when they'd arrived, the shadows deeper and more menacing. The trail back looked less like a path and more like a gauntlet.

They exchanged a glance, unspoken determination passing between them.

They'd come to this island for a fun weekend, for mystery and games and laughter. Now they were armed and walking back into what had become a war zone, where their friends were either victims or suspects, where death waited around every corner.

Together, they disappeared into the woods, the weight of their mission heavy on their shoulders, the weight of the guns heavier still.

Behind them, the shack stood silent, a monument to the killer's depravity.

CHAPTER FORTY-THREE

The atmosphere in the lounge felt as though it were suffocating everyone in the room, the air itself seeming to press against their skin, making it hard to draw a full breath. The dim lighting—someone had drawn the heavy curtains, blocking out the cheerful afternoon sun—cast long shadows on the walls that seemed to move and shift when you weren't looking directly at them. The faint hum of the mansion's air system seemed amplified against the tense silence.

Norma sat curled up on the couch, her knees tucked to her chest in a defensive posture, her arms wrapped around her legs. Her glassy eyes were fixed on the floor, staring at a particular spot on the Persian rug as if she could will herself to disappear into it. Russell had his arm draped protectively around her, though his own face betrayed the storm brewing within—jaw tight, eyes hard, the muscle in his cheek jumping.

Lacy paced the length of the room like a caged animal, her heels clicking against the polished floor with sharp, rhythmic precision that was starting to get on everyone's nerves. Click. Click. Click. Her arms were crossed tightly over her chest, and her jaw was set in a firm line. She was wound so tight she looked like she might snap.

Zoey leaned against the bar with studied casualness, swirling the amber liquid—bourbon, straight, no ice—in her glass. The crystal caught the light with each rotation. Beside her, Gwen sat hunched over on a bar stool, tracing her finger along the rim of her untouched drink, making it sing softly.

"So, they're all across the island?" Zoey's voice sliced through the tension like a razor, her tone casual but her eyes sharp. She'd stopped swirling her drink.

Gwen blinked, startled from her thoughts. "Yeah," she said, her voice a little shaky. "Darren and Alice are at the cabin. I took them there this morning. Curtis and Chelsie were already gone when I got back—probably hiking or exploring or..." Her voice trailed off, uncertainty creeping in. She hesitated, her brows knitting together. "They're fine. I'm sure they're fine. They have to be fine."

Norma broke the fragile illusion with a single, chilling statement delivered in a voice that sounded hollow, disconnected. "Or they're dead."

Norma's words hung in the air like a death sentence, sending ripples of unease through the room. Everyone froze—Lacy midstep, Zoey with her glass halfway to her lips, Gwen's finger stopping its circuit.

She buried her face in Russell's shoulder, her small frame trembling violently. "I can't do this," she whispered, her voice cracking. "I can't. I keep seeing him. I keep seeing Shea's face, his eyes..."

Russell tightened his grip on her, his jaw clenching. "Let's not go there," he said firmly, his voice carrying a warning. "They're fine. We're going to get through this. All of us. Sam and Leroy will be back soon with help."

Zoey downed the rest of her drink in one swift motion and set the glass down with a loud clink that made everyone jump. "We can't just sit here and hope they're okay," she said, her voice rising with frustration. "We have to go get them. Warn them.

What if the killer's already at the cabin? What if they're walking into a trap?"

Lacy stopped mid-pace, turning to face Zoey with an expression that was hard to read. "Or they're the ones we need to worry about," she said sharply, her words clipped and precise.

Russell shot her a cold look that could have frozen fire. "You're not helping," he snapped. "We're supposed to be working together, not throwing around baseless accusations like some kind of witch hunt."

Lacy's eyes narrowed dangerously. "Baseless?" she echoed, her voice rising. "Let's not pretend any of us are above suspicion. Someone in this room could be the killer. One of us. Maybe even you, Russell."

The room erupted in an uproar of voices as tensions boiled over, everyone talking at once, accusations flying.

"Where were you when Kelly died, Lacy?" Russell demanded, his voice cutting through the noise, standing up now. "Tell us exactly where you were."

"Where were you?" Lacy shot back, her voice trembling with barely restrained fury, her hands balling into fists. "You're so quick to point fingers. What's your alibi?"

"I was with Zoey," Russell retorted, gesturing toward her sharply. "We found Kelly's body together. We both saw her. What about you? Where the hell were you?"

Zoey nodded, her gaze steady. "He's right. We were together. Came down the stairs, he jumped out at me like an idiot, we went to the ballroom, and there she was." She looked at Russell, then at Lacy. "So, where were you?" Zoey asked, in a more friendly tone than an accusatory one.

Lacy hesitated, her gaze flicking from one face to the next, suddenly feeling like prey surrounded by predators. The pause stretched too long, became suspicious.

"I was... in the cellar," she said finally, the words coming out defensive. "I found a secret passage. There's a lever hidden behind a brick, and it opens up—"

Russell snorted, the sound dismissive and cruel. "How convenient. A secret passage." He made air quotes. "And I suppose no one can verify that?"

"It's true," Lacy said defensively, her voice getting louder. "I heard the yelling and came up. That's when I saw Leroy and we met you all in the ballroom. I can show you the passage if you don't believe me."

"Sure," Russell muttered, leaning back on the couch with a skeptical smirk. "And the passage didn't happen to lead to the ballroom? Didn't give you convenient access to Kelly?"

Lacy's composure snapped like a twig. "What's your fucking problem?!" she shouted, her voice shaking with anger. "I didn't kill anyone! Just because you found Kelly doesn't mean you're innocent! For all we know, you killed her and came back to 'discover' the body!"

The room fell into an uneasy silence, the weight of Lacy's words pressing down on them all. Everyone was breathing hard, adrenaline flooding their systems.

Russell opened his mouth to respond, his face flushed with anger, but Norma's trembling voice stopped him.

"Please," she said, barely above a whisper, but somehow it cut through everything. "Stop."

Her plea cut through the tension like scissors through paper. She looked up, her tear-streaked face filled with desperation, mascara running in dark trails down her cheeks.

"We can't do this," she said, her voice breaking. "Fighting won't help. It'll only make things worse. The killer wants this. Don't you see? They want us to turn on each other."

Zoey sighed heavily, running a hand through her hair. "She's right," she said, though the words seemed to cost her something. "Enough with the accusations. We're all scared, but we need to stick together. The second we fall apart, we're dead. All of us."

Lacy turned away, facing the window, her shoulders stiff with residual anger and something that looked like shame. Russell exhaled sharply through his nose, his frustration evident, but he said nothing more. He pulled Norma back against him, and she curled into his side like a child seeking protection.

The room descended into an uneasy silence, the air thick with mistrust that you could almost taste. The brief explosion of anger had released some pressure, but underneath it all, nothing had changed.

The fear remained. The suspicion remained.

Zoey leaned back against the bar, her eyes scanning the room, watching everyone. Watching for tells, for signs of guilt, for anything that might give someone away.

Gwen shifted uncomfortably on her stool, her fingers resuming their absent patterns on her glass.

Lacy resumed her pacing, though her movements were slower now, more deliberate. Click. Pause. Click. Pause.

Russell pulled Norma closer, his expression unreadable as he stared at the floor, his mind clearly racing. One hand rubbed her arm absently while the other clenched and unclenched against his thigh.

The group remained together in the lounge, their silence louder than words. Suspicion simmered just below the surface, unspoken but palpable—you could feel it in the way people avoided eye contact, in the way they positioned themselves with their backs to walls, in the way no one fully relaxed.

Each person's thoughts churned with unanswered questions. Who among them was capable of murder? Who had the motive? The opportunity? Who was lying? Who could be trusted?

The questions spun endlessly, creating a dizzying spiral of paranoia that fed on itself, growing stronger with each passing moment.

Even in the company of others, surrounded by people they'd laughed with just hours before, they were all utterly, hopelessly alone. Isolated by fear and suspicion. Trapped with a killer who could be anyone. Could be the person sitting right next to them.

CHAPTER FORTY-FOUR

The lounge doors slammed open with a bang that made everyone jump, Sam and Leroy stepping inside with purpose, their pistols raised and their expressions grim as death. The room collectively recoiled as if they'd been physically struck, the sight of the guns adding a visceral weight to the already oppressive tension.

Zoey's grip on her drink faltered, the glass nearly slipping from her suddenly nerveless fingers, amber liquid sloshing dangerously. "Oh my god," she whispered, her voice barely audible, the glass trembling badly enough that she had to use both hands to steady it. Her eyes were locked on the barrel of Sam's gun.

Sam and Leroy immediately lowered their weapons, recognizing the fear in the room. They tucked the guns into their waistbands, but everyone could still see them—dark shapes that promised violence. The room's fear lingered. Having guns didn't make them safer. It made them more dangerous.

Gwen, sitting stiffly at the bar with her spine ramrod straight, finally broke the silence. "Where the hell did you get those?" she demanded, her voice sharp and accusatory, tinged with something that sounded like betrayal. "Sam, what did you do?"

"Security shack," Sam replied curtly, his tone offering no room for follow-up. "Stubby had them hidden. Ex-military."

Russell leaned back on the couch, his smirk a thin veneer over his unease. "Well," he said dryly, forcing humor where none existed, "I guess that spices things up. Nothing says 'fun murder weekend' like firearms."

Lacy halted her restless pacing mid-step. She turned to face Sam, her whole body angled toward him. "Did you call for help?" she asked, her voice a blend of hope and frustration. "Tell me you got through to someone."

Norma, perched nervously beside Russell on the edge of the couch cushion like a bird ready to take flight, added, "And what about Stubby? Where is he?" Her voice was small, almost child-like. "Is he here?”

Leroy's face darkened as he glanced at Sam before answering, a wordless communication passing between them. "You don't want to know, hun. Trust me." His voice was gentle but firm. "Some things you can't unsee."

The room froze. Even the air seemed to stop moving.

"What do you mean?" Zoey pressed, her voice cracking slightly, rising in pitch. She set her glass down before she could drop it. "Leroy, what do you mean?"

Sam's sigh was heavy, his shoulders slumping. "Stubby's dead," he said flatly, the words coming out emotionless because any emotion would break him. "And the radio's gone. Communication equipment ripped out. Lines cut. We're completely isolated."

The reaction was immediate and chaotic.

Zoey slammed her already-set glass harder against the bar, the sound like a gunshot. "No radio? Are you kidding me? I want to go home. Now!" Her voice rose to a near-shriek. "I want off this fucking island right now!"

"It's not like we didn't try," Leroy shot back, his own frustration bleeding through. "Whoever's doing this made damn sure we couldn't call for help. Destroyed everything. This is all we found." He raised his gun slightly for emphasis. "At least we're not completely defenseless."

Lacy resumed her pacing with renewed agitation, her tone bitter. "So, we're just stuck here? Waiting for a boat that may or may not come? That's the plan? Hope and prayer?"

Sam nodded grimly. "Russell got through to 911 before the line dropped. They're contacting the Coast Guard. We'll have to hold out until morning. Maybe longer depending on weather and how fast they can get a boat here."

Gwen folded her arms protectively across her chest, her expression pale and wary. "Okay, but who's doing this?" she asked, her voice trembling slightly. "Who would do something like this? This is insane."

Sam shook his head, his frustration evident in every line of his face. "I don't know. I guess someone else could be on the island. Could've been hiding here for days."

Lacy stopped abruptly, her eyes narrowing as she focused on Sam with laser intensity. "You don't actually believe that," she said, her voice sharp and accusing. "Do you?"

Sam hesitated, his jaw tightening. He looked around the room, his gaze landing briefly on each person—Russell, Norma, Zoey, Gwen, Lacy, Leroy—before he finally spoke.

"It's always possible, but No," he admitted, the word heavy with meaning. "I think someone's playing their own sick game. And I think it's one of us. Someone who came to this island for this weekend." He paused, letting it sink in. "Someone here is a murderer."

The accusation landed like a grenade, the impact rippling through the group. Faces turned sharply, eyes darting around the room. The silence was heavy, charged with unspoken suspicions and barely contained panic.

Zoey broke it, her voice a mix of fear and anger. "What about the others? Chelsie, Curtis, Darren, Alice? What if one of them is behind this?" Hope colored her words. "What if it's been them all along?"

"It could be any of them." Sam's eyes met hers, and something in his expression made her hope die. "They could be victims also?" he countered quietly. "We need to find them and bring them back here. We need to know."

Russell snorted, leaning forward with a mocking grin that looked more like a grimace. "Still think it's Lacy," he said, nodding toward her dismissively. "All that talk about secret passages and cellars. Convenient, isn't it? Real convenient timing."

"And no one really knows you that well." Norma added.

Zoey glanced at Lacy, her expression conflicted, apologetic but suspicious. "He's not wrong," she said reluctantly. "You don't exactly have an alibi, Lacy. You were alone."

Lacy's eyes flashed with fury, her face flushing red. "Oh, because you and Russell are so trustworthy?" she snapped, her voice rising. "Just because you found Kelly doesn't mean you didn't kill her! You could've done it and come back to 'discover' the body. Classic killer move!"

Russell stood abruptly, his face darkening, hands balling into fists. "Where do you get off, huh? You're the one skulking around alone, finding 'secret passages.'" He made air quotes. "Why would the killer go exploring? Because they already know where everything is!"

"Enough!" Sam barked, his voice cutting through the rising chaos like a whip crack. The room fell silent instantly, all eyes turning to him.

"We're not doing this," he said firmly, his tone tolerating no argument. "We're not tearing each other apart."

Lacy's face was flushed with anger and hurt, tears of frustration gathering in her eyes that she refused to let fall. "You all want someone to blame, fine," she said bitterly, her voice thick. "But I'm done standing here and taking it. I didn't come here to be accused of murder."

Without another word, she turned and stormed out of the lounge, her heels clicking rapidly against the floor. The heavy door slammed shut behind her with enough force to rattle the bottles on the bar.

Sam immediately moved to follow her. "Wait!" he called, but Norma stood abruptly, cutting him off, placing herself between Sam and the door.

"I'll go," she said, her voice shaking but determined. "I shouldn't have said—I was awful to her. Let me talk to her."

"No," he said firmly, his voice brooking no argument. "Sit back down. Gwen?"

Sam turned to Gwen, his eyes pleading with her, begging her to understand what he couldn't say out loud. She rolled her eyes, letting out an exasperated sigh.

"Yeah yeah," she said, standing reluctantly from her bar stool. "I'll go."

Russell's voice cut through the tension, sharp and accusatory. "Why's she so important anyway?" he demanded, gesturing toward where Lacy had stormed off. "Just let her go."

Norma pushed Sam's arm down forcefully, her face flushed with anger and hurt as she pointed at Gwen. "So you trust her and not me?" she challenged, her voice rising. "Why's that?"

Sam was silent, his jaw tightening, his eyes darting away from hers. He had no answer—or at least none he wanted to give.

Zoey downed the rest of her drink in one swift motion, the glass hitting the bar with a sharp clink. She stepped forward, her voice cutting through the awkward silence like a knife.

"Because he's fucking her."

The room froze. No one moved. No one breathed. Even the air seemed to still, as if the mansion itself was holding its breath, waiting to see what would happen next. No one wanted to even blink.

Zoey's lips curved into a bitter smile as she continued, her words landing like bombs. Only the kind a sister could drop.

"And I'm pretty sure he still has the hots for little miss runaway too."

Sam stared silently at Zoey for a long moment, his expression unreadable—caught somewhere between anger, embarrassment, and resignation. His eyes swept across the room, taking in the drooped faces, the shocked expressions, the judgment written across every feature.

Finally, his gaze settled on Gwen. She stood there, unfazed by the revelation, her expression calm. She nodded softly, a silent acknowledgment that said she'd handle this, that she wasn't bothered by being exposed.

"I'll bring her back," Gwen said quietly, her tone matter-of-fact, as if nothing earth-shattering had just been revealed.

She walked toward the door, her movements unhurried despite the tension crackling in the air behind her. Leroy stepped forward, intercepting her path before she could reach the doorway.

"Wait," he said, his voice serious, concerned. "Take this."

He handed her the gun, pressing it into her hands with a look that said *be careful*. She took it, her fingers wrapping around the grip naturally, and gave him a small, grateful smile that didn't quite reach her eyes.

Then she exited, the door closing softly behind her, leaving the lounge in heavy, suffocating silence.

Russell stood, his decision clear. "We're wasting time. Let's go get the others. Standing around here arguing isn't helping anyone."

Sam turned to him, his expression hard, immovable. "No. Someone needs to stay here. We can't leave the mansion completely empty."

Leroy stepped forward, his jaw set with determination. "I'll stay," he offered without hesitation. "You go. I'll hold down the fort."

Sam hesitated, seemed about to argue, then nodded. "Fine.

But everyone else stays put until we're back. Lock the doors. Don't open them for anyone except us."

Zoey crossed her arms, her voice steady and unyielding despite the fear in her eyes. "I'm coming too."

Sam turned to her, his frustration bubbling over. "No, you're not. Zoey, don't be stupid."

Zoey squared her shoulders, her eyes blazing with determination. "Chelsie's out there. My girl, my love, my best friend is out there, Sam. I'm not staying here while she could be in danger. I'm not." Her voice broke slightly. "I can't."

Sam held her gaze for a long moment, a silent battle of wills, before exhaling sharply. "Fine. Let's go. But you do exactly what I say."

As the group prepared to leave, Norma and Leroy exchanged uneasy glances. Norma's voice was quiet but firm. "Be careful. Please."

Sam gave a small nod, his face unreadable. "You too. Lock the door behind us."

The group split, Sam, Russell, and Zoey heading for the door while Norma and Leroy remained behind. The sound of their footsteps faded as they left the lounge, growing distant, then disappearing entirely.

Inside, Leroy and Norma sat in strained silence, the weight of their isolation pressing down on them. The mansion felt bigger now, emptier, more dangerous.

Norma finally stood, breaking the silence. "I need a drink." Her hands were shaking. "A real one this time."

Leroy watched her go to the bar, his expression unreadable, his mind clearly elsewhere. "Make it a double," he muttered, his fingers drumming nervously against the armrest in a rhythm that matched his racing heartbeat.

Alone in the lounge with only each other for protection, both of them thought the same thing but didn't voice it: what if the killer was already here?

What if they'd just locked themselves in with a murderer?

Norma looked at Leroy. "I have to pee."

Leroy rolled his eyes. "You couldn't have said that two minutes ago when the guy with the gun was here?" He stands up and heads for the door.

"Sorry. But also not sorry. I don't think that I can drink enough scotch tonight." Norma said, taking another sip.

Leroy opened the door. "Fuck. Let's go. Stay close to me."

They slowly walked down the empty, quiet hall and into a nearby bedroom. Leroy scanned the room several times before heading to the bathroom door.

He opened the door and scanned the bathroom. "Alright, it's clear. I'll wait right outside."

"Thanks Leroy," Norma said before entering the bathroom and shutting the door.

Leroy crossed his arms and stood tall waiting like a security guard, an impatient, anxious security guard. Then, he noticed the hallway lights flicker.

CHAPTER FORTY-FIVE

The dimly lit theater room smelled of aged velvet and dust. Rows of plush red chairs stretched toward the massive screen, their once-vibrant crimson now muted with age, the centerpiece of a room that seemed frozen in time. Shadows loomed in the corners where the overhead lighting couldn't quite reach, making the space feel both intimate and unnervingly vast.

Lacy moved down one of the aisles, her fingers grazing the soft, worn backs of the chairs, feeling the texture of decades-old velvet. Her eyes flicked toward Gwen, who was walking a row over, gun still tucked in her waistband. Gwen's stride was casual, almost dismissive, as if she owned the room.

"So," Lacy ventured, her voice light but curious, breaking the silence that had settled between them since leaving the lounge, "you and Sam... you're, uh, together?"

Gwen turned her head slightly, her lips curling into a sly smile. "Together?" she echoed, the word dripping with amusement, as if the very concept was naive. "Not exactly. Let's just say we've kept each other company on a few lonely nights. Mutual comfort. No strings attached."

The bluntness of the reply made Lacy's cheeks burn with embarrassment—she'd expected a different answer, something more romantic or at least more ambiguous. But she kept her expression neutral, focusing instead on the texture of the chair beneath her hand.

"Oh," she murmured, her tone uncertain, trying to process this information and what it meant.

Gwen's grin widened as she caught the faint flicker of discomfort in Lacy's posture—the slight stiffening of her shoulders, the way she wouldn't quite meet her eyes. She leaned casually against a chair, crossing her arms. "Relax, darling. It's nothing serious. We're more... convenient than committed. Scratching an itch, you know?"

Lacy stiffened further, unsure how to respond. Before she could muster a response, Gwen's eyes narrowed playfully, knowingly. "And before you start fretting, let me save you the trouble. I'm not in your way."

Lacy blinked, genuinely confused now. "In my way?"

Gwen laughed softly, a sound that was both mocking and oddly kind. "Oh, come on. It's written all over your face. Every time you look at him." She gestured vaguely at Lacy's expression. "You like him. He likes you. It's cute, really. Adorable, even. And for the record, I'm all for it. You two would be good together."

Lacy's face reddened further, heat creeping up her neck. "I don't— It's not—" She stammered, her carefully constructed composure crumbling.

"Sure it is," Gwen interrupted, waving a hand dismissively. Her expression softened slightly, but her words turned sharp, cutting through the embarrassment with cold reality. "But you might want to act on it sooner rather than later. Not much point in being polite if we're all dead by morning. Life's too short, especially right now."

The cold reminder sent a chill through Lacy like ice water down her spine. She opened her mouth to respond, to say something—anything—but no words came. Gwen's bluntness had left her both flustered and unnerved.

"Let's get back," Lacy finally managed, her voice quieter now, smaller somehow.

Gwen nodded, her gaze lingering on Lacy for a moment longer before turning toward the screen. "Probably a good idea," she agreed, pushing off from the chair.

But just as she moved to follow Lacy toward the exit, something caught her eye. A glint in the darkness at the edge of the room.

On a small table against the wall, barely visible in the dim lighting, sat a dusty film canister, its faded label barely legible beneath layers of grime. Gwen's curiosity piqued as she stepped toward it, drawn by instinct. She picked it up, the metal cool and slightly rough against her palms, brushing away a thin layer of grime to reveal the words etched across the surface: MURDER MANSION.

"What the hell is this?" Gwen murmured, turning the canister over in her hands.

Lacy, already near the door with her hand on the frame, paused and glanced back. "What'd you find?" she asked, her tone wary. After everything that had happened, nothing good came from finding mysterious objects.

Before Gwen could answer, a faint click echoed through the room—mechanical, deliberate.

Both women froze, their eyes snapping to the wall beside the table. To their astonishment, a panel slid open with a grinding sound, revealing a dark, narrow passageway that seemed to swallow light.

"Well, that's not creepy at all," Gwen said, her tone tinged with excitement rather than fear. She stepped closer, peering into the shadowy void with fascination. A faint draft wafted out, carrying the musty scent of old stone and damp air.

"Hey," she called to Lacy, her grin widening. "Secret passage. I didn't know about this. Wanna see where it goes?"

Lacy's face twisted in disbelief, her eyes widening. "Another one?" she exclaimed, her voice rising. "Are there any normal walls in this place? What is this, Scooby-Doo?"

Ignoring Lacy's protests completely, Gwen stepped into the passage without hesitation, clutching the canister tightly under one arm. The darkness swallowed her almost immediately, her form becoming a silhouette and then disappearing entirely.

"Gwen, wait!" Lacy shouted, moving toward her, panic rising. "Don't be stupid! We should get Sam first!"

Before Lacy could reach the passage, before her outstretched hand could grab Gwen's shoulder, the wall slid shut with an ominous thud that echoed through the theater.

She froze, her outstretched hand brushing against the smooth, seamless surface that showed no indication it had ever been anything but solid wall.

"Gwen?" Lacy called, her voice rising in panic, her palm pressed flat against the wall. "Gwen! Can you hear me?"

Nothing. Just silence from the other side.

Lacy pressed both hands against the wall, her fingers searching desperately for a way to reopen it, feeling along the edges, pushing, prodding. There was no visible mechanism, no lever or button or seam—just an unbroken expanse of wood and plaster.

"Gwen!" she shouted again, louder this time, her voice echoing in the empty theater. "Gwen! Answer me! This isn't funny!"

Her eyes fell on the table where the canister had been. The faint outline of its dusty imprint remained on the surface like a ghost. She let out a frustrated groan, running a hand through her hair, pulling at the strands hard enough to hurt.

"Great," she muttered under her breath, her voice shaking. "Am I in some twisted escape room? Is this what we're doing now?"

She looked around the theater as if cameras might be watching, as if this was all still part of the game. But the bodies were real. Kelly was real. This wasn't a game anymore.

She took a step back, her mind racing through possibilities. If she couldn't open the passage from this side, she needed to find help. Sam would know what to do. But the idea of leaving Gwen alone—wherever she was, in whatever darkness lay beyond that wall—made her stomach churn.

Leaning in close to the wall, Lacy raised her voice, practically shouting. "Gwen, if you can hear me, stay put! Don't go wandering around in there! I'm going to get Sam or someone. Just stay where you are! Wait for me!"

The silence on the other side was deafening, absolute. Not even the sound of footsteps or breathing. Just nothing.

Lacy straightened, her jaw tightening with determination that barely masked her terror. She turned on her heel and strode toward the door, her pace quickening as her fear threatened to overtake her.

As she left the theater room, nearly running now, Lacy cast one last glance over her shoulder at the seamless wall. It looked like it had never moved, like Gwen had never been there at all.

Her fists clenched at her sides, her heart pounding so hard she could hear it in her ears.

"Hang on, Gwen," she whispered to herself, the words more prayer than promise. "I'll be back. Just hang on."

CHAPTER FORTY-SIX

The air inside the passage was oppressive, thick with the scent of damp earth and decay that clung to Gwen's senses like a wet blanket, coating the back of her throat with each breath. Her breath came in shallow bursts, visible in faint clouds in the cold, stagnant air that hadn't been disturbed in what felt like years. The theater room's dim light had disappeared entirely the moment the wall sealed behind her, swallowed by the suffocating darkness that surrounded her on all sides.

She turned back toward the wall she had entered through, her palms brushing frantically against the cold, unyielding surface, searching for any mechanism, any give, any hope.

Nothing. Just smooth stone.

"Of course," she muttered bitterly, her voice sounding small and swallowed. "Of course it doesn't open from this side. That would be too convenient."

Gwen let out a frustrated sigh that fogged in the cold air, her eyes adjusting slowly to the darkness, pupils dilating to catch whatever ambient light they could find—which was essentially none. In one hand, she clutched the vintage film canister, its metal surface now slick with her nervous sweat. In the other was the handgun Leroy had given her—a weighty reminder of how quickly the weekend had descended into chaos.

The absurdity of her predicament tugged at the corner of her mouth, almost coaxing a laugh. *Film canister and a gun. Walking into a secret passage alone while a killer's on the loose. This is how people die in horror movies, Gwen. You know better than this.*

Almost. Instead, she exhaled sharply, gripping the gun tighter until her knuckles ached.

"Well, Gwen," she whispered to herself, the sound of her own voice oddly reassuring in the oppressive silence, "looks like you're on your own. Again. Story of your life."

The narrow passage stretched endlessly ahead, or at least it felt endless—there was no way to tell how far it went when you couldn't see more than a few feet. Its rough stone walls were damp and uneven, slick with moisture. Gwen kept one hand pressed against the wall, her fingers trailing along the cold surface, guiding herself forward in the impenetrable gloom. The stone was rough, catching on her skin occasionally, leaving her fingertips raw.

Each cautious step sent faint echoes bouncing off the confined space, reverberating weirdly, making it feel as though she wasn't entirely alone. Like someone else's footsteps were matching hers, just out of sync. Just behind her.

Her boots scraped against the uneven floor, occasionally shifting loose stones that clattered and rolled into the darkness. The sudden noise each time made her flinch violently, her breath hitching, her finger tightening on the trigger.

She stopped often, holding her breath until her lungs burned, straining her ears for any sign of movement beyond her own— breathing, footsteps, the rustle of fabric, anything.

Nothing. Only silence. But it was the kind of silence that felt alive, crawling over her skin like insects.

Her thoughts spiraled as she walked, each step taking her further from safety. Was this passage meant to connect different parts of the mansion? Or was it a trap designed to disorient and isolate? To funnel victims into a killing ground?

Her pulse quickened with each step, her nerves fraying as the darkness played tricks on her. The shadows seemed to move, shifting and flickering in her periphery like living things, though no light existed to create them. Her mind supplied shapes—figures standing in the darkness, watching. Waiting.

"Get a grip," Gwen muttered, her voice trembling slightly despite her attempt at bravado. "You're losing it. There's nothing there."

She adjusted her grip on the gun, the cold steel reassuring in its solidity. "Just a passage. Just walls and darkness. You've dealt with worse."

Had she? Right now, she couldn't remember worse.

After what felt like an eternity of aimless wandering—though it could have been five minutes or fifty—a faint glimmer pierced the darkness ahead. Gwen froze mid-step, her heart lurching painfully in her chest as she stared at the speck of light in the distance. It was weak, barely more than a pinprick, but it was enough to reignite a flicker of hope.

Light means an exit. Light means people. Light means safety.

Her pace quickened despite the treacherous footing, boots crunching against the loose debris with less caution now, urgency overriding fear. The light grew brighter as she approached, revealing more of the passage's rough-hewn walls, showing her just how narrow the space really was—barely wide enough for her shoulders in some places.

Finally, she reached the source of the light: a narrow crack in the stone wall, maybe an inch wide and a foot tall, positioned at roughly eye level. Gwen pressed her face against the cold surface, the stone biting into her cheek as she squinted to make out what lay beyond.

Through the crack, she saw a larger room dimly illuminated by the flicker of candlelight—real candles, burning in holders, their flames dancing and casting moving shadows. The space was lined with shelves cluttered with jars, books, and objects that looked both ancient and out of place, like someone had raided a museum and a morgue and combined the collections. In the center stood a heavy wooden table, its surface scattered with papers and strange artifacts she couldn't quite make out.

Gwen's breath caught as she strained to make out more details, pressing her eye socket against the crack hard enough to hurt. Some of the jars appeared to contain dark, viscous liquids—oils, maybe, or something worse. Others held unidentifiable objects suspended in amber fluid. The books were thick and dusty, their spines adorned with strange symbols and faded titles she couldn't read from this angle. And the papers on the table—she could make out what looked like diagrams, charts, maybe blueprints.

"What the hell is this?" she whispered, her voice barely audible over the pounding of her heart. "What is this room?"

It looked like an alchemist's laboratory. Or a killer's trophy room. Neither option was comforting.

Stepping back from the crack, Gwen's mind raced. There was no door visible from her vantage point, no obvious way to access the room—just the crack in the wall and the continuation of the passage ahead. Her fingers instinctively brushed over the gun in her hand, checking its presence like a talisman.

The thought of turning back flitted briefly through her mind. She could retrace her steps, pound on the sealed wall until Lacy—or anyone—came to help. She could wait this out, be smart, be safe.

But something about the room drew her in, a magnetic pull she couldn't ignore. Whatever answers lay ahead felt too important to leave undiscovered. This could be it—the key to everything.

Taking a steadying breath that did nothing to slow her racing heart, Gwen turned her attention back to the passage ahead. The glimmer of light had given her a direction, a goal, but the rest was up to her.

She pressed forward, moving past the crack in the wall, her fingers tracing the cold stone with methodical precision as she searched for an opening or trigger that might lead her into the hidden room—a loose stone, a lever, anything.

The passage curved slightly, and the candlelight grew brighter, spilling from somewhere ahead. She was getting closer.

The faint flicker of candlelight was now her only beacon, its distorted glow her sole companion as she ventured deeper into the darkness. The oppressive silence followed her like a shadow, making the small sounds of her movement seem impossibly loud.

"I'm not going out like this," Gwen whispered fiercely to herself, her grip tightening on the gun until her hand cramped. "Not in the dark. Not without a fight. Not without answers."

She rounded the curve, and ahead, she could finally see it: a doorway, partially concealed but visible now that she was closer, the candlelight spilling from it like an invitation.

Or a trap.

Gwen raised the gun, finger on the trigger guard, safety off now. She approached the doorway slowly, every muscle tensed, ready to fire, ready to run, ready for anything.

CHAPTER FORTY-SEVEN

Norma stood frozen, her back pressed against the doorframe of the bathroom, the dampness of her hands suddenly icy against her jeans as she wiped them repeatedly, trying to dry palms that wouldn't stop sweating. The room was wrong—eerily, unnaturally still in a way that made her skin crawl. Not the peaceful stillness of an empty space, but the held-breath quiet of something waiting.

Leroy, who'd been right outside moments ago—she'd heard him muttering to himself, his presence a comfort through the door—had vanished.

"Leroy?" she called, her voice trembling just enough to betray the facade of calm she was desperately clinging to. She took a cautious step forward into the bedroom, her eyes darting to the corners of the room, to the closet with its slightly ajar door, to the space beneath the bed where shadows pooled thick and dark.

The silence was deafening. It wasn't the comforting quiet of an empty mansion but a predatory stillness, as though the air itself was holding its breath. Her pulse quickened, thudding in her ears like a drumbeat, drowning out all other sound.

"Seriously, Leroy," she said, her voice louder now, more defiant than she felt, trying to fill the terrible silence. "If this is your idea of a joke, I'm going to kill you myself." She forced a laugh that came out strangled and wrong. "I mean it. This isn't funny."

The words hung in the air, hollow and humorless, dying quickly without even an echo.

There was no answer. Only the faint creak of the old house settling, each sound amplified by her heightened senses until every pop and groan sounded like footsteps, like breathing, like something coming closer.

Norma's hands shook as she moved further into the room, her legs feeling disconnected from her body. Her gaze landed on the dresser, and the small decorative statue sitting atop it caught her eye—a heavy bronze piece shaped like a rearing horse, all sharp edges and solid weight.

She crossed the room in a rush, her footsteps barely audible on the plush carpet. Grabbing the statue, she held it tightly, the cool metal grounding her. It wasn't much, but it was something. Something she could use to fight back if she had to.

Her knuckles whitened as she adjusted her grip, her fingers finding the best position to swing from.

"Alright, Norma," she whispered to herself, her voice barely audible over her shallow breaths. "You've got this. Just find Leroy and get the hell out of here. He probably just went to check something. He's fine. Everything's fine."

But she didn't believe her own words.

She turned to the door, her stomach twisting with dread. Her free hand reached for the doorknob, trembling so badly she almost couldn't grasp it, but she hesitated, her fingers hovering just above the metal.

What if something is waiting for me out there? What if the killer is standing right outside, waiting for me to open the door?

Her heart pounded so hard it hurt, but she couldn't ignore the gnawing uncertainty of Leroy's absence. She had to act. Staying in the room wasn't safer—if anything, it was a trap.

Norma twisted the knob and pushed the door open slowly,

the hinges mercifully silent. Her eyes darted into the dimly lit hallway beyond, scanning left then right, searching for any sign of movement. Shadows spilled across the walls like ink stains, stretching and shifting with the flickering light of a swaying chandelier that moved in an unfelt breeze.

"Leroy?" she called again, her voice small against the oppressive quiet.

The mansion seemed alive with silence, the kind that made her feel like she was being watched from every corner. The hallway was empty, stretching endlessly in both directions—too long, impossibly long.

She took a tentative step out, the statue raised slightly in her hand, positioned like a club. Her every footfall seemed deafening against the creak of the old wooden floorboards.

"Come on, Leroy," she muttered, her voice barely more than a whisper now, afraid to speak too loudly. "Where are you? This isn't funny anymore."

A flicker of movement at the far end of the hallway caught her eye, and she froze, her breath hitching painfully. She strained her eyes, squinting into the gloom, but the shadows played tricks on her, shifting and morphing into nothing. Or into something. She couldn't tell anymore.

Her grip on the statue tightened until her hand ached. She edged forward, her back brushing the wall for reassurance.

"If you're hiding," she hissed, trying to sound threatening, "you're going to regret it. I swear to God, Leroy."

As she reached a bend in the hallway, where the corridor turned sharply to the right, a faint noise echoed in the distance. It was subtle—just a soft, muffled thud, like something heavy being dropped, or a body hitting the floor.

She froze, her eyes wide as she stared into the darkness ahead, barely breathing.

"Leroy?" she called out again, her voice faltering, cracking on his name.

The sound didn't come again. The silence that followed was worse, oppressive and suffocating.

She forced herself to take another step, then another, her breath coming in shallow gasps.

Norm stopped as she tried to steady her breathing, tried to slow her racing heart. She took a single step forward, the statue raised high above her head now, ready to swing with everything she had.

Whatever was out there, she wasn't going down without a fight. She'd survived Shea's death. She'd survived finding his body. She could survive this.

She had to.

The hallway stretched on before her, dark and menacing, the chandelier's light seeming to dim with each step she took, as if the darkness itself was challenging her.

And so she did, her feet carrying her forward even as her mind screamed at her to stop, to run, to hide.

She turned the corner, the statue held high, her breath held, her entire body tensed for whatever horror waited around that bend.

The hallway beyond was even darker, stretching into shadows so thick they looked solid.

She reluctantly continued on.

CHAPTER FORTY-EIGHT

The sun descended on the horizon, creating a pinkish glow in the sky that painted the clouds in shades of rose and amber. The full moon lingered overhead, waiting for its turn to shine, a pale ghost against the fading daylight.

Sam pushed through overgrown brush on the path to the cabin, his gun gripped tightly in his hand, knuckles white with tension. One bush retracted back sharply, smacking Russell in the face with enough force to make him stumble. He sputtered, irritation flashing across his features as he swatted at the offending branches.

Zoey kept pace beside Sam, matching his stride. They weren't strolling, but they weren't rushing either—moving with the deliberate caution of people who knew drawing attention could be fatal.

"Hey," Zoey said, breaking the tense silence that had settled over them. "Sorry about all that back there. I shouldn't have said anything. I'm just, I don't know."

Sam looked at her, his expression softening despite the fear etched into his features. "Don't be sorry," he said quietly. "You were spot on. Me and Gwen, it's complicated, but we're nothing more than what we are. As far as Lacy..." He paused, his jaw tightening. "I think you know that's why I invited her here. I'm the one who should be sorry. Getting all of you into this mess."

Zoey shook her head, her voice thick with emotion. "It's not your fault that someone is a maniac. It is scary though. Shea and the maid are dead. God, I hope Chelsie is okay."

Sam touched her shoulder, the gesture comforting but weighted with guilt. "We're all scared, but we'll get through this..." His voice dropped to barely above a whisper. "God, I wish I never invited you."

"What?" Zoey's head snapped toward him, confusion and hurt flickering across her face.

"I mean, I care about you," Sam said quickly, his voice cracking slightly. "You're my sister. I don't like that so many people I care for are..."

He didn't finish. He didn't want to. Instead, he stopped walking and looked up at the cabin, now looming in front of them through the trees, its windows glowing softly in the gathering dusk.

"And to think," he continued, his voice hollow with disbelief, "it's probably one of us. One of those people I care about."

He shook his head, the weight of that realization crushing. He sighed, pushing away the emotions and forcing himself to fill the space with courage he didn't quite feel.

"You ready?" He looked to Zoey, his eyes searching hers.

She took his hand in hers, squeezing it the way they used to as children when they were inseparable, when the world was simpler and monsters weren't real. "I may be your baby sister," she said, her voice steady despite the fear, "but I can still kick some ass."

He smiled, his courage building even higher. He glanced back at Russell, who was barely catching up, breathing hard from the pace.

"Let's go dial up," Sam said, his grip tightening on the gun. "We got some lives to save."

Russell let out a big sigh, his face pale in the fading light.

"After you, Rambo," he muttered, wishing this was over already, wishing he was back on a boat headed home.

Sam carefully climbed the short steps to the cabin's entrance and tentatively knocked on the door, the sound echoing in the stillness. No answer. He tried again, knuckles rapping harder against the wood. Still nothing.

He slowly turned the knob and pushed the door open, the hinges creaking softly.

He peered carefully inside, scanning the room with practiced efficiency, the gun raised and ready. It appeared empty. He cautiously entered, his boots making soft sounds against the hardwood.

The room was bright, all lights blazing as if someone had just been there. A couple of empty glasses sat on the coffee table. Soft music played from somewhere upstairs, the melody faint but distinctly cheerful—wrong for the atmosphere.

The front door thudded shut behind them with a sound that seemed impossibly loud. Sam whipped around, gun raised, finger on the trigger, heart hammering.

Russell stood there, his hand still on the doorknob, eyes wide. "Sorry," he said quickly, holding up his hands.

Sam rolled his eyes, exhaling sharply, and turned back to scan the room. His gaze drifted to the staircase, then up toward where the music was coming from.

"Hello!" he called out, his voice echoing through the empty space. "Darren? Alice?"

"Chelsie? Curtis?" Zoey added, her voice smaller, more hopeful.

Sam checked the kitchen quickly, his movements efficient. Empty. No signs of struggle, no blood, no bodies. Just pristine counters and an eerie sense of abandonment.

He started up the stairs, each step careful and deliberate. Zoey and Russell followed close behind, their footsteps echoing his.

The hall was much dimmer than the living room below,

shadows pooling in the corners. But still easily visible was a long line of candy hearts—pastel pink, yellow, and purple—scattered across the floor like a trail of breadcrumbs.

Sam followed them with his eyes, his stomach dropping. They led to the far bedroom at the end of the hall. It was the same room the music was coming from, the cheerful melody spilling out from the crack beneath the door.

"You two should stay here," Sam said, his voice low and commanding.

Russell looked at him like he'd lost his mind, his face flushing with a mixture of fear and indignation. "Fuck that. Give me the gun and I'll stay here."

Sam looked at the gun in his hand, then back to Russell, weighing the options. Then he continued forward without a word, his decision made.

Zoey and Russell followed, neither willing to be left alone in the dimness.

Sam approached the door, which was slightly ajar, warm light spilling from the crack. He pushed it open slowly with his foot and inched inside.

It was pitch black, the darkness so complete it felt like stepping into a void. Sam whispered back to Russell and Zoey, who stood frozen in the doorway, silhouettes against the dim hallway light.

"Light switch," he said, his voice barely audible.

Zoey slid her hand up the wall, fingers fumbling across the surface until she found it. She flipped the switch.

Light flooded the room.

All three of them froze in horror at what they saw, their bodies locked in place as their minds struggled to process the nightmare before them. Zoey couldn't bear it and had to look away, her head dropping into her hands as a sob tore from her throat.

"Oh my god!" she cried, her voice breaking.

"Wow," Russell breathed, the word coming out strangled, barely more than an exhale.

In front of them, Darren and Alice dangled from the long bedposts, hanged, their faces dead white, skin waxy and lifeless. Their lips were sewn together with crude black thread, as if kissing, creating a grotesque parody of intimacy. Their arms were wrapped around each other in an awkward embrace that looked painful even in death, bound together with wire that cut into their flesh.

Darren wore black boxer briefs with red hearts on them. Alice, pink lace underwear. Rose petals covered the white satin bedsheets below them, scattered like confetti at a celebration of death. It was a truly eerie scene, meticulously arranged with horrifying attention to detail.

But worse—impossibly worse—was what lay closer to the door.

In front of the hanging couple, even closer to where they stood, was a table for two, complete with champagne in an ice bucket, flickering candles that cast dancing shadows, and a box of chocolates with a red ribbon.

In one chair sat Curtis, very dead, dressed only in boxers and covered in blood that had soaked into the fabric and pooled beneath him. His arm was stretched across the table, a bouquet of roses clutched in his stiff hand, reaching toward Chelsie as if offering them to her one final time.

Chelsie sat across from him, topless, her chest ripped open, revealing her heart—which had been cut cleanly in two, the halves separated slightly. One of her arms was propped up to her face, holding a small compact mirror, her middle finger pointed defiantly toward Curtis in a gesture of eternal rejection. Her second hand held a mascara brush to her eye, frozen mid-application. The arm was held up by a metal cord attached from her skull to her elbow, a grotesque puppet string keeping her posed.

The warped music from the record player continued its

diseased melody, skipping over the same phrase: *"...love you forever... love you forever..."*

"Someone is seriously sick," Sam muttered, his voice hollow, drained of emotion because feeling anything would break him completely.

He moved to the record player and turned off the music with shaking hands. The silence that followed was somehow worse, more oppressive. He looked back at his dead friends, his eyes welling with tears that he could no longer hold back.

"I'm sorry, guys," he whispered, his voice cracking. "I'm so sorry."

He looked up at Russell and Zoey, who were beyond words. Zoey was in tears, her whole body shaking. Russell's face had gone gray, his usual confidence shattered completely.

"Let's get back," Sam said, his voice firmer now, forcing himself to take control. "Quick."

They exited, nearly stumbling over each other in their haste to leave the room, to escape the horror.

Russell and Zoey rushed down the stairs followed by Sam, their feet pounding against the wood. Zoey, super freaked out, still in tears, stopped suddenly in the middle of the room, her hand flying up.

"Wait!" she cried.

Sam and Russell stopped and turned to her, both breathing hard.

"What if it's one of them?!" Zoey's voice rose to near hysteria. "Who's doing this? Is there anyone else on this island? Chelsie's dead! My best friend is dead!"

Sam tried to console her, stepping toward her, but he wasn't much better—his own hands were shaking, his face pale. "Calm down," he said, though his voice trembled. "We'll be okay."

"Is there anyone else on the island, Sam?" Zoey demanded, her eyes wild, searching his face for answers.

"No. I mean, I don't think so. I don't know," Sam admitted,

his voice cracking. "But it doesn't matter, even if there is. One of us is doing this."

Russell shook his head violently. "You don't know that."

Sam's pain and anger exploded in his words, no longer able to contain it. "Darren and Alice were hanged and Curtis was stabbed! The same way I killed them! I mean, fake killed them!" He was shouting now, his composure completely gone. "Don't you see? Someone's copying my game. Someone's using my own plans against us!"

They fell silent, the weight of his words settling over them.

Russell's voice was quieter when he spoke. "What about Chelsie?"

"Poisoned. I presume," Sam said, lowering his head, blaming himself for every death, for inviting them here, for creating this nightmare.

Zoey's voice was small, uncertain, bordering tears. "It looked like her neck was broken."

"Maybe," Sam said, his shoulders slumping. "It's all too similar though. No one else should be on this island. It's got to be one of us."

Zoey started to regain herself, wiping at her tears with the back of her hand, forcing herself to think clearly despite the horror. "Okay. Well. There's what—" She counted in her head, her lips moving silently. "Seven of us left?"

"Let's get back, then point fingers," Russell said, his voice urgent, bordering on panic. "If anyone is left."

Sam and Zoey realized the good point and started to move toward the door, their survival instincts finally overriding their shock.

CHAPTER FORTY-NINE

Russell burst through the cabin door first, his feet pounding down the wooden steps in a frantic rhythm, not bothering to check if the others were following. His only thought was escape—getting away from the horror behind them, from the bodies arranged like dolls in some sick Valentine's display, from the realization that they were being hunted.

The path ahead disappeared into deepening shadows as dusk surrendered completely to night. The full moon had finally claimed the sky, bathing everything in cold, silver light that made the trees look like skeletal fingers reaching toward the stars.

Sam and Zoey followed a few steps behind, their footsteps nearly as frantic. Sam's grip on the gun was so tight his hand ached, but he didn't dare loosen it. Zoey's breath came in ragged gasps that sounded too loud in the stillness, each exhale a cloud of mist in the cooling air.

Russell rounded a bend in the path where the trees grew thick and the moonlight struggled to penetrate the canopy. Sam and Zoey rushed to catch up, their eyes straining to keep him in sight in the gloom.

Then—

SWOOSH! THWICK!

The sound was unmistakable—something cutting through air, then the wet, terrible sound of impact.

Sam and Zoey turned the bend and froze.

Russell stood in the middle of the path, wobbling like a drunk, his eyes wide with shock and confusion. An arrow protruded from his chest, the shaft jutting obscenely from between his ribs, the fletching still quivering slightly from the impact. Blood bloomed across his shirt in an expanding circle, dark and glistening in the moonlight.

"Russell!" Sam shouted, rushing forward, his gun raised, scanning the trees for the shooter.

But Russell's legs gave out before Sam could reach him. He fell to his knees first, his hands reaching up to touch the arrow shaft as if he couldn't quite believe it was real. His mouth opened and closed, trying to form words that wouldn't come.

His eyes locked onto Sam and Zoey, wide and terrified and fading fast. With the last of his strength, he managed to force out a single word, his voice barely more than a whisper.

"Run!"

Then he collapsed forward, hitting the ground with a dull thud that seemed impossibly loud. His body went limp, lifeless, one hand still reaching toward them.

Zoey screamed—a raw, primal sound that tore from her throat and echoed through the trees. The sound seemed to break the spell that had frozen them in place.

She darted off into the woods to the left, crashing through underbrush without any sense of direction, driven only by the need to move, to survive.

Sam, unknowingly, dashed off in the opposite direction, into the trees to the right, his boots pounding against the forest floor.

He sprinted through the overgrown brush, his heart hammering so hard it hurt. Branches whipped at his face and arms, leaving stinging scratches he didn't feel. He jumped over fallen logs, dodged between trees, his breath burning in his lungs.

After what felt like hours but was probably only a minute or two, he started to slow down, his body demanding oxygen, his mind finally catching up to his panic. He pressed himself against a thick tree trunk, gun raised, and looked over his shoulder the way he'd come.

Nothing. Just shadows and moonlight and the faint rustle of leaves.

"Zoey?" he called out, his voice harsh and breathless. "Zoey?"

No answer. Just the oppressive silence of the woods pressing in around him.

"Shit," he muttered, his chest heaving as he tried to catch his breath.

He looked around frantically, scanning the woods for any sign of movement, any indication of where she'd gone. The trees all looked the same in the darkness—tall, looming, indistinguishable from each other. He had no idea which direction led back to the mansion, which led deeper into the island, which led to nowhere.

———

ZOEY CRASHED THROUGH THE DARKNESS, her arms up to protect her face from branches that seemed to reach for her like claws. Her foot caught on a root and she went down hard, hitting the ground with enough force to knock the wind from her lungs.

"Sam, I'm scared," she gasped, pushing herself up onto her hands and knees, dirt and leaves clinging to her clothes. "I'm really..."

She looked around, her eyes adjusting to the gloom, and the reality hit her like a physical blow.

She was alone.

"Sam?" she called, her voice small and trembling. "Sam? SAM!"

The woods offered no answer. No sound of footsteps crashing through underbrush. No voice calling back to her. Nothing.

She started breathing faster, heavier, on the verge of hyperventilating, on the verge of another scream that would only give away her position. Tears threatened to spill over but she blinked them back furiously. She had to think. Had to move. Had to do something other than sit here waiting to die.

Her eyes landed on a nearby hill rising above the tree line, maybe thirty feet high. From up there, she could see more. Could maybe spot Sam, or the mansion, or find some way to orient herself.

She scrambled toward it on hands and feet, then found her footing and started climbing.

Atop the hill, Zoey looked down at the woods spread out before her like a dark sea. Much more could be seen from up here—the tops of trees, clearings in the distance, and yes, she could make out the mansion's roof maybe half a mile away, its chimneys stark against the moonlit sky.

Which also meant she was more visible. Exposed. A target.

She didn't care.

She looked frantically for movement, straining her eyes in the darkness, wanting to scream out but knowing what was best. She kept looking, scanning left to right, desperate.

Then she spotted it—a small figure moving through the trees below, maybe two hundred yards away. The moonlight caught them for just a moment before they disappeared back into shadow.

Fuck it!

"Sam!" she screamed, waving her arms high above her head. "SAM!! SAM!"

The small figure stopped moving. Stopped and looked around, searching for the source of the sound.

She waved her arms higher, more frantically, her whole body visible against the sky.

The figure's arms waved back.

Relief flooded through Zoey's terror like warm water, not washing it away but making it bearable. "Thank god," she whispered, tears finally spilling down her cheeks. "Thank god."

———

SAM LOOKED up at the sound of his name being screamed and spotted Zoey atop a distant hill, waving her arms, silhouetted against the moon like a beacon. She was too far away for him to hear her clearly, but he could see her.

He waved back, relief and terror mixing in his chest.

"Jesus, get down, Zoey," he muttered to himself, already looking for a way to reach her.

But deep woods were in the way—thick underbrush and dense trees that would take too long to navigate, that would leave him vulnerable. He turned back around, looking for another route, a clearer path.

"I'm coming," he said to himself, his jaw set with determination. "Hang in there."

He started moving, forcing himself to go slower, to be more careful, to think instead of just react.

———

ZOEY WATCHED as the figure turned and headed in a different direction, away from her, moving steadily through the trees.

"No!!" she screamed, her voice breaking. "Sam!"

She looked in the direction the figure was headed and spotted the mansion more clearly now, its windows dark, its shape hulking against the sky.

He's going back to the mansion, she thought. *He's trying to get to safety. I need to follow him. I need to—*

She took a step forward, starting down the hill.

CRUNCH!

The sound was wet and terrible, accompanied by a searing pain that shot through her jaw and exploded in her skull before she could even process what had happened.

A spear had ripped up through her chin, the sharpened point exiting from the top of her skull with enough force to lift her slightly off her feet. Blood oozed down her face, hot and thick, filling her mouth with copper.

She was dead before her brain could register the pain, her body going instantly limp, her eyes still open but seeing nothing.

The spear held her upright for a moment, swaying slightly, before a pink-gloved hand appeared from behind her and staked the bottom of the spear into the soft ground, planting it like a flagpole.

The hand moved with deliberate care, almost tenderly, and slipped a single red rose into Zoey's mouth lengthwise, inserting it between her lips where the spear held her jaw open. It was easily held in place, the stem resting against the metal shaft. Blood trickled down her face and dripped off the rose petals, darkening them from red to nearly black.

The big moon shone bright behind her, casting her shadow long and distorted across the hilltop. A lifeless, impaled figure silhouetted against the sky—a monument to the killer's work, a message for anyone who might see.

The pink-gloved hands withdrew into the darkness, disappearing as silently as they'd appeared.

And Zoey remained, frozen in death, the rose in her mouth a final, grotesque valentine.

CHAPTER FIFTY

Norma approached the security shack with cautious steps, her bronze statue still clutched tightly in one hand like a lifeline. The small building loomed before her in the darkness, its weathered walls looking more sinister than they had any right to in the pale moonlight that filtered through the trees. The windows were dark, showing nothing of what lay inside, which somehow made it worse—the not knowing, the anticipation of horror.

She stopped a few feet from the door, her heart pounding so hard she could hear it in her ears, feel it in her throat. Her breath came in short, shallow gasps that created small clouds of mist in the cooling night air. Every instinct screamed at her to turn around, to go back, to find somewhere safe to hide.

But where was safe? The mansion? The woods? Nowhere felt safe anymore. Nowhere on this cursed island.

And she needed answers. Needed to understand what was happening. Needed to find something—anything—that could help her survive.

She checked behind her, scanning the tree line with wide eyes, looking for any sign of movement, any hint that she'd been followed. The woods were still, silent except for the distant sound of waves crashing against the cliffs and the occasional rustle of leaves in the breeze. Nothing moved in the shadows. Nothing she could see, anyway.

Taking a deep breath that did nothing to steady her nerves, Norma reached for the door handle. Her hand shook as she turned it, the metal cold against her palm. The door creaked open on protesting hinges, the sound seeming impossibly loud in the quiet.

The smell hit her first—metallic and wrong, the unmistakable scent of death that she'd become far too familiar with over the past hours. Her stomach lurched, bile rising in her throat, but she forced it down and stepped inside.

Her eyes immediately landed on Stubby's remains, and she cringed, turning her face away instinctively. The torso was still propped grotesquely against the desk where Sam and Leroy had left it, candy Valentine hearts spilling from the hollowed eye sockets and gaping mouth in a nightmarish display. The arm was still positioned with the gun.

"God," she whispered, her voice barely audible, trembling. "I'm sorry. I'm so sorry."

But she pushed herself onward, forcing her feet to move despite the horror, despite every fiber of her being wanting to flee. She needed to search the shack. Sam and Leroy had said the equipment was destroyed, the radio gone, but maybe they'd missed something. Maybe there was another way to call for help, some backup system, some emergency beacon.

She started opening drawers with shaking hands, her movements frantic and uncoordinated. The first drawer held only papers—requisition forms, maintenance logs, nothing useful. The second contained a first aid kit that looked like it hadn't been opened in years, the packaging dusty and faded.

She moved to the cabinets mounted on the wall, standing on her toes to see inside. More papers, a few tools, a package of batteries. Nothing that could save them. Nothing that mattered.

Desperate now, her movements growing more frantic, Norma

crouched down to check under the counter, running her hands along the underside, feeling for anything that might be hidden there—a phone, a radio, anything.

Nothing. Just smooth wood and dust.

"Come on," she muttered, frustration and fear mixing in her voice, making it crack. "Come on, there has to be something. There has to be."

As she stood back up, her legs cramping from the awkward position, her hip bumped against the edge of the counter with more force than she'd intended. The impact sent a vibration through the desk.

For a moment, nothing happened.

Then Stubby's torso, already precariously balanced, tipped forward.

It crashed to the ground with a wet, heavy thud that made Norma's stomach turn violently. The impact split the hollowed chest cavity further, and bloody candy hearts spilled out every-where—dozens of them, scattering across the floor in a grotesque cascade of pink, yellow, and purple, their cheerful messages now streaked with dried blood.

"BE MINE" rolled past her foot.

"LOVE YOU" came to rest against the wall.

"KISS ME" landed in a puddle of congealed blood.

Norma jumped back with a strangled cry, one hand flying to her mouth to hold back the scream, the other still clutching the statue so tightly her knuckles had gone white. She gagged, turning away, her whole body shaking with revulsion.

She stumbled backward, trying to put distance between herself and the horror on the floor, and her elbow struck some-thing on the control panel behind her.

A button depressed with a soft *click*.

A mechanical sound filled the shack—gears grinding, some-thing heavy moving. Norma spun around, her eyes wide, expecting another trap, another horror.

The long security desk was moving. Breaking apart at the

middle, the two halves sliding away from each other with a grinding sound, revealing a dark opening beneath. A passageway, leading down into darkness so complete it seemed to swallow light.

Norma stared at it, her breath coming in rapid gasps. A secret passage. Another one. This whole island was riddled with them, like a maze designed to trap and confuse.

Her mind raced, weighing options. She could leave, go back to the mansion, try to find someone—anyone—who was still alive. But the woods were dangerous. The killer could be out there, watching, waiting. And the mansion might already be compromised.

Or she could go down into the passage. See where it led. Maybe it connected to the mansion, gave her a safe route back. Maybe it held answers about what was happening, about who was behind this nightmare.

Or maybe it was a trap. Maybe the killer wanted her to find this, wanted her to descend into the darkness where she'd be completely vulnerable.

She studied the opening, her jaw set with grim determination. Her mind was made up before she even consciously decided. She'd come this far. She'd survived this long. She wasn't going to stop now.

But she needed light.

Her eyes swept the shack and landed on Stubby's lower half, still propped in the corner where it had been positioned. A flashlight was clipped to the belt, its handle visible, the metal gleaming faintly.

"I'm sorry," she whispered again, approaching the remains with reluctant steps. "I'm so sorry."

She reached out with a trembling hand, trying not to look too closely at what she was doing, trying not to think about the fact that she was robbing a corpse. Her fingers closed around the flashlight's handle and she pulled it free from the belt clip with a soft *snap*.

The flashlight was heavy, solid—a Maglite, the kind security guards and cops carried. She thumbed the switch and a bright beam of light cut through the darkness, illuminating the passage entrance.

Stone steps led down into the gloom, rough-hewn and uneven, disappearing into shadows that her flashlight couldn't fully penetrate. The air wafting up from below was cool and damp, carrying that same earthy smell she'd noticed in the other passages, mixed with something else she couldn't quite identify.

Norma took a deep breath, squared her shoulders, and approached the opening. The statue felt reassuringly heavy in one hand, the flashlight warm and solid in the other.

"Okay," she said to herself, her voice steadier than she felt. "Okay. You can do this. Just... don't think. Just move."

She placed one foot on the first step, testing it, making sure it would hold her weight. It felt solid beneath her shoe. She took another step, then another, descending into the passage with the flashlight beam leading the way.

The mechanical grinding started again behind her, and she whipped around just in time to see the desk halves sliding back together, sealing the passage closed with a final, definitive *thud*.

Her escape route was gone. There was no going back now.

Only forward, into the darkness, into the unknown.

Norma turned back to face the descending stairs, raised her flashlight higher, and continued down, each step taking her deeper into the island's secrets.

Behind her, the shack returned to silence, Stubby's remains the only witness to her descent.

CHAPTER FIFTY-ONE

Sam's breath was ragged, tearing from his throat in harsh gasps as he rounded a few trees and began climbing the hill. His legs burned with every step, muscles screaming in protest, but he pushed forward, driven by hope and fear in equal measure.

Near the top, just as he broke through the last line of vegetation, he spotted her.

Zoey.

The sight hit him like a physical blow, stealing the air from his lungs, stopping him dead in his tracks.

She stood upright at the crest of the hill, but unnaturally so—too straight, too still. A long spear pierced her, entering through her chin and emerging from her skull, anchoring her to the ground like some grotesque monument. A single red rose protruded from her mouth, its petals stained with blood that looked black in the moonlight. Her wide, lifeless eyes stared blankly into the night, forever frozen in the moment of her death.

"No!" Sam's voice broke as he sprinted the remaining distance, his feet slipping on the loose dirt and grass. "No! No! Zoey. No."

He reached her and his legs gave out completely. He crumbled to his knees at her feet, his hands trembling as they reached out to touch her arm. Her skin was cold—already cooling, already lost to him.

His baby sister. Gone.

Sobs wracked his body, violent and uncontrollable. Tears streamed down his face, hot against his cold skin, blurring the horrific image before him. He'd held it together through everything—through Kelly, through Stubby, Curtis and Chelsie, Darren and Alice's grotesque display. But this was different. This was Zoey. His sister. His responsibility.

The grief was overwhelming, crushing him under its weight, pressing down on his chest until he couldn't breathe, couldn't think, couldn't do anything but feel the raw, terrible pain of loss.

After a long moment—or maybe it was seconds, he couldn't tell anymore—Sam forced himself to his feet. His legs shook, barely holding him, but rage was beginning to burn through the grief, giving him strength he didn't know he had.

He spread his arms wide and screamed into the night, his voice raw and broken, filled with fury and anguish that echoed across the hilltop and into the forest beyond.

"Who the fuck are you?" he roared, his words tearing from his throat. "What do you want? Me? Here I am, fuckface! Come on!"

He turned in a circle, scanning the tree line, the shadows, anywhere the killer might be hiding and watching. "COME ON!" he screamed again, louder, his voice cracking. "I'm right here! Take me instead! TAKE ME!"

The forest offered no answer. The shadows remained still, indifferent to his pain, to his rage, to his challenge.

Nothing moved. No one came.

Sam's fury faltered, the adrenaline draining away as quickly as it had come. His arms dropped to his sides, heavy and useless. He gave up, his shoulders slumping as the fight left him, replaced once again by the crushing weight of grief.

He sank back down, his sobs quieter now but no less painful, coming in shuddering waves that made his whole body shake.

Finally, through his tears, his gaze drifted to the mansion in the distance. Its dark silhouette loomed against the night sky, windows like dead eyes, the place where this nightmare had begun. Where people he cared about might still be alive. Where the killer almost certainly waited.

The sight of it triggered something in him—a shift, a hardening of resolve. He couldn't fall apart. Not completely. Not yet. There were still people who might need him. Lacy. Leroy. Norma. Gwen.

And there was a killer to stop, who was also probably one of them.

Sam forced himself to think, to push the grief into a locked box in his mind—not gone, never gone, but contained enough that he could function. He took several deep breaths, each one steadier than the last, and slowly composed himself.

His hands still shook, but his jaw was set now with grim determination.

He moved back to Zoey, his movements slow and reverent. He couldn't leave her like this—with her eyes open, staring at nothing. It was the only dignity he could offer her now, the only thing he could still do for his sister.

His fingers trembled as he reached up and gently closed her eyelids, his touch as soft as he could make it. Her skin was cold beneath his fingertips, and the simple act nearly broke him again, but he held on, held himself together through sheer force of will.

He took her hand in his—so small, so cold—and held it tightly, his thumb brushing over her knuckles, over the ring she always wore. The contact felt sacred somehow, this final moment of connection.

"I love you, Zoey," he whispered, his voice barely audible, thick with emotion. "I love you so much."

His throat tightened, threatening to close completely, but he forced himself to keep going. She deserved to hear it, even if she was gone. Even if only the night could hear him now.

"I'll get this fucker," he said, the words a promise, a vow. "I swear to you. I'll make them pay for what they did. For what they did to you, to all of them. I won't stop until they're dead or I am."

He lingered for another moment, unwilling to let go, to sever this final connection. But the weight of his promise—of what he still had to do—finally pulled him away.

He released her hand gently, letting it fall back to her side, and stepped back.

Sam turned around slowly, his eyes locking onto the mansion in the distance. It stood there like a dark monument to his failure, to his arrogance in thinking he could control something like this, in thinking murder could be a game.

But the game was long over now.

This was real. This was murder. This was war.

And he intended to win.

His hand moved to the gun tucked in his waistband, checking it was still there, feeling its weight. It felt different now. Not a prop from his theatrical weekend. Not even a tool for self-defense.

A weapon for vengeance.

Sam's jaw set as he began his descent from the hill, his footsteps deliberate and purposeful now. No longer the filmmaker playing detective. No longer the host trying to solve a mystery weekend.

Now he was something else entirely.

Now he was a man with nothing left to lose.

The forest swallowed him as he made his way back toward the mansion, back toward whatever hell waited there. He didn't know who the killer was. Didn't know if anyone else was still alive. Didn't know if he would survive the night.

But one thing was certain, crystallized in his mind like steel:

He would not stop until the monster who had taken Zoey—and everyone else—was brought to justice.

Or until he was dead trying.

CHAPTER FIFTY-TWO

Norma's footsteps echoed faintly as she moved cautiously through the narrow passageway, each sound magnified in the confined space. Her flashlight cast a jittery beam across the damp, uneven walls that glistened with moisture. The air was thick and musty, carrying the faint scent of decay—something organic that had been left to rot in darkness for too long. The oppressive darkness pressed against her like a living thing, trying to smother her.

The low ceiling forced her to duck slightly, her shoulders hunched, making her feel even more vulnerable, more trapped. Each step forward was an act of will, pushing against the fear that wanted to freeze her in place, that wanted to make her curl up and hide.

She stopped at a fork in the tunnel, her breath catching in her throat as indecision froze her. The light from her flashlight flickered ominously, the bulb threatening to die, sending shadows dancing along the walls like phantom figures.

"No, no, no," she whispered, gripping the device tightly, willing it to keep working. "Not now. Please not now."

She glanced down each path, trying to decide which offered better odds. The left tunnel curved slightly, disappearing around a bend, a faint breeze whispering from its depths. The right appeared to dead-end just beyond her line of sight, the darkness absolute.

Taking a shaky breath that did nothing to calm her racing heart, she made her choice, veering left into the unknown.

Please let this be right. Please let this lead out.

The tunnel twisted and turned, each corner revealing more darkness, more uncertainty. The air grew cooler with every step, raising goosebumps on her arms. Norma's heart pounded against her ribs as doubts began to creep in. Had she chosen the right path? Would she find a way out—or only more danger?

Just as the questions began to overwhelm her, threatening to spiral into full panic, a glimmer caught her attention. A thin sliver of light shone through a crack in the wall ahead, like a beacon in the suffocating dark.

Relief surged through her, warm and intoxicating. She scurried over, her steps quickening despite her exhaustion, her fingers fumbling for the crack, finding purchase. She pushed against the wall, and it gave way with a low groan—ancient hinges moving—and she stumbled forward into an open space.

Norma found herself in a sprawling wine cellar, much larger than the passageway. She shone her light around, the beam illuminating dusty wine bottles stacked on towering shelves and large oak barrels that looked centuries old. The faint glow of an emergency light in the corner barely pierced the darkness.

She recognized this place—Lacy had mentioned finding a passage down here. She was back in the mansion. Back to where people might still be alive. Was Lacy the killer? She needed to warn the rest.

Her flashlight flickered again, the beam stuttering like a dying heartbeat. Then it went out completely, plunging her into near-total darkness.

"Fuck," she hissed, smacking it against her palm hard enough to hurt. "Piece of crap."

Nothing. The flashlight remained stubbornly dead.

She felt around aimlessly in the darkness, her hands groping for orientation, for balance. Her breathing quickened, every creak and drip amplified until they sounded like footsteps approaching. Finally, her fingers closed on the edge of a shelf, rough wood against her palm. She held it, using it to guide herself, trying to adjust her eyes to the dim emergency light.

She moved carefully along the shelf, each step tentative, testing the floor before putting her weight down.

A shiny knife flashed in the dim light, slashing through the air with a whistle.

Norma moved just in time, throwing herself backward, back-pedaling frantically. Her feet tangled and she tripped, landing hard against a barrel with enough force to knock the wind from her lungs.

The knife plunged toward her again, aimed at her chest.

She moved—rolling, falling on her back—and the blade missed her by inches, searing into the barrel instead with a solid THUNK.

Red wine spurted from the puncture like blood from a wound, drenching her in its sticky flow, soaking her clothes, filling her mouth and nose with its sour-sweet taste. The liquid poured over her face, into her eyes, making it impossible to see.

She scrambled to her feet, slipping on the wine-soaked floor, and ran for the nearby stairs she could barely make out in the darkness. Her only thought was escape—getting away, getting upstairs, finding help.

A massive shelf toppled over with a tremendous crash, knocked deliberately from behind.

It caught Norma mid-stride, the full weight slamming into her back and driving her forward and down. She hit the ground hard, her head cracking against the stone floor with a sickening thud that made stars explode behind her eyes.

Bottles crashed all around her, glass shattering, wine exploding in sprays of crimson. A jagged piece of glass sliced deep into her arm, cutting through fabric and skin, and she screamed—a raw, terrible sound that echoed through the cellar.

The shelf pinned her down, its weight crushing, making it impossible to breathe, impossible to move. Wine and blood pooled around her, mixing until she couldn't tell which was which.

A pink-gloved hand appeared in her blurred vision, reaching down with casual ease. The figure threw the shelf aside like it weighed nothing, tossing it away with a crash that sent more bottles shattering.

Norma tried to crawl backward, her injured arm dragging uselessly, leaving a trail of blood. But she was too weak, too hurt. Her head spun from the impact, consciousness threatening to slip away.

The pink-gloved hand reached for the wall, pulling an axe from its mounted hook—decorative, antique, now a weapon. The blade gleamed menacingly in the faint light.

Norma looked up at her murderer, her vision swimming, trying to focus through the pain and the wine and the blood. All she could make out was a blurry cupid mask. She grasped her bleeding arm, applying pressure that did nothing to stop the flow, and stared up at the figure looming over her.

She was too weak to fight. Too hurt to run. She knew this was the end.

"You," she whispered, her voice trembling, breaking. "Who are you?"

The figure said nothing. No explanation. No justification. No answer.

They simply raised the axe high above their head, both hands gripping the handle.

"Please—" Norma started, tears streaming down her face, mixing with wine and blood.

The axe came down with brutal force.

The blade split her head open with a sickening crunch that

echoed through the cellar, the sound wet and terrible and final. Her scream cut off mid-sound, silenced forever.

The killer stood over Norma's lifeless body, the axe still embedded in her skull. Blood pooled around her head, seeping into the wine-stained floor, mixing until crimson became indistinguishable from crimson.

Her wide, unseeing eyes stared up at the ceiling, at nothing. Her final expression frozen in terror.

The killer wrenched the axe free with a wet, sucking sound and stepped back, tilting their head as if admiring their work.

The Cupid mask stared down at the corpse, that frozen plastic smile grotesque in its cheerfulness.

Satisfied, the figure stepped back into the shadows, their pink gloves stained dark now.

CHAPTER FIFTY-THREE

Sam entered through the open front door, his footsteps echoing in the cavernous space. The foyer was eerily silent, the chandelier above casting fractured light across the marble floor. He looked around for anything abnormal, his gun raised and ready, his finger resting on the trigger guard.

Everything looked the same as it had hours ago—the ornate furniture, the paintings on the walls, the grand staircase sweeping up to the second floor. But it felt different now. Emptier. More menacing. Like the mansion itself had become complicit in the murders.

"At least you got a gun," he muttered to himself, though the words offered little comfort. The weight of it in his hand was reassuring, but he'd seen what the killer could do. A gun might not be enough.

He moved cautiously toward the lounge, his steps measured and deliberate, checking corners, scanning shadows. His heart hammered in his chest, adrenaline keeping him hyper-alert, his senses heightened to the point where every sound seemed amplified.

He entered the lounge.

Nothing.

The room was completely empty.

Furniture sat undisturbed, the bar still stocked with bottles that gleamed in the low light, the fireplace cold and dark. But there were no people. No bodies. No signs of struggle.

Where is everyone?

A chill ran down Sam's spine. The silence was worse than screaming, worse than blood, worse than bodies. The not knowing was its own special kind of torture.

He heard loud footsteps running in the hall—frantic, desperate footsteps pounding against hardwood.

Sam whipped around, his gun raised, finger moving to the trigger.

Lacy, out of breath, appeared in the doorway. Her hair was disheveled, her clothes torn and dirty, her face streaked with tears and grime. She looked like she'd been through hell.

Sam directed his gun at her, the barrel aimed directly at her chest.

She threw her hands up immediately, her eyes wide with terror. "Don't shoot, Sam, it's me!" she gasped, her voice hoarse and desperate.

He didn't lower the gun. His expression was hard, unreadable, his jaw set. "They're all dead," he said, his voice flat, emotionless. "There's not too many people left it could be."

Lacy's face crumpled, hurt flashing across her features. "I didn't kill anyone, Sam," she pleaded, her voice breaking. "Just please, put the gun down. Please."

A bookshelf suddenly shifted with a grinding sound, swinging open to reveal a dark passage behind it. Another secret passageway.

"Shit," Lacy breathed, her eyes snapping to the opening. "Who did that?"

They both froze, staring at the opening, waiting for someone to exit, weapons ready, hearts pounding.

No one did.

The darkness beyond was complete, impenetrable. Nothing moved. Nothing made a sound.

Sam glanced at Lacy, then back to the passage. He lowered the gun slightly—not all the way, but enough—and moved slowly toward the opening, his steps cautious.

He looked in, squinting into the pitch black, trying to make out any shapes, any movement.

Nothing. Just darkness.

"Fuck that," he said, starting to back away. "Let's get out of—"

THUD!

A short sword plunged through the air, embedding itself in the bookcase inches from Sam's head with enough force to make the wood splinter. The blade quivered from the impact, gleaming in the light.

Sam and Lacy backed away furiously, stumbling over each other, their hearts in their throats.

A pink-gloved hand reached out from the darkness, wrapping around the sword's handle. The killer pulled it free with a sharp yank, the blade sliding out of the wood with a scraping sound that made their teeth ache.

Then the killer stepped through the secret passageway.

They wore black pants and a black hooded sweatshirt that concealed their build, making it impossible to tell if they were large or small, male or female. The pink gloves stood out starkly against the dark clothing, delicate and obscene. But worst of all was the mask—a creepy Cupid doll mask with painted cherubic features twisted into something grotesque, lifeless eyes staring out from painted sockets, a smile stretched too wide.

The killer stood before them, sword in hand, and blew them a kiss—a mocking, theatrical gesture that made Sam's blood boil.

BANG!

Sam fired his gun, the sound explosive in the confined space, deafening.

The killer flinched slightly but was otherwise unharmed. The bullet had done nothing.

Sam's eyes widened in disbelief and growing horror. He fired again.

BANG!

The killer started toward them, moving with deliberate, unhurried steps. Still unharmed. Still coming.

BANG! BANG! BANG!

Sam emptied the remaining rounds, each shot doing absolutely nothing. Not a scratch. Not even a mark on the clothing.

"Fucking blanks!" Sam shouted, rage and terror mixing in his voice. "Let's go!"

He chucked the useless gun at the killer with all his strength, the weapon spinning through the air and hitting them dead-on in the chest. The killer didn't even stumble, didn't even pause.

Sam grabbed Lacy's arm and ran like all hell, pulling her toward the hallway, toward anywhere that wasn't here.

Behind them, the killer followed, sword in hand, that horrible Cupid mask watching them flee.

CHAPTER FIFTY-FOUR

S am and Lacy raced down the hall, their feet pounding against the hardwood, their breaths coming in ragged gasps. Behind them, they could hear the measured footsteps of the killer, unhurried but relentless, following them like death itself.

They burst into the ballroom, not slowing down, not looking back.

Kelly's body still lay where they'd found her hours ago, the blood pooled around her now dried and darkened, her lifeless eyes staring at nothing. Sam and Lacy sprinted over her without hesitation, leaping over her outstretched arm, making a beeline for the kitchen on the far side of the room.

BEEP! BEEP! BEEP!

A smoke alarm blared to life, the shrill sound piercing through the mansion, adding to the chaos of their pounding hearts and labored breathing.

Steam floated under the kitchen doorway like fog, thick and white, accompanied by the sound of sizzling—meat cooking, pots boiling.

They flipped around, checking for the killer, scanning the ballroom entrance behind them.

The killer wasn't there yet. The hallway was empty.

But they could still hear those footsteps. Getting closer.

Sam and Lacy looked at each other, their faces pale, eyes wide with fear and confusion. Something was very wrong. But they had no choice. Nowhere else to go.

They pushed through the kitchen door.

Smoke filled the room like a thick curtain, making it hard to see, hard to breathe. Stovetop pots boiled violently, water and steam spilling over the edges, hissing as they hit the hot burners. Meat sizzled on the grill, the sound wet and obscene, fat popping and crackling.

Sam and Lacy covered their noses immediately, the smell hitting them like a physical blow—burned flesh, charred meat, something sweet and rotten underneath that made their stomachs turn violently.

"Oh god," Lacy choked, her voice muffled behind her hand.

They moved deeper into the kitchen, their eyes watering from the smoke, squinting to see through the haze.

Then they saw them.

Severed body parts, neatly arranged on plates like a grotesque meal preparation. Arms on cutting boards. Fingers lined up like vegetables being prepped. Everything organized with horrible, meticulous care.

A hand boiled in one of the pots, the flesh pale and bloated, fingers splayed open like a flower. The sight was hypnotic in its wrongness, impossible to look away from even as every instinct screamed to run.

A leg sizzled on the grill, the skin blackened and split, blood and fat spitting and hissing as it cooked.

Lacy turned, her hand still covering her mouth, and her eyes landed on something that made her scream into her hands—a sound that was half-horror, half-denial.

Leroy's head hung from a meat hook above the prep station, his eyes half-open, his mouth slack, a trickle of dried blood running down his neck. His usually animated face was frozen in death, all the warmth and humor gone.

Sam turned at Lacy's muffled scream and cringed at the sight, his stomach heaving, bile rising in his throat. But there was no time to process it, no time to grieve, no time to do anything but survive.

He grabbed Lacy's arm and pulled her toward the back door, practically dragging her as she stared at Leroy's remains.

"Move!" he shouted, yanking her with him. "We have to move!"

They flew out the back door, bursting into the night air.

Sam and Lacy choked and gasped, sucking in fresh air as the smoke poured out the door behind them like a toxic cloud. They bent over, hands on their knees, coughing violently, trying to clear their lungs, trying to breathe.

The cool night air had never felt so good, so clean, so—

Gwen came racing around the corner of the mansion, moving at a full sprint, her face twisted in terror.

"Gwen!" Lacy cried out, relief flooding through her at the sight of another living person, someone who wasn't dead, someone who could help.

But Gwen didn't slow down. She didn't look relieved. She looked horrified, her eyes wide and wild, focused on something behind her.

"Run! Run!" Gwen screamed as she sprinted straight at them, waving her arms frantically. "He's coming!"

Sam and Lacy didn't need to be told twice. They didn't look back to see what was coming. They didn't hesitate. They just ran.

Sam spotted the stairs leading down to the cellar as they took off, a brief thought flashing through his mind—*We could hide there, we could lock ourselves in*—but Gwen and Lacy had already passed him, their terror contagious, their momentum pulling him forward.

He followed, his legs pumping, his lungs burning.

Gwen slammed open the gate to the backyard, the metal clanging loudly as it hit the fence, and rushed through without slowing.

CHAPTER FIFTY-FIVE

S am and Lacy burst into the backyard, their hearts pounding from the chase. The scene before them was almost surreal —the pool's surface was carpeted with floating rose petals, creating a pink-tinted mirror that reflected the moonlight. Gwen stood beside it, catching her breath near a decorating table.

The table itself was a Valentine's Day fever dream: pink and red decorations scattered across its surface, a giant pink cake that looked untouched, two broken heart-shaped knives, and a gun. Gwen's hand moved toward the weapon—the same one Leroy had given her earlier in the weekend.

"We've got to keep moving," Sam urged, his voice tight with urgency. "The Coast Guard should be here soon."

Gwen looked up at him, and Sam felt something cold settle in his chest. There was no fear in her eyes. No panic. Just a calm, almost amused confidence.

"It's okay," she said softly, her fingers closing around the gun's grip. "I've got this."

Sam's mind raced. "It won't work. They're filled with blanks."

He noticed Lacy stiffen beside him, her body language shifting as she began to understand something he didn't. She was trying to catch his attention, but his eyes were locked on Gwen.

Gwen raised the gun, pointing it directly at them. A small smile played at the corners of her mouth. "Is that so?"

BANG!

The shot exploded through the quiet evening. Lacy flew backward, her shoulder erupting in red as she crashed into a small cupid statue. The statue toppled with her, and she lay motionless on the ground.

"Lacy!" Sam lunged forward, but froze when Gwen swung the gun toward him.

"Ah, ah, ah. I don't think so, stud." Her voice was light, almost playful.

Sam's pulse hammered in his ears. He forced himself to focus, to think. Maybe he could talk his way out of this. "Gwen, put the gun down."

"The hell I'm putting the gun down." She laughed, the sound sharp and brittle. "You think I went through all of this for nothing? Planning two Murder Mysteries this weekend. Being your little lap dog. Sucking your dick. It's about time for the payoff."

Sam held up his hands in a peaceful gesture. "Come on Gwen, it's just you and me. We can find a way out of this."

"Just you and me, huh?"

"If you want money, or the company, there's no way you'll get anything if you kill me. I can give you whatever you want. You don't have to do this."

Gwen actually laughed at that, her whole body shaking with genuine amusement. "I don't have to do this? No shit... Sherlock."

She seemed very pleased with her own joke, grinning at him.

"Yeah Perry Mason," a voice called from behind Sam. "You got it figured out yet?"

Sam whirled around toward the gate they'd entered from. Standing there, silhouetted against the fading light, was the killer in the creepy cupid doll mask. The figure stared at him for a long moment before reaching up and pulling off the mask.

Russell's face emerged, very much alive.

Sam's world tilted. His mind struggled to process what he was seeing—Russell, who should be dead, standing there with that familiar smirk. Sam looked from Russell to Gwen and back again, his thoughts spinning uselessly as he tried to make sense of it.

Russell walked past him casually, moving to stand beside Gwen.

"Gwen didn't have to do anything," Russell said, his voice carrying that same easy confidence it always had. "Hell, she just wanted to."

"It was fun," Gwen added with a shrug. "Even the sex wasn't that bad, rock star."

Russell politely took the gun from her hands. "I'm the one that had to do it. The situation had to be rectified, and what better way to do it than at your own mystery weekend, huh?"

Sam stared at him, completely lost. Nothing made sense anymore.

Russell saw the confusion on his face and chuckled. "I'm really disappointed, Sam. The master of the macabre, Mister Mystery himself doesn't get it."

Sam opened his mouth to speak, but Russell cut him off with a raised hand.

"Well, I'll spell it out for ya. You're not the only one who deserves the family fortune. As a matter of fact, you don't deserve jack shit! I deserve it!"

"Russell, you can have whatever you—"

"Emilia White," Russell interrupted, his voice suddenly serious. "She was your Aunt. Well, she was my Aunt too."

The words hit Sam like a physical blow. His face went slack with shock. Even Gwen looked surprised by Russell's intensity.

Russell's smirk returned, his eyes gleaming with dark pleasure. "Starting to make sense now? Meet your half brother, Sam."

"No." The word came out as barely a whisper.

"Yes. Our daddy dearest didn't only fuck your mom. He had a little fun on the side, with my mom. Knocked her up. Then they both decided they didn't want me. Adoption sucks balls, Sammy!"

Sam felt like the ground had opened beneath him. "I didn't know."

"Of course not. No one knew."

"This whole time we've known each other..."

"I always said we were like brothers." Russell's grin widened. "Literally."

Sam's voice came out hoarse. "What do you want, Russell?"

"All I wanted was a piece of the cut, but your Aunt didn't like that idea. She left every fucking dime to you, even after I told her the truth."

"You can have it all."

"I plan to."

"That was the plan all along, Sammy poo," Gwen chimed in cheerfully.

Disgust rolled through Sam's stomach. "You're both sick."

Russell's grin turned sinister. "Yeah."

The pieces were falling into place now, each one worse than the last. "She never had a heart attack, did she? You killed her."

"Bingo."

"And when you didn't get what you wanted, you devised a morbid mystery of your own, to kill off all of my friends. Brought Gwen here along for the ride. What did you do to manipulate her?"

"Like I said, it was all on her own accord. She's crazier than me."

Gwen smiled, clearly taking it as a compliment.

Russell continued, "Quite the help though. Of course, I did give her a little something she wanted."

He looked at Gwen with exaggerated seductiveness. She smiled back, playing along.

"I guess that makes us eskimo brothers."

"We're not any kind of brothers," Sam said through gritted teeth.

"Either way, she's not needed much anymore." Russell turned to Gwen with an apologetic shrug. "Sorry babe."

He pointed the gun at her. Gwen's smile faltered, confusion flickering across her face before morphing into fear. He wouldn't—

BANG!

The shot caught her square in the chest. Gwen soared backward, her body hitting the ground hard.

Sam stared in horror, the reality of Russell's insanity finally sinking in completely. Russell turned back to him, the gun swinging in his direction.

"Looks like this is it. Down to you and me, just the way it was planned. Face it, my mystery kicked your mystery's ass."

Russell let out a huge laugh, genuine and unhinged.

Sam's eyes darted around, desperate for a plan, any plan.

"Did you like the mask? Awesome, huh? Designed by..." Russell glanced at Gwen's motionless body on the ground. "...our dead bed buddy over there. Very helpful. My acting wasn't bad either, huh? The Coast Guard bit should earn me an award. And how about the cupid's arrow?"

Russell pressed his index finger to a spot on his chest. With a theatrical flourish and sound effects, an arrow appeared to penetrate through his body, the tip emerging from his back. Sam felt a sick recognition.

"My death vest."

"Filled with an arrow instead of a blade."

"Clever."

"Like I said, kicked your ass. Now, let's cut the crap and finish this thing, shall we?"

Russell raised the gun just as a moan of pain cut through the tension. Both men looked toward the sound. Lacy was stirring, very much alive.

Russell's face twisted with annoyance. "Damn it. This is why I hate guns. Cutting is so much more effective."

His eyes moved to the knives on the table.

That split second of distraction was all Sam needed. He launched himself forward, his shoulder driving into Russell's midsection. They crashed to the ground together in a tangle of limbs, the gun flying from Russell's grip and skittering across the concrete toward the pool.

Sam's fist connected with Russell's face once, twice, three times. Blood splattered from Russell's nose, but he managed to flip Sam over, his elbow cracking down into Sam's face with brutal force.

Pain exploded through Sam's head, making the world spin. Through his blurred vision, he saw Russell grab one of the half-heart knives from the table. Russell raised it high, preparing to plunge it down into Sam's chest when—

CRACK!

The cupid statue connected with the back of Russell's head. He toppled sideways, dazed. Lacy stood behind him, barely upright, the statue clutched in her good hand.

Suddenly Gwen barreled into Lacy from the side. Both women crashed into the bed of roses, their bodies moving with the sluggish desperation of the badly wounded. They fought viciously but slowly—biting, slapping, pulling hair like high school girls in a parking lot, each movement clearly agonizing.

Russell staggered to his feet. Sam pushed himself up, his head still spinning from the elbow strike. Russell sliced at him with the half-heart knife, the blade whistling past Sam's face by inches.

Sam grabbed the second knife from the table. They circled each other, slashing and stabbing, their movements growing more frantic. Neither could land a hit.

Near the roses, Gwen shoved a handful of dirt into Lacy's face. Lacy spit soil from her mouth, her free hand scrambling across the ground until her fingers closed around a brick. She swung it with every ounce of strength she had left, connecting with Gwen's temple. Gwen's eyes rolled back and she collapsed.

Sam swiped his knife at Russell. Russell sliced back. The

blades met in midair with a metallic ring, then separated. Russell's frustration was evident on his face. This wasn't working.

He made his decision in an instant, dropping his knife and diving for the gun on the ground.

Lacy's hand shot out, grabbing Russell's discarded knife. As Russell spun around, gun in hand, both Sam and Lacy thrust their blades forward with everything they had.

The knives sank deep into Russell's stomach, right next to each other. Blood splattered across all three of them, hot and sticky.

Russell let out a high-pitched squeal of agony. He stumbled backward, the gun falling from his hand as he grabbed at the knives protruding from his torso. The two half-heart blades sat side by side, forming one complete heart.

Russell's knees buckled and he crumpled to the ground, his eyes wide with shock and pain.

Sam stared down at his former friend's body, his former brother's body. "Asshole."

A sound made him turn. Gwen was on her feet again, charging toward him with the cupid statue raised high above her head, her face a mask of rage and desperation.

BANG!

Lacy's shot caught Gwen in the heart. Her momentum carried her forward two more steps before she plummeted into the pool, her body hitting the water with a splash that sent rose petals flying. The clear water began turning red almost immediately.

"Bitch," Lacy muttered.

Sam nudged Russell's body with his foot. It was completely limp, lifeless. He picked up the gun from where Russell had dropped it and hobbled over to Lacy. They came together in an embrace, both of them shaking, their wounds screaming in protest but neither caring.

"You okay?" Sam asked, his voice rough.

Lacy looked up at him, their faces close enough that he could feel her breath. "Besides the bullet in my shoulder, yeah. You?"

Sam simply nodded, not trusting his voice.

Together, they collapsed into a couple of nearby chairs, their bodies finally giving out. They sat in silence, waiting, surrounded by carnage and Valentine's decorations, two survivors in the wreckage of Russell's twisted revenge plot.

CHAPTER FIFTY-SIX

The yacht cut through the water with a steady, rhythmic motion.

On the top deck, the morning breeze was gentle and cool, carrying with it the salt spray and the promise of distance—distance from the island, distance from the blood and bodies and betrayal they were leaving behind.

Sam sat with his arm around Lacy, a blanket draped over both of them. Her shoulder was secured in a sling, the white fabric stark against the colorful pattern of the blanket. Neither of them had said much since they'd boarded. There wasn't much to say.

Sam turned to look back at the island. It was already growing smaller in the distance, its dark silhouette becoming less defined with each passing minute. From here, it looked peaceful. Almost inviting. No one would guess what had happened there, what horrors had unfolded in that sprawling mansion among the Valentine's decorations and mystery game props.

His chest felt tight as he stared at it. Everyone he'd invited—everyone except Lacy—was dead. His good friend had been his half-brother. His aunt had been murdered for money that Sam would have given away freely if anyone had just asked. The entire weekend had been a trap, an elaborate revenge plot disguised as the very thing Sam loved most.

He'd probably never host another mystery weekend again. The thought sat heavy in his stomach.

Lacy shifted slightly beside him, and he tore his eyes away from the island to look at her. Something in his chest loosened when he met her gaze. The sadness didn't disappear—he didn't think it would for a long time—but it became more bearable. She was here. She was alive. That had to count for something.

Her face was soft with understanding. She could see his pain as clearly as if he'd spoken it aloud, and beneath it, she could see the other thing too—the love that had been there all along, hidden under years of bad timing. Her good hand moved to his arm, rubbing it gently, the touch grounding him in the present moment.

Sam managed a small, bitter smile. "Well. Happy Valentine's Day."

Lacy let out a quiet breath that might have been a laugh under different circumstances. "Next year, we are staying in and eating chocolates."

"Deal."

The word came out rough, his throat tight with emotion. But as he said it, he felt the faintest smile form on his face. It was real, even if it was small. Even if it hurt.

She was all he had left. But maybe that was enough. Maybe she was more than enough.

He squeezed her tightly against him, careful of her injured shoulder, and turned his face back toward the sunrise. The sky behind them was erupting into brilliant colors now—deep purples fading to pink, orange bleeding into gold where the sun kissed the water. It was beautiful in a way that felt almost wrong after everything that had happened.

But they were here to see it. They had survived.

Lacy leaned her head against his shoulder, and together they watched the island disappear into the distance as the yacht carried them toward whatever came next. The nightmare was over. The mystery was solved.

And for the first time in days, Sam allowed himself to simply breathe.

EPILOGUE

He'd been sitting here for an hour, unable to start, unable to put that night into words. His therapist had suggested writing it down, processing it through the one thing he'd always been good at—storytelling.

But this wasn't a story. This was his life. His trauma.

His phone buzzed. A text from Lacy: *How's the writing going?*

It's not, he replied.

Want company?

Always.

Twenty minutes later, she slid into the seat across from him, two coffees in hand. "Still stuck?"

"I don't know where to start," Sam admitted.

Lacy looked at his screen, at the cursor blinking on Chapter One. "Start with the truth," she said. "Start with what happened."

Sam stared at the screen for a long moment. Then, slowly, he began to type:

The invitation arrived on a Tuesday, delivered by courier with a wax seal and a sense of theatrical flair that should have been my first warning...

The words came slowly at first, then faster. The story

pouring out of him like poison from a wound. Lacy sat across from him, reading over his shoulder, occasionally squeezing his hand when the words got too hard.

He wrote about Kelly. About Shea and Chelsie and Curtis. About Leroy's kindness and Norma's fear. About finding Zoey on that hill.

He wrote about Russell's betrayal and Gwen's madness.

He wrote about surviving.

Hours passed. The sun set. The café closed around them, but they barely noticed.

Finally, Sam typed the last line: *And somewhere in the mansion, a killer walked free, their blade still wet with Kelly's blood.*

He sat back, exhausted but somehow emptied in a good way.

"It's good," Lacy said softly. "Really good. Dark as hell, but good."

"Think anyone will want to read it?"

"I think people need to read it," she corrected. "Not as entertainment. As a warning." She paused. "What are you going to call it?"

Sam thought for a moment, then smiled sadly. "Murder Mansion: A Valentine's Day Nightmare."

"Perfect."

————

Six months later, Sam held the first printed copy of his book in his hands. The publisher had called it a "gripping true crime thriller unlike anything they'd ever read." It had sold to a major house. There was talk of a documentary.

He'd donated all the proceeds to victims' families. He didn't want to profit from their deaths.

But writing it had helped. Had given him a way to honor them, to tell their stories, to make sure they weren't forgotten.

The book's dedication page was simple:

For Zoey, Kelly, Shea, Chelsie, Curtis, Leroy, Norma, Darren, Alice, and Stubby. You deserved better. You deserved to live.

Sam set the book down and walked to his window, looking out at the city. He though back to that weekend and the chaos that it became.

The memories remained. He would carry them forever—the weight of survival, the guilt of living when so many had died.

But he would carry them forward, into a life worth living. It's what Zoey would have wanted.

His phone buzzed. Lacy: *Dinner tonight? To celebrate?*

Sam smiled and typed back: *Sounds perfect. But nowhere with a mystery theme.*

Obviously, she replied. *How about Italian?*

Perfect.

As he pocketed his phone, Sam looked at the book one more time. At the cover. At the words that told the story of the worst weekend of his life.

Then he turned away, grabbed his jacket, and walked out the door.

Into the light.

Into life.

Leaving the darkness of Rose Island behind him.

Finally.

THE END

Jesse Dylan Young is a screenwriter and novelist based in Long Beach, California. *Murder Mansion* is his debut novel, adapted from his award-winning screenplay that came close to production years ago.

Inspired by Kevin Williamson's *Scream*, Jesse has been honing his writing craft for years, drawing influence from Williamson, Dan Brown, and James Patterson. When he's not writing, Jesse creates real-life treasure hunts, DJs and produces music, and travels the world in search of his next creative obsession.

Murder Mansion is the first in what promises to be a thrilling career of twists, turns, and exciting stories.

@jessedylanyoung